"*How I envy you!*" *Her words seemed to hang tangibly on the air, drifting around the pillars of the chancel arch, echoing eerily in the vaulting of the roof. Suddenly she was overcome by that weightless detachment that comes with the feeling that this particular moment of one's life has been lived through before. A sudden pause in the rage of the hurricane brought a silence that was even more ominous than the previous clamour, then the pandemonium resumed in redoubled fury. A jagged spear of brilliant energy stabbed directly at the chrysoberyl, glowing now in its magnetic bed with a weird iridescence it had not shown before. The whole world erupted in one vast holocaust of cold blue flame. The jewel completely disintegrated, as fragments of the shattered dagger rained down upon the altar. The icy fire whipped back upon itself, a huge swirling cobalt spiral. For an eternity of seconds, Lucy stared into the depths of its chill, hypnotic coils. Again that lethargic, indescribable sensation of déjà vu, and then a blast of exquisite agony swept her into the bitter blue vacuum, dissolving body and soul into absolute nothingness.*

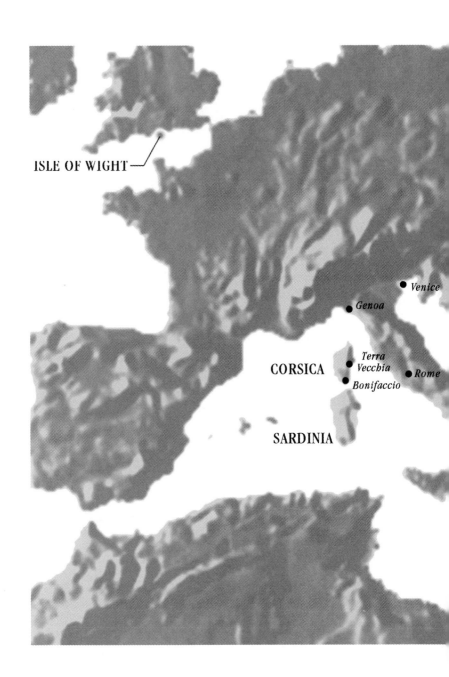

ISLE OF WIGHT

Venice

Genoa

CORSICA

Terra
Vecchia

Bonifaccio

Rome

SARDINIA

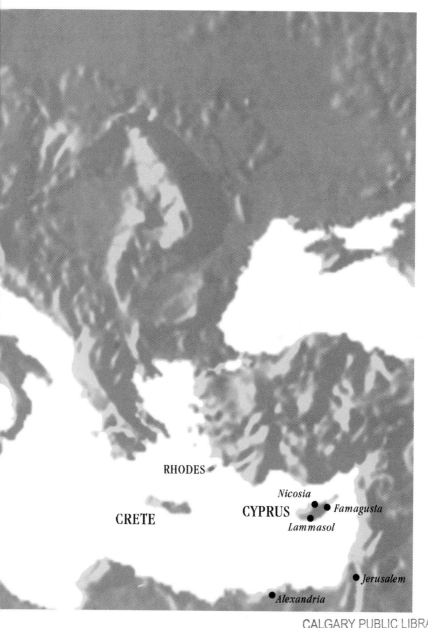

RHODES

Nicosia

CYPRUS ● ● Famagusta

CRETE

Lammasol

● Jerusalem

● Alexandria

I have been here before,
But when or how I cannot tell:
I know the grass beyond the door,
The sweet keen smell,
The sighing sound, the lights around the shore.

Dante Gabriel Rossetti.

The Grass
BEYOND
The DOOR

Cicely Veighey

FRONTENAC   HOUSE
Calgary

Canadian Cataloguing in Publication Data

Veighey, Cicely, 1917 -
  The grass beyond the door

  ISBN: 0-9684903-0-1

  1.Title.
PS8593.E346G72 1999   C813'.54   C99-910158-7
PR9199.3.V44G72 1999

Book design by Kevin Berggren

Cover picture: "Destiny" by J.W. Waterhouse, 1900

Printed and bound in Canada

Published by Frontenac House Ltd.
1138 Frontenac Ave S.W.
Calgary AB   T2T 1B6
Canada
Ph: (403) 245-2491 Fax: (403) 245-2380
E-mail: frontenachouse@telusplanet.net

1 2 3 4 5 6 7 8 9   03 02 01 00 99

This book is dedicated to the memory of my husband David and to my family. It would not have been possible without their help.

1

The ancient body of Nona Lucina sat on the bench outside her home in Terra Vecchia, on the island of Corsica, watching her grandchildren and great-grandchildren playing in the afternoon sunshine. Her spirit, still youthful, still vibrant, chafing within its jail of withered flesh, stared impatiently through faded, dim-sighted eyes, toward the village church, where her husband lay in the tiny graveyard. There, when the time came, she would join him. She was more than ready.

She closed her eyes, recalling his beloved face, and the little Italian song he was always whistling, or singing:

"If I were fire, I'd burn the world away,
  If I were wind, I'd turn my storms thereon …"

and always when he came to the last verse:

"If I were Me …
  I'd pick the prettiest girls to suit my whim,
  And let the other fellows have the rest!"

He would roll his eyes, and leer so ridiculously, that she could never keep from bursting into laughter. He had such wonderfully expressive eyes. She'd noticed that the first time she saw him. That was …

Monday, June thirteenth, eighteen thirty-one.
Mistress Lightfoot stood at the front door of Stoney Meadow Farm, in the Bowcombe Valley, on the Isle of Wight, England. A fine

Cashmere shawl protected her plump shoulders from the early morning breeze. She smiled as Lucy climbed from the whitewashed mounting stone by the gate into the saddle of her restive chestnut hunter. With loving pride she watched her pretty daughter ride down the lane and out of sight and, had she but known it, out of her life, forever.

Trotting along the tree-lined road, Lucy passed girls of her own age, and children with but half her years, working in the fields. She was thankful to have been born the only child of well-to-do, loving parents. Proud of their beautiful, popular daughter, the Lightfoots had given her the best of educations and denied her nothing, within reason, that added to her pleasure and enjoyment in life. This morning she was on her way to spend the day at Chillerton Farm with her best friend, Marjorie Braithwaite. There was to be a total eclipse of the sun and the two girls planned to watch it together.

Her gray eyes sparkled with anticipation and delight as her thoughts lingered on the wonderful news she had to share with Marjorie. Last night, quite out of the blue, Papa had looked up from his newspaper and harrumphed. That was the only word that could describe the peculiar sound that signalled to his wife and daughter that he was about to surprise them with "one of his wild schemes"! Mama had laid down her tatting, and Lucy had looked up expectantly from her seat on the hearth rug, where she was teasing her kitten Sooty with a piece of paper tied to a ribbon.

Papa had glared sourly at them, and growled, "All those French and Italian lessons I've spent a fortune on – what on earth are they good for, if you never use 'em?"

"Oh, but I do, Papa!" Lucy returned blithely. "Marjorie and I speak French together all the time – especially when we want to tell secrets."

"Pah! Schoolgirl secrets! All that good coin gone to waste," he mourned. But neither of his ladies was deceived by his gloomy countenance. They regarded him alertly, waiting with undisguised interest for him to continue.

"As I see it," he resumed, "There can be only one solution. After the harvest is in, I shall have to escort you both on a tour of Europe. It's the only way," he sighed, "to determine if I have received my money's worth."

"Papa!" Lucy screamed, throwing herself onto his lap. "Do you really mean that?"

"Unlike some people I could name, I am not in the habit of spinning Banbury tales." He attempted to sound insulted and severe, but the wicked twinkle in his eye betrayed him, and he succumbed under a deluge of excited questions from his wife and daughter.

Now, riding dreamily through the pleasant morning, Lucy was busily concocting her own plans. She and her best friend would lay siege to Squire Braithwaite, and persuade that gentleman that it would be to the utmost advantage of his daughter and everyone concerned that he allow Marjorie to join the Lightfoot entourage.

If Marjorie were to accompany them, that would really be the top of the boughs! What fun it would be to explore foreign shops and markets together, as they so often explored the streets of Newport and other island towns on market and fair days. She recalled the pleasure of last year's Saint James' Day Fair at Yarmouth. It had been a heavenly July day – blue skies and bright, warm sunshine, with just enough of a gentle sea breeze to keep them comfortable.

As was customary on fair day, a big stuffed hand protruded from the upper window of the old town hall, its fingers half open, indicating that, for this one day, the hand of the Law was relaxed and a blind eye would be turned to such minor misdemeanors as over-indulgence at one of the several taverns.

While their mothers shopped and chatted with friends, Papa had escorted the girls around stalls that offered food, ribbons and cheap jewelry and other tempting and fascinating fairings.

As entranced as the town urchins, all scrubbed to Holy Day cleanliness, Lucy and Marjorie watched the knife grinder's foot-operated grindstone hurl showers of sparks from the carving knives and scissors brought by white-aproned housewives. They laughed hysterically at the farm and fisher lads, attempting to walk the greasy pole that leaned out over the water, in an effort to grab the flag at the far end before falling into the sea. A piglet was the coveted prize to be awarded to the winner.

There were foot races, swimming and boat races, and wrestling bouts, with many entertaining and comic events in between – jugglers, clowns and musicians, and a treacle bun race where the contestants, hands tied behind their backs, had to devour a treacle-covered bun suspended from a string.

The "Battle of Trafalgar" had been the funniest show. Men and boys, dressed in weird and wonderful costumes, crewed two old boats. Using shovels for oars they bombarded one another with paper sacks, filled on one side with flour and on the other with soot, all the while trying to knock their rivals overboard or sink their craft. Lucy smiled at the memory.

Oh, it had been tremendous fun, even if they did have to leave early before the games became too rough! As a consolation, Papa had bought them yards of coliquet ribbons (that their mothers had never let them wear!) and chunks of gilded gingerbread. He had even permitted them to have their fortunes told, supplying them with a shilling apiece for crossing the gypsy's hand with silver, on pain of dire and dreadful reprisals should they ever betray him to their Mamas!

Marjorie had been first, and the fierce-visaged, dark-skinned woman had brought warm blushes to her face, foretelling of a handsome lover, a wealthy marriage and bonny children. But as she bent her gaudily wrapped head over Lucy's small hand, the gypsy's manner abruptly changed. She started, and looked up into the bright gray eyes with a strange expression – almost, thought Lucy, as if she were scared. The dark eyes wavered and dropped.

"A far journey, a foreign land, far from here and now," she uttered, grimly. "Two men to love, and to love you – one mild and fair, but a doughty warrior – the other dark and wild, a man of the sea."

She released the girl's hand with a gesture of dismissal, obviously intending to say no more. The woman's manner had been so peculiar! Lucy felt again the cold thrill that had passed through her body, as if the sun had suddenly gone behind a cloud.

"Fustian! A pack of nonsense!" her father had growled, hustling his charges away from the glowering Romany woman.

Seeing that he was mentally castigating himself for indulging them in such a disturbing pastime, Lucy promptly began to make fun of the bizarre prophecies, mimicking the gypsy with exaggerated imitation, catching her father's hand, and pretending to see weird and wonderful happenings in his future, such as self-milking cows, talking sheep, and other amazing curiosities, until she had both her listeners shaking with laughter.

After a day of two, she had consigned the whole affair to the back of her mind, but today for some reason the memory resurfaced, to puzzle her again. She shrugged off the vague feeling of disquiet it aroused, returning her thoughts to the pleasures she expected to enjoy today. Hidden beneath the long sleeves and high neck of her stylishly cut new yellow riding habit she was wearing her gold jewellery. Carefully packed in her saddle bag was her brand new muslin, in her favourite yellow, sprigged with dainty green leaves and white daisies. It was the very last stare in fashion, made from a pattern imported straight from France – she suspected by courtesy of the "Gentlemen" (the euphemistic name for "'Free Trade"). At any rate, it had appeared simultaneously with Papa's latest consignment of cognac – but, of course, one never asked awkward questions!

There would be quite a gathering at Chillerton – the Braithwaites were famous for their hospitality – and she and Marjorie had agreed that today they would outshine even that odious, high-in-the-instep anti- dote, Daphne Fielden, and the London "creations" that she flaunted so nauseatingly. It was fortunate that the fribble considered herself so high- ly. It was for certain that no one else did!

A masculine hail interrupted her reverie. She turned her head, to see George Brewster, a young farmer from the nearby village of Chale, fol- lowing her. A mischievous impulse urged her to ride Dandy at a gallop, giving her pursuer no chance to overtake her, until she reined in at the gate of St. Olave's churchyard.

"What's the hurry?" he grumbled in his slow Island drawl. "Where bist thee off to, so 'arly? B'aint ten o'the clock, even yet."

"Chillerton Farm," she told him. "To the Braithwaites. I'm watch- ing the eclipse with Marjorie."

"Ar! Thee better be careful about that, now. They say lookin' at the sun, direct like, can blind 'ee."

"Oh, we shall be all right. Rufus is going to smoke bits of glass for us to look through."

"Huh! And help 'ee look through en, I'll be bound!" George's ruddy face turned an even deeper red.

"Oh, cut rein, George! Don't be such a gudgeon." Lucy leaned over to hitch Dandy to the churchyard railing, and slid from the saddle, adroitly avoiding the young man's outstretched arms. George was a sweet boy, but such a rustic!

"I'm going into the church for a while," she dismissed him.

"Better not hang around too long. I don't like the looks o' that sky. Big storm comin' up, I reckon."

"Oh, I hope not! It could spoil the eclipse!" Lucy looked up to see thick, yellowish clouds stretched above the treetops. An eerie light slanted through long narrow rifts, striping the grass with light and shadow. The air was heavy with the scent of bluebells; not a bird, an insect, nor a rustling leaf disturbed the unnatural calm. The church, nearly six hundred years old, standing so serenely in its setting of grand old chestnuts and sturdy English oaks, in full, glorious summer foliage, might have been a painting on a darkened canvas.

"It does seem peculiar," she agreed. "Something to do with the eclipse, I expect." She shrugged, and tripped lightly along the path toward the church.

George Brewster watched, as she paused for a moment, her butter-coloured habit bright against the darkness of the doorway. Then the sombre shadows seemed to gather her in.

He wished he had the nerve to follow her, even to drag her away from this place, holy church though it might be. Something was definitely out of joint this day. In spite of the humid warmth of the air, the brooding stillness and the gathering gloom sent a wave of icy chill through his veins.

Like most of the other young bucks of the neighbourhood, he had been head over heels in love with the bright-eyed Lucy ever since she had arrived in the Bowcombe Valley more than a year ago. But she favoured none of them. Instead, even as a hundred years in the future her twentieth century counterparts would lay their hearts at the stamping feet of raucous "pop stars", so young Lucy had conceived a mad infatuation for the oaken effigy of Sir Edward Estur, fourteenth century Crusader, entombed in this, his family church.

George turned away in disgust. Who in bloody hell could compete with a damned ghost? Reluctantly he remounted his horse. The whole sky was now hidden by the strange ochreous clouds, and the first distant rumble of thunder could be heard.

Standing by the recess in the north wall of the sanctuary, Lucy gazed dreamily down at the reclining likeness of the medieval knight. She knew every carved line by heart, from the small cherub guarding his peaceful, handsome head, to the carved dog nestled at his feet, and the slender hands that enfolded the hilt of his own steel dagger, clasping it like a crucifix to his breast.

She patted the head of the tiny wooden dog, wondering if it were really true, as the country folk maintained, that once in a hundred years the little fellow came to life. It could only happen, they believed, if a full moon and Midsummer Night coincided. Then, the legend said, the dog could be seen dancing along a moon-lit path, to a mystic gathering place in the woods, to meet those strange entities that dwell in the hollow hills around the Chillerton Downs. There the Eldritch company would spend a few hours in gossip, story telling and ghostly revelry, until the dawn chased them back to their abiding places.

Midsummer was only a few days away. Eleven, to be precise, to that magical shortest night of the year, when the inhabitants of the occult world held sway. Would this be the year of the little dog's brief liberation? She must remember to check the Almanac, to find out if the moon would be full. How wonderful if her dear Sir Edward could join his small pet in that moonlit frolic! With one slender bare finger, she caressed the cool, yellow-green loveliness of the chrysoberyl, gleaming fitfully against the intricate lodestone setting, that ornamented the dagger's crossbar. There were still people who believed that lodestone held great magic, and that the shattering of a crystal could release immense occult powers.

She sighed. Being in love with a statue could be very unsatisfactory at times. For example, when her father, laughing comfortably, would assure her mother that their little maid's attachment to a lump of wood was just a girlish fantasy, to be out-grown with adolescence. In the meantime Lucy knew that it suited him well enough. He was in no hurry to have his darling enamoured of a real flesh and blood hero.

People just did not understand. Only Marjorie knew exactly what Lucy meant, when she explained, "I love to imagine that I am with him sharing his adventures, and following in the train of King Peter of Cyprus, on his great crusade to free the Holy Land from the grasp of the Infidels."

Neither of them was quite sure what an Infidel was, but Marjorie was a most satisfactory confidant. She thought her best friend's hopeless devotion was so wonderfully romantic, and so sad.

Lucy wandered around the little church that she knew so well and loved so much for his dear sake. When she knelt at the Communion rail, in a different place each Sunday if she could manage it, she hoped that she might be kneeling in the same spot that his knees had once pressed. She regretted that he could not have sipped from the same chalice as she, but the famous Henry VII Gatcombe Communion Cup had not been presented to Saint Olave's Church until 1540, two hundred years after her hero's lifetime.

She wished she had more knowledge of her Crusader's life and adventures. Mr. Worsley, the Vicar, said that only the knight's name was on record, that he had served under Pierre de Lusignan and was known merely because he had been a member of King Peter's personal group of friends, The Companions of the Order of the Sword. It was the short, dagger-like sword of his initiation into the order that his wooden likeness clasped in its hands.

She laid a tender hand on one of the slightly sunken arched panels of the old Purbeck marble font. Also of thirteenth century origin, it had probably been installed when the church was built, so her beloved must certainly have been baptized in holy water from its octagonal bowl. If only she too could have been christened here! What a lovely bond that would have forged between them.

The Estur family had erected the church as a Manorial Chapel to their ancestral home, Gatcombe House, a hundred years before even Sir Edward's lifetime. Remembering their Norman roots, the Esturs had adopted the great Scandinavian Saint Olaf as their own patron, and dedicated the church to him. Many changes had been made to the old building through the ensuing centuries. Originally, there had been no tower, nor had one existed in Sir Edward's time. It had not come into being until the fifteenth century, when Carisbrooke Castle, later to become the prison of the ill-fated Charles the First, was being built.

The south side windows were also of that era, with angels pictured in the leaded lights. Lucy's favourite was the feathered angel, balancing on the wheel of life, as he guides mankind through the ups and downs of earthly existence.

A chill draft recalled her wandering thoughts. Heavens! How dark it had become. Could the eclipse already have started? Totality was supposed to be at ten past eleven. She peered at the golden face of the dainty watch pinned to her lapel, hardly able to discern the hands in the deepening gloom. Almost half past ten! She should be at Chillerton Green by now. She hurried to the open door, just as great drops of rain began to burst in crown-sized splashes on the stone step. As she hesitated, the shower became a cloudburst, whipped into an impenetrable gray curtain by a raging wind that bent trees and shrubs almost to the ground. A searing flash of lightning, and an almost simultaneous sky-splitting crash of thunder, sent the girl scurrying inside. Groping her way back to the tomb, she heard, faint against the rising tumult of the storm, the whinny of her frightened horse. Poor Dandy! She hoped, with some guilt, that the gelding would not be too scared, but storms terrified her. She dared not brave the appalling fury of nature to go to his aid.

Inside, the tiny building was so dark that she could scarcely see. The noise was nerve-shattering. A shrieking wind racketed around the building, tearing at corners, prying at roof slates. It hurled batteries of rain against the stone walls, and beat on the stained glass windows with frantic tendrils of dislodged ivy. The thunder was continuous. Lightning flashes followed one another in rapid succession, giving the feathered angel a simulated life, and the reclining warrior the appearance of illumination by flickering candlelight.

A small whirligig of fear began to spin in Lucy's stomach. Perhaps this really was to be the end of the world, just as that shabby old preacher Marjorie and she had seen on a Newport street corner last market day had predicted. She shivered as she remembered his ferocious eyes, peering through his prophet-like hair and beard, and his raucous, chastising voice, urging indifferent passers-by to repent while there was yet time. What if he had been speaking the truth? Was she to face the last trump, all alone? She wished they had not giggled and joked behind the old man's back.

Seeking comfort, she crept close to Sir Edward's tomb, impatient to escape into her favourite day-dream — the one in which, by some unexplained miracle, his carved lids would blink open, revealing dark, reckless brown eyes, with lashes as long and black as her own. The stiff wooden hair would start into springy black curls, and the lean brown face would be enlivened by an endearing grin.

Her hand brushed against the familiar contours of the little dog. She whispered, "Ah, Flaçon-Caprice! How lucky you were to have known him – to have heard his voice and walked in the gardens with him. How I envy you!"

"How I envy you!" Her words seemed to hang tangibly on the air, drifting around the pillars of the chancel arch, echoing eerily in the vaulting of the roof. Suddenly she was overcome by that weightless detachment that comes with the feeling that this particular moment of one's life has been lived through before. A sudden pause in the rage of the hurricane brought a silence that was even more ominous than the previous clamour, then the pandemonium resumed in redoubled fury. A jagged spear of brilliant energy stabbed directly at the chrysoberyl, glowing now in its magnetic bed with a weird iridescence it had not shown before. The whole world erupted in one vast holocaust of cold blue flame. The jewel completely disintegrated, as fragments of the shattered dagger rained down upon the altar. The icy fire whipped back upon itself, a huge swirling cobalt spiral. For an eternity of seconds, Lucy stared into the depths of its chill, hypnotic coils. Again that lethargic, indescribable sensation of déjà vu, and then a blast of exquisite agony swept her into the bitter blue vacuum, dissolving body and soul into absolute nothingness.

For the next four hours, a most terrible storm, of a severity never before known on the Island, devastated the countryside, keeping even the most foolhardy from venturing out of doors. Then the turmoil ceased as suddenly as it had started. As a strange calm settled over all, Henry Worsley, Rector of Saint Olave's, fared forth to ascertain what damage had been sustained by his church and his parish. He found a bedraggled but familiar horse hitched to the churchyard railing, and muttered an extremely ungodly epithet. That girl had obviously been mooning over the Estur effigy again and had been caught in the tempest. Just what he needed to complicate this mess, an hysterical female on his hands. Strange, this peculiar fixation of hers. In all other ways, she seemed a normal, sensible young maid, a shade more intelligent than most, and quite pretty manners. Well educated, too – fluent in French and Italian, and of all things, Latin. She'd borrowed a Latin book or two from him concerning the Crusades. He had taken it upon himself on several occasions, however, to chide her for her unhealthy attachment to the graven image of the Estur Crusader.

"Why do you stand so?" he had demanded during one of her daily visits to the church. She had merely raised those bewitching dark gray eyes to his, murmuring, "I love to be with him in my thoughts and dreams," a reply which did absolutely nothing to help his bewilderment. How was a man to deal with that? Females! He had let it lie.

At the church door, he was joined by a somewhat concerned George Brewster. "Miss Lucy be inside, parson," he told the clergyman. "Saw her come in, I did, before the tempest. Come back to see if her was all right. Horse is still outside, all of a dither, so to speak. Poor beast."

Worsley strode past him. The church was empty. He exchanged a puzzled look with the young farmer, and shrugged. Making his way to the chancel, he peered into each pew, in passing, then stopped dead in his tracks. Everything was in perfect order, except – the Crusader's folded hands were empty! Shards of steel from his demolished dagger lay scattered on the altar, but the jewel that had adorned it was nowhere to be seen – and neither was Lucy Lightfoot.

2

Lucy opened her eyes, and looked into the dear familiar face of – a man she had never seen before! She was lying on wet sand, with the stranger's arm supporting her shoulders. Bewildered, she struggled to her feet, steadied by his firm grip on her elbow.

"How did I get here?" she asked.

The man, apparently a seaman of sorts, must have understood her meaning, although it was in French that he explained that he'd only just found her.

"I was about to go fishing," he said. "Tomorrow being Friday, I can sell everything I can catch at the camp. Then I found you, lying here."

"Tomorrow is Tuesday," she corrected him, automatically using the same language.

"Friday." He bent his head courteously but his black eyes sparkled with amusement.

Friday? Did the man have windmills in his cockloft? Of course, he was a foreigner – he was probably confused, perhaps not very bright.

Speaking slowly and distinctly, she told him, "Today is Monday, June the thirteenth, eighteen hundred and thirty-one."

Now he was looking askance at her, as if she were the crazy one.

"Today is Thursday, June thirteenth, thirteen hundred and sixty-four," he answered, gently, in the same deliberate tone she had used.

Lucy pressed a hand to her throbbing head. "Please," she whispered. "Will you take me home? I live at Stoney Meadow Farm, in Bowcombe Valley."

"With pleasure, my lady, if you will direct me. I am not a native of this island." This made her smile. Obviously he was not! Then he added, "I am Corse. The army camp and parts of the coast are all I know of Cyprus."

"Cyprus!"

The unknown man caught her as she fainted.

*   *   *

The second time Lucy recovered consciousness she found herself in a strange room, where she lay for several days in the vague half-awareness of delirium. From the muted conversations that penetrated her fever-stricken understanding, she gathered that she was indeed on the Island of Cyprus, that the year was definitely 1364, and that she had been brought to the home of Will and Roberga Salter by Lionallo Momellino, the young Corsican fisherman who had found her lying on the shore.

Finally accepting, although reluctantly, that for better of worse some bizarre happening had tumbled her back through time to the place and era she had most dearly longed for, she was at first panic-stricken.

But when she learned that Will Salter was an armourer in the service of a wealthy English knight, and that this knight was enlisted in the army that Pierre de Lusignan, King of Cyprus, was raising to drive the Mamalukes out of the Holy Land, she realized that her longed-for miracle had, in some occult fashion, been granted her. She recalled with foreboding the old adage, Be careful what you pray for – it may be given unto you!

Practical worries assailed her. How was she to exist, misplaced in time and space? How would she support herself? She examined the small pile of possessions set out meticulously on the stool beside her pallet. Her watch had not survived the transition, but her jewellery – locket, earrings, ring and bracelet – was intact. How fortunate that her vanity had prompted her to wear her "baubles", as Papa called her golden trinkets, to impress Daphne Fielden. The gold should pay her way for a while.

No one could have treated her more kindly than Roberga and Will, but she felt she could not impose on her new friends indefinitely. They did their best to convince her, in view of her light-headed babblings of a terrible storm, that she must have been swept overboard from a passing ship. Her claim to have come from the future was dismissed as the feverish delusions of a temporarily deranged mind. Until she became accustomed to it, Lucy found their English, even mixed with some basic French, hard to understand, so she gave up talking of her past (future?) to anyone, save the young Corsican fisherman who, to her surprise, believed every word she told him. Indeed, he insisted that since it was he who had found her, cast up at dawn upon a deserted beach, Fate had obviously destined their meeting so she should marry him, then and there!

Attractive though she found the young Corsican, she was convinced that her incredible journey through space and time was for the express purpose of uniting her with her Crusader. She tried to explain this to Lionallo, but he merely retorted, "And I know the miracle was for me – I knew it the moment I looked into your eyes!" Not all her protests, arguments or denials could change his mind one whit. He stood by his guns. Fate had cast her into his arms, and sooner or late she would know it was so.

"And I trust it will be sooner," he grinned. "I am not a man of unlimited patience!"

3

W hat is it?" mumbled Lucy, rousted from slumber by Roberga's excited chatter as she vigorously shook her young guest into wakefulness.

"Sir Edward! Sir Edward is coming to see you, that's what! Do wake up, Lucy! You must hurry and dress. You cannot receive him in your shift!"

Lucy had already inquired about Sir Edward, learning, to her intense relief, that although for the moment he was absent from Famagusta, he was indeed on the island. She sat up abruptly.

"Sir Edward? Sir Edward Estur? Coming here?"

"Yes! Yes!" Roberga almost shouted with impatience. "He arrived home last night. My Will's master told him about you, and that you come from his parish. He sent his page to beg permission to call on you. I told the lad, 'Yes.' Hurry! Hurry!"

"Oh, dear! Mercy be with us!" wailed Lucy. "Do help me dress, Roberga, my sweet."

She rolled out of bed and a willing Roberga helped her into a pretty blue gown, chosen from the charitable offerings donated by some of the ladies of the court who had heard of the English girl's plight. Roberga brushed and combed her patient's rippling russet curls, letting them fall like a shimmering cloak around her shoulders, pinning the hair back from her face with a pair of her own carved bone combs. If hair was worn down, she told Lucy, it must fall free. Plaited hair was always pinned around the head or stuffed into gold net crespines. She stood back to admire her handiwork.

"You look lovely."

"Do you really think so?" Lucy was suddenly timid. "Do you suppose he will think so?"

"Sir Edward? He will worship at your feet," declared Roberga, catching her hand and leading her to finally meet the gallant knight who had for so long held her girlish heart in thrall.

Lucy had to admit that Sir Edward's limp, sandy hair, round, freckled face, and shy naiveté were hardly what she had envisioned, but the graciousness with which he promptly placed his purse, his sturdy right arm, and his innocent heart at her disposal was most gratifying.

"My deepest regret, my dear lady," he told her, bashfully, "Is that I was not here to greet you, on your unexpected arrival." That was certainly one way of referring to her sudden eruption into this strange world of her romantic fancies, Lucy thought! He, too, spoke in French, which she recalled was the court language of nearly all Europe, including England, in the fourteenth century.

"Being somewhat bored with the inactivity here, I journeyed to Nicosia to visit and gossip with old friends. Now that I am returned, I am determined that you shall lack for nothing that I am able to provide for your comfort and well being." He waved both her doubts and her thanks aside, assuring her that it was no more than his bounden duty, as well as the epitome of pleasure, to protect and serve a lady in distress. All the more so, since that lady came from his own parish. Moreover, he brought with him, addressed to the Lady Lucy, a request, nay, a Royal Command, from Her Most Gracious Majesty, Eleanor, Queen of Cyprus and Jerusalem, to take up her abode among the Ladies of the Court – an invitation he was sure would be seconded by King Peter on his return to the kingdom. The King, she learned, had been absent for two years attempting to drum up support and attract more recruits for the holy cause to which he was devoting his life. Pierre de Lusignan devoutly believed that he was chosen of God to rescue the Holy Land from the occupying Infidel.

Lucy was received by Her Majesty with formal kindliness, and soon discovered that she was an object of intense curiosity, not only to the Queen but to the entire court. In an environment that thrived on speculation and rumour, her dramatic arrival on the island had provided them with an endless, and prolific, source of gossip and conjecture. The fact that Sir Edward had taken her under his protection, and that she claimed to come from his own home parish, added a certain spice to the theories and assumptions of the court. Lucy found her company very much in demand. She was perfectly willing to answer their questions, as far as she was able.

Lucy had long given up hope of having her true story believed by anyone but Lionallo. She contented herself with insisting that she had lost all memory of how and why she had come to be there. It was presumed that she had been on a ship that had been lost without trace off the coast of Cyprus, casting her fortuitously ashore in Famagusta Bay, which everyone supposed had been her intended destination.

In spite of her scandalized denials, it was also taken for granted that she and Edward had been lovers in England. She could never convince them that they had never met before, even though she pointed out that, considering the years that had elapsed since the knight had left his native land, she would have been only a babe at the time.

Estur himself was the soul of knightly chivalry, so no one cared to repeat the slander in his hearing, and Lucy did not choose to inform him. She wanted no duels fought on her behalf! Her hero's behaviour to her was beyond all things irreproachable, and she was thrilled to be the recipient of his courteously romantic attentions. He and his fortune, he repeatedly assured her, were hers to command, assuming, over her worried protests, full responsibility for all her financial needs. Secretly, she was extremely relieved, since, save for her jewellery and the one golden guinea Mama had always made her carry in case of an emergency, she was at *point-non-plus*, pockets entirely empty. She had been under grave apprehension as to how she was to survive, penniless, in this strange situation into which, *bon gré, mal gré*, she had been hurled.

When he shyly made his tentative offer of marriage, Lucy had accepted. Even though he was not exactly as she had imagined, he was charming and lovable and, after all, she had been devoted to him for simply ages, hadn't she? Of course, as he diffidently explained, it would be some time before the wedding could actually take place. He would be bound by his vows of celibacy until he returned from His Majesty's Crusade against the Mamalukes in the Holy Land.

Lucy assured him that she would willingly wait. She was in no hurry, and since she was here, where she had so often declared she wanted to be, she was going to make the most of her opportunity to experience the adventure of a Crusade. When the time came, she would insist on accompanying Sir Edward to the wars. It was not unusual for women to join their men folk on a military expedition. Many high born ladies, she knew, had travelled with earlier Crusades. Richard Coeur de Leon's lady Berengaria was an illustrious example. Like many Regency ladies, her own aunt had travelled to Portugal, where her husband had served in the Peninsula wars against Bonaparte. Now she, Lucy Lightfoot, was determined to follow the drum. Whatever would the Vicar think of that? she wondered, with a slightly hysterical giggle. Poor Mr. Worsley!

Thinking of Henry Worsley brought memories of Papa, and Mama. She truly grieved for the loss of her parents and friends, but, in the back of her mind, she could not bring herself to believe that her situation was really permanent. One fine morning she would wake up and find that this was all a weird and wonderful dream; even as now her earlier life seemed to be fading into the misty reaches of imagination, so she would explore this new life to the full while she had the chance.

Only when she talked with Lionallo did her old memories sharpen into reality. No one else, not even Roberga, could be convinced that they were anything more than feverish hallucinations caused by her illness.

Sir Edward, having been so long away from his home, was naturally most anxious to hear any news she could give him, concerning his old acquaintances and neighbourhood. To satisfy his curiosity, she had to stretch her ingenuity to its limits. Fortunately, she had always enjoyed her history lessons and the historical novels among the books her father was accustomed to read to her and her mother as they worked at their embroidery on winter evenings. She found that she could chat most convincingly about world events and the wars in France, even slipping in little anecdotes about the Prince of Wales – the Black Prince, as her history book had called him. But she had to improvise when giving him "local" news.

Luckily, descendants of some of the old families still lived in the Gatcombe area, some even answering to the same Christian names as their forbears. Thus, calling discreetly on her fertile imagination, she was able to gossip quite easily about the Worsleys, Firebraces, and other ancient dynasties. She could also tell him that the church incumbent that he had known, William de Hull, had been replaced by Mr. Thomas

Lambyn. Some good had come of the time she had spent searching old records for information on her Crusader!

In return, flattered by her genuine interest in all his travels and campaigns, Sir Edward entertained her with tales of his own adventures, when, with the permission of his own monarch, England's third Edward, he had fought under de Lusignan on an earlier crusade in Asia Minor.

It was because he had performed so creditably in the battle for Adalia that the King had inducted him into his own elite corps as a Companion of the Order of the Sword. This she learned from his fellows knights, Edward being too modest to admit to more than mere duty. That was, for Edward, the highest of honours. Only those knights who had distinguished themselves with exceptional courage and chivalry in the King's service in the Holy Land were admitted to the Order, and he displayed his insignia to Lucy with shy pride.

Lucy immediately recognized the sword. She had seen it so many times before, clasped in the hand of his wooden image, in the tiny church of Saint Olave's back home in Gatcombe.

"It is called a misericord," her knight told her, as she once again rubbed an exploring finger over the smooth, gleaming crystal in the hilt. "The stone is a chrysoberyl." He added what she already knew.

Lucy suppressed a shudder and quickly removed her hand. Misericord meant Mercy of God. She had read about such daggers but had not realized that this was one. Not so much an actual combat weapon, its main use was to quickly dispatch a fallen foe or, if the occasion warranted it, to mercifully relieve a fatally wounded comrade from prolonged suffering. With an inward shiver, she wondered how often Edward had been forced to use it.

"It is a thing of beauty, is it not?" Edward sought her admiration, unaware of her sudden revulsion. "It holds great power. It is not as other swords. See … " He stroked the elaborate setting. "This ornamentation is crafted from true lodestone, which bears strong magic. Then there is the jewel – and no one knows what alchemy may be locked within such a crystal. There are those philosophers who reason that if, under certain circumstances, such a stone could be shattered, the occult forces released might well set the universe a tremble."

"I can believe it!" Lucy recollected the lightning playing on the jewel just before her violent transmission from her own time to this. She listened with only half an ear as Edward showed her the remaining articles of the Order – the Silver Collar, and the Silver Buckle, inscribed with the motto *C'est pour loiauté maintenir*, thinking him rather vague as to its meaning, although he waxed quite eloquent regarding the history of the Order.

"His Majesty was given his Quest by a vision, imparted to him at Stavrovouni when he was a very young man," he went on to explain. From the wistful look in his eyes, it was evident that his innocent soul envied his liege lord that marvelous spiritual experience. "In the Church of the Holy Cross. That was when he was inspired to found an Order of true knights who would follow him loyally on his life's work, driving the Infidels out of the Holy Land. I am one of those oath-bound to serve him until his quest is achieved," he finished, pride beaming from his face.

"And you will return with honour," his lady assured him, remembering, gladly, that he had returned in the end to live long and happily in his native land. Then it occurred to her that there was no tomb for her beside his, in that far distant future, when she had first given him – would give him – her admiration. "Admiration?" Now why had her mind balked at saying "love"? She was very fond of Edward, she admonished herself, belligerently. No – not just fond. She loved him. She was sure of that. Didn't she have the same tender feelings, when she looked into his doting blue eyes, that stirred in her heart when she held Roberga's youngest in her arms, its tiny face nestled into her throat, and its small, bald head thrust damply under her chin?

That was love! Not the unsettling, sometimes antagonistic excitement that was so disturbing to her self-possession whenever Lionallo made his silly claim that Fate had destined them for one another.

Lucy had good cause to bless her father's indulgence that had allowed her to make the most of her linguistic gifts. With her fluency in French, which seemed to be the common language of the Cypriote Court, and Italian as well, she was able to converse with the ladies of the men recruited from Sicily and Italy by the King's agent, John of Verona. At first the accent and some of the antique words gave her trouble but she had a quick ear and soon adjusted to the differences.

For a while, Lucy felt she was participating in a *Grand Bal Masqué*.

But as the weeks went by the strange clothing she and her new companions wore seemed commonplace and unremarkable. She became accustomed to the rush-strewn floors of the Great Hall and the long table where the whole household took their meals. At the head, ensconced in a throne-like chair at the High Table, sat King Peter's brother Prince Hugh, who was in charge of the kingdom as Regent while His Majesty travelled abroad. Beside him was Eleanor, Peter's queen. With them sat their favourites and more important members of the court, while the rest of the establishment occupied backless benches, according to rank, at long tables stretching the length of the hall.

Lucy sat with the court ladies, while Sir Edward ate with his fellow knights at their own table where they discussed hunting, weaponry, and similar topics of masculine interest. They devoured huge chunks of meat as they talked, occasionally tossing orts and bones to their hounds, who had the run of the hall. She wondered what Mama would have thought of the table manners. There were no forks. One simply gnawed on a bone, or gripped a chunk of meat between one's teeth, and sawed off the excess with a small sharp knife. Lucy owned a very pretty personal knife with an embossed silver handle, a gift from Lionallo, who had acquired it by barter from an Arab trader. She soon became quite adept in its use. It took longer to get used to the fleas that leapt out from among the rushes and attacked her ankles!

Although she now lived at Court, Roberga remained her close friend and Lucy managed to visit her almost daily. Often she might meet Lionallo Momellino, who would creep up behind her, catch her up in his brawny arms, and swing her dizzily around, before planting a solid buss on her cheek.

"Ha! My Star of the Sea!" he would salute her. Her scolding protests he laughed away, insisting, "I found you. You belong to me, like it or not."

Lucy did not tell him that at home, in her own time, such behavior was so disgraceful that, if they were seen, they would be expected to marry immediately! She had no wish to arm him with another weapon to aid his peculiar courtship! It was in vain that she reminded him of her betrothal to Sir Edward. He merely grinned his annoying grin and said, "We shall see."

4

Philippa L'Mesurier, a cheerful French girl of her own age, had appointed herself Lucy's court mentor and confidant. When Sir Edward insisted that his betrothed must have a wardrobe at least equal to that of her new companions, Philippa over-rode Lucy's qualms and, to Estur's gratitude and satisfaction, declared that she would make sure that his lady's apparel should be second to none.

For the next few days, life became a hectic round of measuring, fitting, and choosing of colours and fabrics. Lucy was astonished at the quality and variety of the materials, and found it delectably difficult to choose among the vibrant hues, the magnificent oriental silks and the velvets displayed for her benefit. Eventually, with Philippa's urging, she was as fashionably outfitted as any other lady of her acquaintance. If that antidote Daphne Fielden could see her now!

Edward was charmed when she wore her new gown for his approval – a daffodil yellow kirtle beneath a leaf green bliaut of fine-spun wool. "You remind me of Springtime in our home copse," he told her as he bowed elegantly over her hand, and touched his lips to her fingertips.

"Oh! Did you gather daffodils there too?" she asked, nostalgia sparking her eyes with unbidden tears.

"Aye, and sweet violets, and primroses by the brook," he sighed. "But none so fair or sweet as you, my lady."

Lucy blushed becomingly. She knew the actual words and form were merely standard courtly flattery, such as every knight was educated to use, but Edward's face was an open book. He was totally unable to mask his true feelings. It was plain to see that he meant every word of his chivalrous little speech and she was touched.

Scandal was rife and morals tended to be lax in the Cypriote court, and the Queen's ladies kept a rather shocked Lucy up-to-date on the latest *on-dit*. Philippa in particular imparted choice bits of gossip often adding her own slightly wicked speculations just to enjoy her friend's scandalized embarrassment. Lucy, born at the end of the Regency decade, knew that it was tacitly accepted that gentlemen should have *petits plaisirs* and extra-marital affairs, but not, definitely not, ladies!

"But how can men have lovers if women may not?" Philippa was genuinely perplexed. Lucy was not too well-informed on the subject, as she was not supposed to be aware of such ladies' existence, but at school there were always girls who knew all sorts of interesting things, and if one kept quietly in the background, when Mama's friends came to take tea – well, one could accidentally overhear some rather peculiar anecdotes. But she did know that there was a class of women who accepted the "protection" of gentlemen and were rewarded with jewellery and other expensive gifts. Not, she hastened to explain, that she had ever met such a woman. Such persons were not admitted to respectable society, where they were referred to as ladybirds, light skirts, barques of frailty, and Cyprians. Odso! She'd better not mention that last referent in present company!

"Such creatures are quite beyond the pale, you must know," she continued.

"I understand that," agreed the French girl. "But it seems unfair, when the peccadilloes of married ladies are carefully ignored."

"Surely not!" Lucy was aghast. "That would be adultery!"

"Pah! If one's spouse does not find out, and no one is hurt, where is the harm? Where have you been hiding all your life, *ma petite innocente, hein*? Everyone does it. Even the Queen!"

Lucy was scandalized. "I cannot believe that. Not Her Majesty!"

"I assure you, *ma chère amie*," Philippa insisted. "Everyone."

"Don't tell me your Mama … ?" Lucy, tongue in cheek, suggested, wickedly.

"*Maman*! Philippa turned a face, scarlet with outrage, to meet Lucy's teasing giggles. "Oh you monster!" she grinned. "You know that *Maman* is all that is proper, in every way. She would no more think of betraying Papa than she would walk to Mass in her shift! She could never be anything but a true wife."

"Nor can I imagine your dear Papa playing the giddy goat," chuckled Lucy. Philippa joined in her laughter. "But seriously, I am sure you must be mistaken about Her Majesty."

"Hah! Then you must be blind! Do you mean to tell me that you have never noticed the rapport between the Queen and John de Morphou?"

"You mean the Count of Roucha?" Lucy queried, disbelief sharpening her tones. "Surely you are joking. They would not dare – the King ..."

"Marie's Mercy, Lucy!" Philippa clucked, impatiently. "The King himself is no monk, I assure you! He has at least two mistresses travelling in his entourage."

But I thought he adored Queen Eleanor. Did you not tell me that he carries her shift with him at all times?"

"True -- but what has that to do with apples? He is big, handsome and virile, and attractive enough to lure any woman. Even if he were not Royal, he is so handsome and romantic that there are few females who could resist him." Philippa sighed wistfully. "They say he is a lover *sans pareil.*"

"Philippa! Surely you would not ... " Lucy was horrified.

Philippa shook her head, with a rueful laugh. "Oh, no! Not I! I have no wish to die an early death. It would be a race, between *Maman* and Eleanor!" She laughed at Lucy's bewilderment. "Our Lady Queen is not one to allow another to trespass on her territory with impunity." Clapping her hand over her mouth, she looked hastily around, suddenly aware of her rattling tongue. She lowered her voice. "But let us go for a walk, and enjoy the fresh air."

Once outside, the French girl held her tongue until they reached the shore. As they wandered along the sands, looking perfunctorily for shells, she harked back to their earlier conversation.

"It is well known that Eleanor is violently jealous of any woman King Pierre favours. Ill fortune often befalls them, especially if they are of lower rank or unprotected. Several young women to whom he has paid attention have fallen victim to strange maladies. At least one has died, and they say that others have mysteriously disappeared, though none speak of such things openly. So far, she has not dared to harm either Echive de Scandelion or Joanna l'Aleman, his two favourite paramours.

Did she so, there is no knowing how hard His Majesty's wrath might strike." She sighed. "They are both so very beautiful, one can hardly blame him."

Lucy gasped. "Not blame him? It is scandalous!"

Philippa shrugged. "*Chacun à son goût!*" she muttered. "But perhaps you will believe that I speak truth, when you see Pierre de Lusignan for yourself."

"Enough of this fustian! It is too glorious a day for such gloomy nonsense!" Lucy caught her friend by the hand, and they ran happily along the strand, until they came to a small rock outcropping. Scrambling to the top, they lay prostrate on the sparse, sun-warmed grass, resting their chins on folded hands.

"Tell me about your home. You have not always lived in Cyprus, have you?" Lucy was truly curious about her new friend's background.

"*Non, non!* We are from Montpellier. We came here only a few months before you. It was rather horrible, at first," Philippa muttered, with a shudder. "It was terribly dreary and empty. Not a lot of people around — not even *des paysans*. On account of the plague, you know. It came two years running to Cyprus. It started here, in Famagusta, and spread to Nicosia. We were lucky. We just missed it." She looked into Lucy's disturbed gray eyes, mistaking shock for fear. "But do not be afraid, *ma chère Lucy*. All is well, now. I have heard that the Regent was very capable. He ordered masses, and processions, and prayers for the dead and dying, and supervised all the hospitals and burials and everything. He's a very able man. Things would have been much worse but for him."

"Why did you come here in the first place? Surely your Papa is not a military man?"

Philippa laughed. "Papa a warrior? How droll! No. You must know that for years, ever since anyone can remember, Montpellier has traded through Cyprus. We are peaceful people and have always been on the best of terms with everyone, not like the Sicilians and the Genoese, always stirring up trouble. All we want is our fair share of honest trade. A large sum of money has always been held in trust here, as a guarantee of our honorable intentions. But things were not as they should have been. We were not accorded our due rights, so, when King Pierre came to France last year, our citizens petitioned him."

What happened?" Lucy's eyes sparkled with eager curiosity. "Did he promise to look into the situation?"

"More than that. Much more." The French girl was triumphant. "He not only confirmed the agreements we have always had, he gave us new privileges – and protection, too!"

"Oh, I am so glad!" Lucy was surprised to find that if Peter of Cyprus had not been so just and generous, she would have been decidedly disappointed! Apart from the stories of his amorous adventures, which the narrators seemed to think added to the stature of his reputation rather than otherwise, she had heard his praises sung continually since she had come to his kingdom.

"I don't understand all the where-to-fores and here-in-afters, and all that roundaboutation, but certainly Papa and his friends were very excited about the whole affair. All I know is that it was settled that our Consul should have a lodge here, in Famagusta, and that he could appoint deputies. Papa is one of those deputies."

"How fortunate for me!" Lucy gave her companion an affectionate hug. "How lonely and miserable I should be were it not for you and Roberga. But tell me, do. Is the King really as handsome as they say? Or do people speak of him as they do, merely because he is Royalty?"

"They do not in the least exaggerate. You must understand," confessed Philippa, "that I have never really met him. But I have seen him, quite close, riding through Montpellier, and he is everything a king should be. He looks regal. Exceeding tall. He stands quite above most other men. The shoulders so broad, so muscular. Then there is the hair, of a blond that is like gold in the sun. I speak the truth!" she interrupted herself, indignantly, offended by Lucy's amused giggles.

"Of course you do, dear Philippa," Lucy soothed. "I beg your pardon – please go on."

Her friend regarded her with suspicion, but, caught up in her romantic recollections, continued. "But it is the eyes that are so *magnifique*. They are of the bluest blue one can imagine!" She clasped her hands, and gazed heavenward, with a dramatic sigh. "Truly, he is a *chevalier sans pareil*."

"I have heard that Pope Urban calls him the Athlete of God."

"Indeed, he does, and rightly so," replied Philippa.

The English girl stood up, silently gazing upon the deep blue

Mediterranean Sea. This rocky island was so different from the one she called home – the Wight, with its green, green grass, flaming gorse, and snow-white, wind-dancing moon daisies, where one could stand on the windswept heights of the downs and view the whole diamond-shaped expanse of the Island. You could see from Saint Catherine's Point, at the southernmost tip, to the swift flowing Solent channel, bright with gamboling "white horses", forcing its way between the Wight and the English mainland; and from Ryde in the east to the treacherous Needles, lying viciously in wait for unwary mariners, off the multi-coloured cliffs of Alum Bay on the jutting west coast.

She was jerked summarily out of her daydreams by the sight of a well-known vessel plying toward the land.

"There is Lion's boat," she exclaimed "He has returned!"

"The Dolphin? You are mistaken, *ma petite choux*. That is not the boat of your *bon ami*."

"Of course it is! Lucy was quite alert, now. "I would know the cut of her jib anywhere, anytime."

"*Non*! This time you are in error. This is not the 'Dolphin'. Do you not see the name on her bow? She is called the 'Stella Maris'."

Lucy gasped and felt the warm blood rush to her face, turning her cheeks scarlet. It was Lionallo's boat. She had no doubt about that. Every line of the craft was too familiar for her to have been mistaken. How many times had she stood on the shore, searching the horizon for this same ship to bring him back to harbour only to dash off, once assured of his safety, to Roberga's home the moment she sighted it. There she could be legitimately visiting her friend, unsuspected of timing her visit to coincide with his arrival. He would not know how much she missed his comforting presence when he was gone, nor how thankful she was for his safe return.

It was not that she had more than a sisterly affection for the cheerful fisherman – that was only natural, was it not? After all, it had been he, her first friend in this strange and alien world, who had rescued her on that dreadful day of terror. But still, there was no need to give him ideas! He was impudent enough, as it was – in no need of unnecessary encouragement!

"Stella Maris." That meant Star of the Sea. Lionallo had renamed his boat for her! Suddenly, Lucy had no wish to meet him in Philippa's company. She did not want her new friend to witness the ebullient greeting she knew she could expect from Lionallo – the incurably romantic French girl would certainly read more into it than mere friendship!

"Come! We shall be too late to watch the squires practising if we do not hurry," she urged, grabbing Philippa's arm, to hustle her back to the palace.

"*Arrête! Arrête!*" gasped Philippa, breathlessly, as she was dragged mercilessly along the littoral. "Since when have you been so interested in the squires? You have never wanted to watch before when I have asked you."

"But Sir Edward will be there today, I collect. I am sure I heard him promise Geoffrey that he would give him some personal coaching this forenoon." Lucy mentally crossed her fingers, praying her guardian angel would help her out.

Her plea was answered. When they reached the jousting field, where the weapons masters trained the pages and squires, Sir Edward was indeed there watching the proceedings with several of his friends. He smiled shyly as he noticed the two young women and came toward them, followed by Sir Guy Bouvier, who was know to have a *tendresse* for the Lady Philippa. After expressing their pleasure at the ladies' interest in the proceedings, they provided them with seating, by the simple process of upending a wooden bench in a corner of the practice yard that was noisily occupied by a few boisterous young pages. After some courteous chit-chat, the knights excused themselves to attend to their duties, and the two friends settled down to watch, each primarily interested in her own admirer and his protégé.

There was tremendous activity all over the field. In one area the young pages, in the charge of an assistant weapons master, were valiantly menacing one another with wooden swords with tremendous energy and great enjoyment. Such a welcome change from fetching and carrying for the court ladies and serving their masters at table on bended knee – all part of the education the little boys had been sent away from their parents to acquire under the supervision of foster parents. The custom of fostering served more than one purpose. A foster father was in honor bound to educate his charge in all the knightly virtues, physical, social, and spiritual, under a discipline he might not receive from over-fond parents in his own home. There was also a political significance. With his vulnerable children scattered like hostages among his neighbors, a truculent or disgruntled Lord would think carefully before giving offense.

Lucy and Philippa concentrated their attention on the section where the squires were working out. At the moment, Geoffrey and Sir Guy's squire, Onfroi, were attacking the quintain, a contraption that hung like a balance from a tall pole. On one side of the crossbar hung an effigy of the Sultan, the Christians' avowed foe, and on the other a bag of straw. The intention was to ride at top speed down the course, hit the Sultan and carry on to spear a ring suspended near the end of the run. But there was a catch – when the target was hit, the crossbar spun around. If the rider was not speedy and skillful, he was soundly thumped by the counterweight.

The two girls watched both young men successfully negotiate the quintain, although neither managed to collect the ring. Their mentors strode purposefully to the other end of the course and could be seen talking earnestly to their respective squires, who paid deferential heed to the advice given them before returning to their places in line for a return tilt at the Sultan.

This time, both Geoffrey and Onfroi assaulted the target with much more expertise, but only Geoffrey triumphantly hooked the iron ring, to the discomfiture of his rival. The English lad's understandable inclination to crow over his friend was promptly nipped in the bud by his master. As Sir Edward pointed out, such taunting was not only unworthy of a gentleman but extremely foolhardy. It was most unwise to offend a man who might be in a position, in some future fray, to save one's life. He who aspired to be a true knight should therefore practise courtesy and chivalry at all times. The young gallant was suitably apologetic and abashed. Onfroi was generous in his forgiveness, but could not himself refrain from a little sly teasing, which resulted in some rambunctious horseplay as their respective knights returned to their ladies.

The two couples watched with interest, with occasional cries of apprehension from the females, as the youths were set to sword practice. Their weapons, although blunted, were the genuine article, not the wooden counterfeits used by the small pages, who were gathered at one side of the yard, avidly watching and cheekily criticizing their seniors.

Both knights kept a sharp eye on their own squires and after a while, Sir Edward consigned the women to the care of a very willing Sir Guy, and made his own way onto the field.

They saw him remove his immaculate tunic, and hand it to an awed and honoured little page, who looked ready to guard it as fiercely as the robes of King Peter himself. Lucy was surprised by the muscular arms and torso thus revealed. Edward's apparent slenderness was deceptive. He had neither the powerful breadth of shoulder nor the thickness of biceps and neck that she had seen Lionallo display as he worked bare-chested and barefoot on his boat, but Edward's leaner build and corded muscles gave promise of equal strength and stamina.

When she saw him take up his great sword, she understood how this could be so. Continuous exercise with weighty weapons, and the wear-ing of heavy mail over a period of years, could not help but develop the considerable strength such a life would demand. She wished she could hear his conversation with Geoffrey as he engaged the lad in swordplay, turning away the youth's every thrust with what was obviously gentle criticism and knowledgeable advice. She noticed that not many of the knights were as conscientious as Estur. Although there probably were occasions when they gave their dependents personal attention, for the most part they appeared content to leave their instruction in the hands of the weapons masters, rather than engaging in such sweaty and grub-by exercise themselves.

As Lucy looked about her, one of the onlookers in particular caught her attention. For some time she had been aware of his brooding gaze. When her eyes met his, he neither looked away nor bowed in acknowl-edgment. A frisson of alarm shivered down her spine, as she quickly lowered her own eyes. She decided to ask Sir Guy who the hard-eyed blond man was, but when she looked again he was gone. Chiding her-self for stupidity, she shrugged off the feeling of foreboding from her mind, and returned her attention to the field.

After the lesson, Sir Edward returned to suggest that, after he had made himself presentable, the four of them might go riding, a proposi-tion hailed with enthusiasm, especially by Lucy. She was an accom-plished horsewoman, and secretly rather despised the gentle palfrey her knight had given her as being most suitable for a lady. What she hun-gered for was a heady, uninhibited, and unladylike gallop on her beloved chestnut hunter Dandy. Poor Dandy! What had become of him? Had he survived the storm? But how could he, when he didn't even exist yet?

As they ambled through the bridle paths of the nearby woods, Edward Estur mused upon the blessing heaven had suddenly seen fit to cast upon him. He could, of course, in common with every man who had been educated as a knight, compose a few flattering lines of verse to honour a lady, and accompany himself reasonably well on the lute as he sang a love ballad. But he had always been far too shy and retiring to actually press his suit on any particular woman. His vow of celibacy, taken for the duration of Pierre de Lusignan's crusade, was actually a Godsend to him, as an unassailable excuse from paying particular attention to any one lady. Fearless on the battlefield, he had often wondered, wistfully, if he would ever be able to summon up the courage to seek a wife, although he supposed that a marriage of convenience could be arranged for him. But now, out of the blue, Heaven had sent him the Lady Lucy. Honour had induced him to offer his protection, and his name, to a distressed lady from his own parish in a precarious situation. That she should be possessed, not only of youth and beauty but also a pleasant, lively nature and a disposition to enjoy his company and, even more incredible, an apparent fondness for his person, was more than any man had a right to expect. Truly he was thrice blessed! Tonight he would light a candle to his family's patron saint, Olaf, and one to the Blessed Virgin as well!

5

Quietly Lucy rose from the bed she shared with her French friend in the large sleeping room assigned to the junior ladies of the court, and made her way to the guarderobe. During her first days in this era, she had been appalled by the primitive sanitary arrangements. It was not so much the actual plumbing system. After all, even in her own time, sanitation for most people was still quite primitive. It was the alternative for toilet paper that so disgusted her – a curved piece of wood, that Roberga called a gomph-stick, and Philippa a *torche-cul*, kept in a basket! She had soon worked out her own modification. There was scrap cloth a-plenty available, linen, cotton and wool, often bundled up and sold to the rag pickers. Some of this she appropriated and snipped into small squares to cover the business end of the stick, hoping that no plugging of the drains, which ran down through the thick stone walls, would result.

How fortunate that some of the upper class ladies enjoyed frequent baths, often making the occasion a social event. Tub-like wooden baths, provided with stools and often with gay little canopies as well, were kept in a room near the kitchens. Lucy's modesty was sorely tried at first, but she soon began to enjoy the luxury of soaking in warm, rose-scented water, listening to the latest court *on-dit*. The soap, though, left much to be desired. Made in the court workshops from mutton fat, wood ash, and soda, it was very soft and had little cleansing power. But Dame Agathé, in charge of the still room, had taken quite a fancy to Lucy. The older woman appreciated that, if an herb must be picked at the full of the moon or, conversely, at the dark of that same moon or exactly at dawn, Lucy could always be relied upon for company. It was comforting not to be alone on such excursions. And so she was not averse to sparing *la p'tite Anglais* a small bag of meal and rose petals with which to scrub herself, and a tankard of ale for the weekly laundering of her hair.

Lucy thoroughly cleaned her teeth with a "brush" made from a shredded willow twig, then polished them with a woollen rag. She had no wish to lose any of them as early as some of the ladies she knew here! This morning she would not risk any of her new gowns. She was going to the shore on an errand she considered pleasant and that would please Dame Agathé, who had a multitude of uses for the seaweed she would gather in the wake of the ebbing tide. She chose an old green morning gown from the dresses the court ladies contributed before Sir Edward had provided her with a wardrobe of her own. Her hair covered with a bright red kerchief, she crept stealthily from the room and on to the kitchens, where she picked up a basket and a chunk of manchet bread, coaxed from a bleary eyed scullion, and skipped lightly on her way.

A moon-pale sun was slowly burning away the early morning mist as she wandered along the wet sand, seeking the particular weeds she required. With a small crow of satisfaction, she seized upon a clump of purple dulse, a familiar delicacy from her own experience. Sprinkled with grated cheese and baked to a crisp, as her mother had prepared it, it made a wonderfully toothsome snack. She speculated as to how the French woman would use it. For medicinal purposes, perhaps, or for a dye, or maybe it would be sent to the kitchens to be added to soups or stews. It did not take long to fill her basket with the pick of the tide's choicest bounty, but Lucy did not want to return at once to the palace. She relished the time spent away from the constant clatter and chatter of the crowded buildings.

Turning from the beach she climbed a slight incline to a sandy elevation of a few feet above the shoreline. There she sat, hugging her knees, gazing out at the Mediterranean, free from mist now, blue and silver in the bright sunlight. Below she could see the "white horses" as they sped across the waves, whipped into sparkling action by the same stiff breeze that tugged at her hair, urging her to pull off the confining scarf. This was her favourite retreat. It was here that she came to indulge in sad memories, and tears of regret for her lost life. Not that she was truly unhappy, she told herself. Wasn't this the where and when she had so often insisted that she wished to be?

But not like this, her inner self lamented. She had never wanted to leave Mama and Papa behind! Nor Marjorie, and Dandy, and all her other friends and relatives. Nor all the things and places she knew and loved. Right now, she wanted to be standing on a grass-topped chalk cliff, with the white capped Solent whipped into heaving gray-green pyramids by a damp salt wind, and the misty outline of the New Forest lining the far shore. She wanted scented soap, and soft kid boots, and afternoon tea in fragile china cups, and ices in the pastry shop! She wanted long white gloves, and fine lawn underwear, and beaux to flirt with, behind chickenskin fans, in a properly genteel manner. She wanted to dance civilized dances, waltzes and quadrilles, and ride to church, and make courtesy calls in a glossy, well-sprung carriage behind her father's fine gray team. And none of that was ever going to happen again, she knew with dreadful certainty.

Her head drooped forward onto her knees as despair overwhelmed her, sending shuddering sobs through her huddled frame while she grieved for her loss. Absorbed in her own misery she did not hear Lionallo's approach, and so was totally unaware of his presence until he dropped down behind her. Drawing her back against his chest, he gently rocked her, murmuring soft Italian words of comfort and endearment. With a valiant effort she managed to regain her self control.

Ashamed to be discovered in her grief – for she had always endeavoured to hide her small attacks of unhappiness from others – she would have apologized for her weakness. But correctly guessing the cause of her sorrow, he softly hushed her, and turning her face toward him, wiped away her tears with the heel of his hand. With a sigh, she laid her head on his chest. How his heart thundered against her cheek. He was strong, she realized, not only physically, and somehow he was sharing that strength with her. She snuggled closer, as he lifted her chin to brush her lips lightly with his own, then slowly deepened the kiss to a tender caress, loving and gentle, leaving her warmed and comforted.

"It is foolish of me, I know," she confessed, "but I do miss my father and mother, and it grieves me to think of how bitterly they must be sorrowing for me."

"Now that they are not!" Lionallo stated with such confidence, that Lucy felt insulted. Her parents would indeed be grief stricken! He laughed at her shocked expression, and added, "My Star – how can they possibly be mourning for you? They do not even exist, as yet. It will be almost five centuries before they can be born!"

"That is part of the whole horrible dilemma," groaned the girl. "If they do not exist, then I have never been born. So how can I be here, in this time and place?" She picked up her discarded kerchief, and scrubbed, vigorously, at her face.

Her companion considered, then dug into the pocket of his coarse seaman's smock to pull out an orange. He then drew a sheath knife from his belt. Lucy watched, as he carefully peeled the fruit from flower scar to stem, without a break. He held up the twisted strip of rind by one end, and asked, "What have I here?"

"A long piece of orange peel," was her pert reply.

"A spiral," he corrected her. "Now this is my theory. Let us suppose that time has a shape – that it too is spiral."

"Like the stairway to a church belfry, or to the top of the keep tower," put in Lucy, helpfully.

"Exactly! Now, say you were here." With the tip of his dagger, he indicated a point about three fourths of the way up the spiral. "There is a sudden, unnatural calamity, of tremendous magical force . . ."

She decided to ignore the word "magical", although even in the enlightened nineteenth century, there were still people who believed in magic. Lots of people claimed to know witches, and everyone knew that gypsies had dark powers. It was not wise to offend them, even though Papa laughed at such ideas, and teased Mama for her fears. But hadn't that gypsy woman foretold her of the very adventures that had now befallen her? "A far journey, a foreign land, far from here and now." Closing her eyes, Lucy could still see that strange dark face. "Two men to love you – one fair and mild, but a doughty warrior." Sir Edward, of course. "The other dark and wild, a man of the sea." Lionallo. And there was the demolished sword and its shattered crystal and lodestone, both supposed to contain terrific occult powers! There might be a perfectly rational explanation for her fantastic journey through space and time, but if there was she had no idea what it could be.

"The storm, and the eclipse, and the lightning bolt," she offered.

"It could be," the young Corsican agreed. "Then this supernatural force might have tilted the whole structure of time, by an infinitesimal fraction, toppling you down through the centre, to land on a lower level, in a different time and space. He touched the inside of the spiral further down on the loops, looking inquiringly at Lucy, seeking her opinion of his theory, and met her admiring gaze with his usual engaging grin.

"Lion!" He noted and approved of her abbreviation of his name. She always spoke to that Estur fellow very formally, addressing him as Sir Edward. "That is amazing! It does sound as good an explanation as any." Her smile faded. "But that could mean that I will never get back home. I shall never see Mama and Papa again." Her eyes filled, and he quickly grasped her hand.

"Ah, but you will!" He grinned mischievously. "See – we are here. But not forever." He traced the upward curve of the rind. "Time goes forward, and one day it will reach your century, and you will be born again, to your same parents. You must just have a little patience."

"Five hundred years worth of patience!" Lucy managed a small, tremulous laugh. "That is a long time to wait."

Lion shrugged. "A long time indeed." He paused a moment, regarding her obliquely before continuing. "You will give your parents joy, again, before you come tumbling back to me."

His words hit Lucy like a blow to the stomach. "Oh, no!" she gasped, white faced. ""You cannot mean that it will happen again!"

"It has happened," he pointed out. "For all we know, many times before, which may be why I have known, since the day I found you, that you were for me. It is our destiny. It is a story we shall tell our grandchildren, when we are too old to work, and sit in our garden of a summer evening."

"But there will be no grandchildren – not for you and me!" Indignation restored Lucy's spirits. "You know I am betrothed. If I am to have grandchildren, they will be Sir Edward Estur's."

His smug grin was infuriating. "We shall see, my Star. Fate sent you to me I shall not easily relinquish my claim."

Lucy picked up her basket, and lifted her chin, defiantly. "You have no claim on me, save that of friendship, and my gratitude for rescuing me, which will be yours forever." She marched off, stiff-spined, resisting an almost overwhelming urge to look back.

The young Corsican watched her go. He had followed her here, intending to press his claim to her hand, but found that he could not take advantage of her moment of sorrow and vulnerability. He sighed, lowering himself to the scant grass, picked up the scarf she had forgotten, and ran it idly through strong brown fingers. There would be other opportunities. He would make sure of that. In the meantime, he stretched out, supine, on the sun-warmed earth, covering his face with his darling's forgotten kerchief. Clasping his hands behind his head, he closed his eyes to dream of teasing that saucy little temper of hers to exasperation, before quenching its fire with passionate kisses, that would reduce her to pliant clay in his competent hands. A treasure such as his Stella Maris would be wasted on that chilly Englishman. That laggard could never give her, or draw from her, the excitement and the passion that he, a Corsican of Corsicans, could already feel pulsing between her and himself each time they met. Married to Estur, she would certainly be a faithful and affectionate wife – and find herself bored to distraction for the rest of her life. No. He had no misgivings. He knew, as surely as he knew that the sun would rise in the east tomorrow morning, that God, Fate, Providence, call it what you will, had sealed their twin destinies for all Eternity. A smile of anticipation lingered on his lips, as he drifted into contented slumber.

6

"A re you ready?" Lucy asked Philippa. They were planning an outing to the docks. There were so many interesting people and things to see there, when the trading ships from all over the world came into port. At least, as much of the world as was civilized in this century, Lucy reminded herself.

"I cannot make up my mind," the French girl fretted. "Shall I wear the red, or the blue, over this kirtle?"

"Oh the red by all means." advised Lucy. She knew her friend. Since Philippa would certainly reject her advice, and was already wearing the blue bliaut, much time would be saved. For good measure, she added, "The red gives you such a high colour – a good healthy glow."

"Does it really? Merciful saints! I have no wish to look like a *paysanne*," she frowned. "I think it had better be the blue." Catching Lucy's grin, the maid who had been assisting with their toilettes winked and hurriedly whipped the other gowns off to the guarderobe, where they were kept, on the assumption that the strong smell of ammonia would discourage the omnipresent fleas. Unfortunately, the clothes so stored did tend to smell rather unpleasant, so Lucy was in the habit of retrieving her choice for the day ahead of time, to be left in the draft of an open window for a while.

Now she was anxious to be on their way. "Come!" she cried. "We shall miss the fun!" She raced quickly down the stairs and out of the castle, collecting Geoffrey from the great hall where he waited to escort them.

The day's business was well under way, as they crossed the courtyard. Servants were holding impatient horses, while their masters chatted with friends and men at arms clanked about their duties with cheerful shouts.

A lovely day, thought Lucy, revelling in the warmth of the morning sunshine. She was about to say so aloud to Philippa when she saw him – the sombre stranger she had seen at the squires' practice. He was staring at her again, in that same offensive way. He did not look away when their eyes met, but inclined his head, a mere suggestion of a bow.

She shuddered. This man, she knew instinctively, was evil. Whoever he was, he bore her no good will. She forced herself to turn away. She was being ridiculous, of course. There was absolutely no reason to suspect the man just because he stared at her. But she had to know who he was.

"Don't let him see you looking," she murmured to Philippa, "but who is that man in the brown surcoat, next to the knight in green?"

Philippa peeked, discreetly. "I think his name is l'Amoureux. I have never met him."

By now they were through the gates, but had hardly left the castle before they met Lionallo with an empty basket slung over his shoulder. Obviously he had disposed of the last of his night's catch and was on his way back from the market.

He stopped to greet them. When he heard of their intentions, his familiar grin was replaced by a disapproving frown.

"No!" He objected, forcibly. "You must on no account go near the docks at this time. It is far too dangerous."

"Fustian!" snapped Lucy. How dared he dictate to her? He had no earthly right whatever to order her comings and goings! "We are merely going to watch the ships unloading. What possible danger can there be in that? And we have Geoffrey's protection."

"The Regent has business with the Genoese." The cryptic utterance was made to the young man accompanying them, rather than to the ladies. Geoffrey paled.

"Then you are indeed correct," he agreed. "This is no place for ladies." He began to shepherd them back the way they'd come, Philippa joining forces with him to overcome Lucy's irate protests. He was glad to see the Corsican fellow fall in behind them. He looked like a desirable backup to have in reserve if a tricky situation should arise.

Safely home, Lucy lingered behind Philippa and the squire, to demand that Lionallo explain his high-handed conduct.

"If you paid more attention to the real news, instead of frippery court gossip, you would have known better than to place yourself in such jeopardy, you foolish young witling!" was his less-than-flattering retort.

Lucy gasped. How dare he speak so to her! It was so ungentlemanly. Before she could gather her wits to frame a suitably shattering setdown, he went on, "You must have known that there were more than Venetian traders in port."

"Of course, but what does that signify? All kinds of ships come, from everywhere, every week."

"But the Genoese are here, too."

Lucy turned a blank stare on him. He wanted to shake her. Didn't she know what that meant? What did they talk about, up there in the castle, anyway?

"Oh, Maria ha' pity! Ask your precious Estur to explain the facts of life to you!" He spun on his heel and strode angrily down the path to Roberga and Will's place.

She watched him go, with a sick feeling of bereavement. Squabbles and arguments were nothing out of the ordinary for them, but were not to be taken seriously. Never before had he left her without a smile. This was so unlike Lion – he was genuinely upset. What was so significant about more than Venetian ships coming in? Particularly the Genoese, as he named them? She would ask Sir Edward.

But Sir Edward, as she might have expected, was not very forthcoming. He answered her with courtesy, but told her nothing. Such dreadful occurrences were not for a lady's delicate ears, he assured her, and he would certainly not assault hers with unpleasant matters. She must not concern herself. Hah! That was a man for you! Papa would have driven her to distraction, too, saying, "Don't worry your pretty little head about it!"

Sir Edward agreed that her friend had been right to advise against visiting the docks, and she must promise him to stop entertaining such a notion. She promised, knowing that Lion would not have raised such a fuss if he had not truly believed there was danger. But she was determined to discover what was this unspeakable menace.

Roberga's Will, she decided, would be her best source of information. Although he had no formal education, and could not read or write other than sign his own name, Will was a man of intelligence and perception.

He had a fair grasp of contemporary politics and was quite willing to give Lucy a history lesson.

He told her that Venice, long a powerful City State, had had a trade agreement with Cyprus for many years. In August of 1360, the year after Pierre de Lusignan's coronation, the Venetians had taken advantage of the occasion to send an ambassador to the Cypriote capital, Nicosia. On the surface their purpose was to convey congratulations and many valuable gifts, but their real intent was to renegotiate their trade agreement of 1328. Among other things they managed to gain jurisdiction over all maritime and criminal cases involving Venetians. In return, they were to guarantee that none of their ships would carry contraband, that their ship's Masters would not allow non-Venetians aboard without special permission from the King, and that they would compensate for any injury caused to a King's subject.

"That sounds fair enough," Lucy commented, when Will had explained all this in his usual, concise, rather dour style. Will's reply was a derisive snort. "Was it not?" she queried.

"Hah! Fair enough for those tricksters," he growled. "But when the shoe was on the other foot, it was a different story."

"Why, what do you mean, Will?"

"Just that when the King expected the same prerogatives for his own people in Venice, they gave him a flat 'No!'"

"Oh, but that's not fair! How could they?"

"Hunh! Said if they granted it to us, everyone else would want it too. They have the power."

"Us?" thought Lucy. Will spoke as if this were his own country. "How long have you been here, Will?" she asked, aloud.

"Since '56. My Lord fought with the King in the Holy Land. He and Queen Eleanor are also the crowned King and Queen of Jerusalem."

"Yes. I had heard that," admitted Lucy. "Then none of your children, except young Willy, were born in England."

Her mentor chuckled. "Not even Will. He was born at sea, on the voyage here."

"How exciting!" Lucy's eyes sparkled.

"Roberga didn't think so," remarked her husband dryly.

"Indeed, then I did not, "Roberga conceded, "But it makes for interesting gossip now."

"Then Alyse, and Ned, and baby Eleanor were all born here?"

"Yes," their mother grimaced. "Which accounts for the three years between Alyse and young Will. My dear husband left me rusticating here on a strange island, while he went gallivanting off to the wars, and having a rollicking good time too, I'll be bound."

"Following the drum's no life for a woman," grunted Will.

"But I shall go with Sir Edward," declared Lucy. "Lots of women accompany their men to war. My Aunt Lucinda followed my uncle all over the . . ." She almost said "Peninsula", but caught herself in time, and changed to "Continent". Now was the time of The Hundred Years War, she recollected, so that would serve to cover her slip. Oh, dear! It was so difficult, keeping her one life's memories out of the other. Only when alone with Lion could she let down her guard.

But to return to her muttons, "Why did Lion say that it was dangerous for Philippa and me to go down and watch the ships? That is what I cannot understand. He said something about the Genoese, but what has that to do with anything?"

Will frowned, and was silent for a long moment. When he did speak, it was with some seriousness.

"Genoa is also a City State, as you know. They have privileges, same as Venice. Goes back more than a hundred years. King Peter renewed their contract last year, when he was there. But a different breed of cat, they are. The Venetians are only interested in trade, and travel, and the glory of Venice. For that they will sacrifice everything, even honour."

"Yes! Of course! Marco Polo." Whoops! Had she made another blunder? She tried to recall the explorer's time frame, and was relieved when Will said. "Ah! I've heard about him, lass. A real man, he was. Went as far as Cathay, they do say. But these Genoese, now. A troublemaking, rambunctious lot, they be. You'd best take Lion's advice, and stay away from the docks for a while."

"But we would not have had anything to do with the men, and we did have an escort. Sir Edward's squire, Geoffrey. I shall go, anyway. I will find someone else to accompany me." She had forgotten her promise to Estur.

Will grunted. "I suppose I'd best tell what's going on, or you'll be poking that curious little nose of yours in a wopsy's nest." He looked at Roberga. "It's not a pretty tale, my love."

Roberga sat up straight, startled. Will never bestowed endearments on her in public.

"That's all right," she assured him.

"These four galleys the Regent, Prince Hugh, is fitting out for the King . . ." he began.

"Yes!" interrupted Lucy. "For the defense of Cyprus and Adalia. That was part of what I want to see."

"No you don't," she was told. "Seems that a couple of the crew deserted, but they were caught. They claimed to be Genoese, but Prince Hugh had them flogged, and their ears cut off, anyway. Did you not hear the clamour the trumpets were making, yester forenoon? That was meant to cover their screams."

He paused, noting with a certain grim satisfaction that Lucy's complexion was as green as Roberga's, and stretched out a warm hand to comfort his wife. Her fingers clung to his as he continued. "They say there is another Genoese galley coming in to port, so there's likely to be big trouble brewing."

He was right, as they soon discovered. A few days later Onfroi dashed excitedly into the pleasance where Lucy and Philippa with other ladies of the court were enjoying a stroll in the gardens. He made but the sketchiest of bows, breathlessly inquiring for his master.

"He is not here, Onfroi," Philippa told him. "But why are you so excited? Have you news of interest or importance?"

"Nothing that you should hear, my lady." With an even briefer obeisance, he backed away with as much haste as he had entered.

With one accord, the ladies gathered up their skirts and hurried off to the great hall, chattering and speculating as to what news could possible be too dreadful for their "delicate" ears! Sorting through the wild rumours flying through the Court, it was finally disclosed that the crew of the newly arrived Genoese galley, under charter to Cyprus to carry supplies to the forces left in Adalia, had attacked one of the Regent's galleys. They had murdered those of the ship's company who were Cypriotes and then fled to Chios with the valuable and much needed, cargo. It was the beginning of a series of horrible atrocities. The court positively seethed with nightmarish stories, both true and false. It took a while to sort fact from fiction until the real picture, ghastly as it was, could be revealed.

"How terrible!" Lucy exclaimed, as she listened to Lionallo and Will discussing the disgraceful affair. "How can Christians treat their fellow men so shamefully?"

"There will be worse to come," grunted Will, pessimistically.

The Corsican, serious for once, agreed. "The Regent has already ordered that all Genoese be arrested. He has demanded return of the stolen goods. William Ermirio, -- he's the Genoese Podestà, their local Governor, " he explained for Lucy's benefit, " has sent a caique to Chios, to bring back the runaway galley and the stolen provisions. Perhaps that will cool a few tempers."

Alas! Affairs were not to be settled so easily.

"Did you hear what has happened now?" Philippa, returning from a morning spent at her family's home, was bursting with her news. The Court ladies gathered around her, expectantly – urging her to tell – quickly!

"They have brought back the runaway galley. But as soon as she docked, Sicilian mercenaries from the Regent's galleys boarded her, and killed several of her crew."

She paused, while her listeners exclaimed, and cried shame on the murderers.

"But that is not all, is it?" The query came from Lucy, who knew her friend well enough to read her face. The French girl shook her head.

"No." she admitted. "One side is as evil as the other, I fear. The Genoese struck back by abducting a Pisan sailor from one of the Regent's ships. They said he was Genoese, but he wasn't. When he insisted, that awful Podestà creature had the poor fellow's tongue cut out!"

There was a collective gasp of horror before everyone began to talk at once, shocked and horrified by the dreadful cruelty and viciousness of the whole situation. They were only distracted by one of the younger girls sliding gently to the floor, in a dead faint. There was a rush to aid her, one reviving her with the pungent smoke of burnt feathers, while others applied vinegar-soaked cloths to her head, chafed her hands, or brought wine for her to sip. Lucy slipped quietly away to the armourer's cottage.

The Corsican was there, a mug of ale in his hand, watching Will sharpen a throwing dagger. Roberga handed Lucy a wooden cup of citrus juice and gestured her to a low stool next to her own. They both listened avidly, as the men discussed the latest news.

"You say that the Sicilians and the Genoese were actually fighting at the Podestâ's place?" Will asked.

"That's what I heard, and I believe it to be true." Lion took another swallow of ale. "I know that Admiral John le Sûr went with John de Soissons to the Podestâ's loggia. The Admiral was in a towering rage, they say, and told Ermirio that if he didn't disarm his men and send them to their homes he'd set his troops on them."

"Who is John de Soissons?" asked Lucy.

"The King's Bailey," answered Will, distractedly. "How did the Genoan take that?" he asked Lion.

"Do you have to ask?" the Corsican chuckled. "He was just as infuriated as le Sûr. Screamed that his countrymen were not the Admiral's serfs, and that he might kill every one of them in Famagusta, but there would always be more, come to avenge them."

"I'll wager that went down well!"

"What will happen now, I wonder?" worried Lucy.

"Nothing good, I'll be bound," muttered Roberga.

*   *   *

All three protagonists, the Podestâ, the Sicilians, and the King's Bailey, de Soissons, took their complaints to the Regent. Prince Hugh tried his best to please everyone, so succeeded in satisfying no one. He chose four knights, and sent them, with two monks from every monastery in Famagusta, to negotiate with William Ermirio.

"Time and effort wasted," the word went around. The Podestâ would listen to no one. In a flaming rage, he dashed down his Staff of Office, and ordered all Genoese citizens to leave the island by October.

Philippa was able to tell Lucy and their knights, "The Regent said that any Genoese who so wished, might remain in Cyprus in complete safety. Now they say that the Podestâ has stormed off home, to complain to the Government."

"Yes, That is true," Sir Guy affirmed. "Prince Hugh has sent word of the fracas to the King, delivered by the hand of their brother Prince James, the Constable of Jerusalem, and their cousin Bohemund de

Lusignan, whom the King has summoned to join him in Germany."

"And the Doge has ordered all Genoese back to Genoa," put in Philippa. He is preparing an armed galley to send against Cyprus."

"Nought to fear, dear lady," Sir Guy took her hand, reassuringly. "We are more than able to defend the island."

7

"Some good news, at last," Sir Edward told Lucy one day, as they were riding to the hunt. It was not the kind of hunt that Lucy had known in her other life. Her new friends had introduced her to their own favourite sport, hawking.

On her gloved wrist perched a small species of hawk called a merlin. A leather hood covered its head, and scarlet streamers hung from its jesses. She thought it very pretty, but could not work up much enthusiasm for the pastime. Chasing a fox was exhilarating, but more often than not the wily animal outwitted hounds and hunters, and even if he did not, one need not witness the kill. But with hawking, beautiful as the bird's soaring attacks were to watch, she found it rather revolting when it returned with a small bloody body in its claws.

She turned eagerly to the knight riding beside her, an inquiring smile lighting her eyes. He gazed dotingly down at her.

"The Pope has been told of our troubles with Genoa and Sicily and is taking a hand in the business."

Urban V, who desperately wanted Pierre de Lusignan's Crusade to succeed, did intervene. He urged Peter to punish the offenders. He forbade the Doge to attack Cyprus, promising, if the King would not pay compensation, to make up Genoa's losses himself.

"And the King is on his way home!" Edward was really up in the boughs! "He will stop at Venice, to give the Venetian Ambassadors to Genoa the authority to represent him, until his own envoys arrive; then there will be nothing to delay him further, nothing more to block our way!"

Pierre de Lusignan wisely chose that holy man, Peter Thomas, as his envoy. In spite of his failing health, Thomas accepted the burden, taking his physician, Guy de Bagnolo, with him. The King's Chancellor, Phillipe de Mézières, accompanied them, and later wrote of the reception they received as being extremely unpleasant, giving him the feeling that their lives could be in danger.

In Famagusta, the assembled army waited impatiently. Negotiations were long drawn out and acrimonious, while the Venetians, concerned only for the safety of their trade, secretly circulated false rumours that the Crusade was to be abandoned. In this way they hoped to sabotage King Peter's efforts to raise more European support, causing many of his intended followers to disband their armies and return to their homes.

*   *   *

"Finished at last!" rejoiced Lucy, as she held up the heavy silk garment she had been embroidering.

Several ladies of the small company sewing in the bower left their own work to inspect hers. One of the older women took it from her and moved over the window, to examine it in a better light.

"Excellent work, my dear," she commended. "Sir Edward shall be justifiably proud to wear such a splendid tabard."

Lucy flushed with pleasure. She was quite proud of herself, and of the hundreds of tiny stitches she had sewn in the embroidering of the Estur coat of arms, especially after the shocking discovery that there were no scissors in this medieval world. She had to use an awkward implement, rather like garden shears, similar to the ones used to trim hedges and topiary in her "own" time. Even hair and beards were clipped with such barbarous tools!

"Much credit must go to you, dear Madame," she replied. "Without your help, I could never have cut out the garment in the first place."

"Ah, but I have had many years of practice," smiled Lady Tiphainé. "When you have cut as many gowns and jupons as I have, you will be able to work blindfold, *non*?" She chuckled, then said, "And who is this young man?" indicating a very small page, probably about seven years old, standing in the open doorway, timidly scratching at a door panel.

"My lady!" The tiny lad made a prim little bow. "I have a message for the Lady Lucy."

He turned bright eyes in that young lady's direction, and piped, "The noble knight Sir Edward Estur does beg that she will honour him with her gracious presence, as he has news of great import he wishes to share with her. He awaits her pleasure in the Hall." As he finished his speech, delivered without pause or inflection, he gulped a huge breath and sighed with relief.

"Important news? I wonder what it can be!" Lucy jumped to her feet, and handed her needlework to Philippa. "Be an angel, and take care of this, for me," she begged, and curtsied to the senior lady. "With your permission, Madame?" Hardly waiting for that lady's benevolent smile of consent, she gathered up her skirts and fled from the bower, to find her betrothed patiently awaiting her in the Great Hall. No grown or even adolescent male was ever permitted to enter the female quarters of a gentleman's establishment, save only the master himself.

"My dear lady," he informed her, his face alight with excitement and pleasure as he bowed over her hand. "I have just heard the splendid news, and hurried to share my joy with you! The Regent has received orders for us to join His Majesty at the Island of Rhodes. The Crusade is to begin, at last! This is the day for which we have all waited for so long." Seriously, he added, "My one concern now is for your safety and comfort during my absence."

"But you must take me with you!" Lucy begged. "Please! It is my dearest wish to accompany you."

Estur was shocked. "My sweet Lady," he exclaimed. "That of all things is beyond permission! I could never expose a lady to such danger and discomfort." Nor could all her pleadings, tears, and even tantrums cause the slightest wavering of her gallant's determination. It grieved him to deny her slightest whim, but in this he was adamant.

"I am flattered, dear one, that you should wish to stay by my side, but I must know that you are safe, or I shall not be able to devote myself whole-mindedly to my duties."

Since no other ladies were to go – even those who had made the lengthy European voyages with the King's entourage had been returned to Famagusta by the same ship that brought the royal call to muster – Lucy decided to make a virtue of necessity and graciously accede to her knight's wishes.

No one knew just exactly where Peter intended to attack the

Mamalukes, but rumour favoured Syria, as he had sent orders to the Prince of Antioch and Queen Eleanor to forbid all trade with that country. This accorded with the King's plans very well, as he did not trust the Venetians. Although he had the blessing of Pope Urban on his enterprise, he feared they would protect their own business interests by betraying his intentions to the Sultan, as Frederic II had done on an earlier occasion.

Lucy and Philippa attended some of the Masses that were read for the safety and success of the Crusade and its warriors, and sometimes lingered afterwards with Sir Edward and Sir Guy to admire the beauty and the treasures of the Cathedral, lighting candles for the safety of their chevaliers.

The English knight proudly drew their attention to the Ikon of Saint Nicholas.

"Admiral Sir John le Sûr brought it back from Myra, as spoils of war," he told them. "It looks well here, does it not? And it is especially appropriate that it should adorn this particular church, The Cathedral of Saint Nicholas of the Latins!"

"That was the second time we had to teach the Tekke Bey a lesson," grinned Sir Guy. "The first time, we were with the King when he took Adalia. Saint Bartholomew's Day – sixty-one, was it not? That was a magnificent battle!"

"Yes," agreed his friend, with a fine air of complacence. "I rather think we surprised them that day. They had fitted out quite a fleet, intending to attack us here on Cyprus."

"But we had a larger!" chuckled the French knight, reminiscing, as Lucy listened with avid interest. "Grand Master Roger les Pins' four galleys of Hospitallers, two from Pope Urban, at least a dozen privateers, not to mention all those ships from Cyprus and other countries. What was it? One hundred and twenty vessels, all told, I believe. *Merveilleux!*"

"Indeed! We landed at Adalia, you will recall, and you and I went forward with the Regent's powers. We could have taken the place then and there with ease. But Prince Hugh wished to save that honour for his brother, so we took it by storm, under Peter, the next day."

"We were invincible!"

"Ah! But you must admit that the Bey was absent from his fortress when we captured it," Sir Edward reminded him, with scrupulous fairness. "There is a story that he managed to creep in secretly after the battle, but seeing the banner of the Holy Cross flying from the battlements, he realized that all was lost and fled."

"We were lucky that time"

"Especially so since we missed the plague at Famagusta."

Sir Guy shuddered. "I would rather face ten thousand pagan infidels, than that unholy scourge!" His face brightened. "And now we hie us forth once more, on our Holy Quest."

8

The next weeks were pure chaos. The streets of Famagusta were filled with archers and men at arms, and a host of camp followers – an army in themselves, of hawkers, jongleurs, tumblers, dancers, buskers and tricksters of all persuasions. Philippa's father assigned two of his retainers to accompany the girls whenever they went out, as the young squires now had other, more important duties to attend to. However, their masters managed to find time to visit their ladies and sometimes ride out with them.

Lucy could not help secretly thinking that her knight was of much more aristocratic bearing than Sir Guy, who displayed a definite lack of taste in apparel. He favoured parti-coloured affairs: one side of his clothes in one colour and the other in sharp contrast, with the hues of the tunic in opposition to those of the stockings. The toes of his shoes were so exaggeratedly curled they were nicknamed "harlots" by irreverent pages, and the whole was topped by a short velvet cloak of dazzling scarlet, thrown back to display its gaudy yellow silk lining. His legs, one red and one yellow, looked ludicrously elongated beneath the short tunic, which barely covered his derrière.

And that ridiculous pointed hat! Except for the over-long liripipe that dangled from its tip, matching the tippets hanging from his elbows, it resembled a dunce's cap that small children in disgrace had been made to wear as they repented their sins sitting in a corner, back – oh dear! Should it be forward? – in her early schooldays.

Sir Edward looked every inch the English gentleman. His elegant but understated cote-hardie of burgundy velvet was worn over a dark green knee-length tunic and hose, topped by a stylish velvet cap, a single feather pinned to one side with an emerald and diamond brooch. His only other ornaments were a heavy gold chain suspending an emerald-studded cross, and a gold ring engraved with the Estur crest. Sir Guy, on the other hand, wore several sparkling rings and arm bands as well as a diversity of gold chains adorned with a dazzling array of jewelled fobs and medallions.

Suddenly ashamed of her snobbish reflections, Lucy berated herself for her ungracious thoughts concerning the French knight. After all, his behaviour toward her had always been beyond all reproach, everything that was friendly and chivalrous. And in spite of the war between their respective kings, he was Edward's best friend. Surely his foppish attire should be a matter of small concern to her. It was Philippa's opinion that counted, and she thought her suitor perfect!

Once the knights who planned to join King Peter at Rhodes were leaving from Famagusta, the entire court would be moving to Nicosia, the capital, for the duration of the Crusade. Will's master was among the Crusaders and as his lady was moving with the court, Roberga too was journeying to the capital in her train.

As she helped her friend pack her scant possessions – a minimum of clothing, a large iron seething kettle, and a flat iron griddle – Lucy was extremely grateful that, thanks to Sir Edward's gift of the pretty palfrey, she would not have to travel in one of the springless wooden carts in which the non-riders and baggage were to be transported. That would indeed be a miserable experience. Roberga had been through it all before, and appeared to be rather philosophical about the whole affair. But though she presented a bright, cheerful front to the world and her husband, neither Will nor Lucy failed to note the taut apprehension that shadowed her usually laughing eyes. Of course, Lucy mused, Roberga did not have the reassurance of prior knowledge that her man would not only survive but live to return to his native land to enjoy a long and happy life.

She would miss Philippa, who would not be going to Nicosia. Her father had declared that his place was here in Famagusta, and he had no intentions of allowing his daughter to accompany the Court, away from his supervision. Both girls were devastated at the mere thought of the coming separation, but M'sieur l'Mesurier was determined for once. Not all Philippa's tears and wheedling could change his mind. So Lucy was astonished to see her friend rushing to meet her, with a dazzling grin illuminating her plump, pretty face.

"Ah! *Ma chère Lucy!*" She grabbed the English girl's hands, and swung her around in a joyous fandango. "We are not to be parted after all!"

"We are not? Your Papa has relented, then? You are to come with us?"

"Non, non! Even better. You are not to go. You will stay here with us. Papa and your dear Sir Edward have arranged everything!"

"And to your satisfaction and approval, I hope, my dear lady." Philippa's exuberant greeting had prevented Lucy from noticing Sir Edward's more dignified approach. "If it pleases you, Monsieur l'Mesurier has proposed that you join his household during my absence. It would give me great peace of mind to know that you were under the protection of such an honourable gentleman. He has also agreed to act as my man of business while I am away, so you will want for nothing. You may draw on him for anything you need. And prithy, my sweet lady, do not stint yourself. It would grieve me to think that you lacked anything that was in my power to supply."

"Dear Sir Edward! The only thing I shall lack is your presence." Lucy was touched by his diffident smile. How could she have survived without this kind man's generosity? "And certainly I could wish for nothing better than to accept Monsieur l'Mesurier's hospitality, and enjoy the company of my dearest Philippa. I shall pray every day for your success and safe return in every church in Famagusta!"

He burst in a hearty laugh. "I think, my fair lady, you will be very busy. Know you not that there are three hundred and sixty five churches in this town? One for every day of the year!"

"Oh!" Lucy was taken aback, but soon recovered her aplomb. "Well, I shall pray every day in the Cathedral, and at as many other churches as I can fit in."

"And so shall I," declared Philippa. "We shall pray for the success and well-being of the whole army, but particularly for you and Sir Guy."

On the day before they were to set forth on their Holy War, the army gathered outside the town to be reviewed, with great pomp and pageantry, by the Prince of Antioch, under whose leadership they would embark the next day. An open-air Mass was to follow.

Lucy and Philippa were taken by the French girl's parents to enjoy the spectacle. Everywhere, great pavilions were set up, surmounted by the banners of the Houses whose noble scions they sheltered. The ladies were fascinated by the colourful hues of the tents, as well as the flags and pennants, which rivalled the clothing of spectator and warrior alike in dazzling the unsophisticated eye. M'sieur l'Mesurier, being a personage of some consequence, had been able to procure excellent seats for his party on one of the temporary platforms set up near the reviewing stand for the gentry.

An elderly blacksmith friend of Will's stood among the peasants near them. Knowing Lucy well from her visits to Roberga, he took it on himself to enlighten them. Lucy had long become accustomed to old Matthew's peculiar English accent.

"Now thon's the archers," he told them. "English archers. Edden't none to beat 'em, says I! Thee can tell 'em by them round iron caps. Zee, they wears sword an' dagger too. But it's the good wold longbow, made of true English yew, that'll win the war. Zee yon lad, now. A's bow es tall as enself, and a's arrows es the length of a cloth yard. Fletched wi' the gray goose feathers, they be, none o' y're peacock feathers and suchlike fancies for en!"

Lucy dutifully studied the archer in question. He certainly did look smart and efficient in his green tunic and leather armour, strengthened with disks of metal, even if his helmet was rather like an upside-down cooking pot.

"They arrows 'as a barbed iron tip, that once 'tis in, 'll not come out again without the chirurgeon's knife!" went on their self-appointed instructor. "An' young Ned there can loose 'em off, a dozen to the minute, and never miss the bull's eye, even if it be as much as two hundred an' forty yards! Bests they arbalest things, every time!"

He broke off as a military band marched by: two nakirs, three flutes, and a bagpiper, all kept in time by a drummer, followed by a troop of men-at-arms carrying pikes, battle axes, and daggers. They carried, Lucy noted, the colours and crest of a Sicilian knight she had met through the l'Mesuriers.

Near each pavilion, knights in full armour were milling about on restless mounts, their high-held lances draped with limp pensiles barely fluttering in the still air.

Old Matt began to chatter again, naming the different families represented in the host. "Not that most of them bi'st Heads of Houses," he explained. "The chiefs'll be in France wi' the Prince of Wales. These be younger sons, and cadet branches o' the Great Houses. Zee y' there! That be the crest of one o' the northern Houses. Look to be the Percys, they do."

"And that pretty blue and white one, over there, with the wavy lines – whose is that?" inquired Lucy.

"Azure an' argent, lady – that's how thon heralds call the colours. I reckon that bi'st the Stourtons o' Wiltshire, though there be Stourtons in Cheshire, too. Bi'st a 'Ampshire man, m'self. Come out with young FitzClarence, as was liege-man to Lord Burleigh."

Lucy chuckled. "Then you are a Hampshire Hog!"

"*Ma chère Lucy*" reproved Madame l'Mesurier, who, in her travels, had acquired a smattering of English, enough to follow the conversation.

"Oh, it's only a joke, Madame," Lucy hastened to explain. "People from Hampshire call themselves that. We of the Island are know as calkheads, although there has been a joke going around lately that brands us as Isle of Wight Calves."

Madame shook her head. The mad *Anglais* again! One would never understand them.

"But why, Lucy?" asked an intrigued Philippa. "Why should one refer to oneself as a baby cow?"

"Oh, it is quite simple my dear, in more ways than one! The story is that an Island farmer found his calf with its head stuck through the bars of a gate. He called a friend for advice, and after due consideration, the second man told him, "There be only one thing to do, Jarge. We'm goin' to ha'ta cut off 'is 'ead to save 'is loife!""

"Oh Lucy!" Laughing, Philippa slapped at her friend's hand. "You do talk such nonsense." She turned to the old man. "That one over there, Matthew – the gay red and silver flag – do you know that one?"

"Ar, that I do, little lady. Worsley of Appuldurcombe, another 'Ampshire family."

"Oh, no, no, no, no, no! You are wrong there, Matt my old gossip!" chortled Lucy, gleefully. "The Worsleys are no grockles. Appuldercombe is on the Wight."

"B'aint no terbul divr'nce," shrugged the smith.

"No difference! Matthew, it would take a very bold or a very foolish man to make such a statement in the hearing of an Islander!"

The old man sniggered. "Ar! I knows that. Done it avore, many a time, when ai was a young rapscallion – to stir up a bit o' action in a tavern, loike, on a dull night!"

"And, I pray thee, what is a grockle?" demanded Philippa.

"Any one who is not an Islander," grinned the other girl. "And mainlanders who have come 'over' the Solent to live on the Island are called 'overners'." Her attention was diverted. "Oh, look! Over there, by that scarlet pavilion! I am sure that must be Sir Edward! Although one cannot be sure that is Thor, Sir Edward's destrier, underneath all those trappings! But certainly it is Geoffrey, standing beside him. How fearsome they look!"

"*Magnifique!*" mumbled the French girl, absently, as her blue eyes sought eagerly for another gallant.

"It is Sir Edward!" Lucy cried, excitedly. "I can see now – he is wearing the tabard I made for him."

"And there is Sir Guy," announced Philippa, with a sigh of satisfaction. "Do not they both look handsome and brave?"

The two friends sat silently, holding hands, admiring their admirers, a little over-awed by the knightly splendour so handsomely displayed, their pleasure somewhat dampened by the realization that this majestic grandeur was the prelude to the departure to the battlefields, possibly to glory, but possibly also to maiming or to death.

After the various companies were lined up in their appointed places, the Regent, Prince Hugh of Antioch, rode out to review the host. It was a dazzling spectacle. Each noble lord, in full panoply, his armour brightly gleaming beneath a tabard magnificently embroidered with his family crest, sat astride his elegantly caparisoned destrier, in front of his powers.

What an abundance of sand and vinegar, not to mention elbow grease, must have been used to achieve such brilliance! Lucy grinned, as she recalled Geoffrey's and Onfroi's recipe for polishing chainmail. They had stuffed their lords' gorgets into a stout leather bag, with a fair amount of vinegar and sand, which they then tossed back and forth like one of the medicine balls she had seen on an outing to Bournemouth.

The young squires had been having a high old time when she saw them, seemingly trying to annihilate one another with their awkward plaything.

The great horses were as richly apparelled as their riders, in voluminous skirts of rich and elegant weavings, and harnesses ornamented with gold or silver, inset with precious stones.

Flanking each leader, and slightly to the rear, were his standard bearer and his herald, with his aristocratic cohorts ranged behind them. To their rear were the lowlier men-at-arms.

The two girls watched intrigued as the Prince and his escort rode from group to group, waiting for him to reach the companies that held their own attention. Lucy was thrilled to see that when His Highness singled out an occasional man, speaking a few friendly words to each, her own knight was one of those so honoured. Of course, she recollected, Sir Edward had campaigned with King Peter before, in the Holy Land. He was a member of the coveted Order of the Sword, so it was not surprising that Prince Hugh, being the King's brother, should know him well.

After the review, an altar was set up in the field, and the Archbishop proceeded with the Mass. It was a startling experience for Lucy to hear the great masculine roar that rose to heaven, as the congregation made the age-old responses. In spite of the dreadful deeds some of them would perform, and probably not for the first time, they were all devout Christians, according to their own standards. They would no more have gone into battle unshriven than fight without their weapons and armour.

The ceremonies over, Lucy and Philippa were delighted to observe their heroes advancing in their direction. Lucy watched with pride as Sir Edward paid his respects to her host and hostess, before turning to her. How bright his armour shone! Geoffrey must have spent hours polishing off every minute speck of the ubiquitous rust that burst forth at the merest suspicion of dampness. She remembered the rust stains on the under-jupon which the young squire had smuggled to her for use as a pattern. She had taken fastidious care in fashioning the two new gambesons she had made for Edward from soft quilted cotton, as Geoffrey had explained what awful discomfort the smallest wrinkle could cause beneath that weighty iron.

Armed *cap-à-pie*, Sir Edward looked every inch the noble warrior, from his conical bascinet to his spur straps and sollerets. Lucy felt proud of her handiwork as she studied the fit of Sir Edward's tabard. The garment could hold its own in magnificence against any other on the field. How grateful she was now, that her mother had insisted she become an expert needle woman. That called to mind her dear Papa's extravagant praise of the embroidered waistcoat she had presented to him last Christmas, bringing a lump to her throat and unbidden tears to her eyes.

Too soon for the ladies, if not for their warriors, the day of departure dawned bright and sunny. In the company of M'sieur l'Mesurier and every other able-bodied resident of Famagusta, Lucy and Philippa made their way to the docks, to wish the expedition Godspeed.

The horses and their gear had already been taken aboard ship. There were so many! Each knight had at least one great war-horse, one or two riding beasts, and a pack horse. It must have taken hours to load them all. Then there were the weapons and all the other supplies the army would need, both for the voyage and on their arrival in Smyrna. Every one of the 108 vessels gathered in the bay would be required. They were scheduled to rendezvous with the King at Rhodes, where he would meet them with another 31 galleys from Cyprus, Venice and Genoa, and four galleys and a hundred knights sent by the Grand Master of the Knights Hospitallers. Lucy had little or no knowledge of this Crusade, having found information about it extremely hard to come by in her other lifetime. She only knew that Sir Edward had returned to his native Island, to enjoy a pleasant and lengthy life. She wasn't even quite sure where Smyrna was. Later, she promised herself, she would ask Philippa's papa. He had some fine maps in his accounting room.

Now, the last of the men at arms were boarding and it would soon be time for Sir Edward and Sir Guy to leave.

Philippa sobbed openly as she bade farewell to Sir Guy, who did not let slip the opportunity to comfort her, clasping her in his arms and murmuring encouraging endearments. Although they were not officially betrothed, they both knew that her father would not refuse the offer Sir Guy intended to make for her hand if he returned safely from this adventure. Nor would his aristocratic family object to a merchant's daughter, especially if she came with such a fortune as that with which Philippa's father would endow his darling.

Even though she knew of the certainty of her own betrothed's safety, Lucy found her eyes, too, sting with unbidden tears as he took both her hands in his and gently kissed her fingertips. He had such an exalted look in his eyes as he spoke of his quest, and he begged her, his own dear lady, not to mourn if he should not return. "Could any man wish a nobler death," he said, "than to die fighting for the glory of his Lady, and in the service of his God?" Overcome with tenderness, she rose on tip-toe to link her hands behind his neck and kiss him lightly on the lips.

"For luck!" She gave him a tremulous smile and pressed her favourite blue silk scarf in his hand. The blush that flooded his face matched hers, as a bashful grin of surprised delight spread across his dear features.

"When we return," he told her, shyly, "I shall seek absolution from my vows."

"And I shall be waiting!" Lucy assured him, carried away by the emotion of the moment.

She watched him wind the sheer length of silk around his gorget. Then he turned to Geoffrey, standing by with his lord's sword and shield and his mailed gloves lined with yellow leather, and took from the waiting squire a black eye patch. "My lady," he formally announced, "I am hereby resolved to wear this patch, and not uncover my eye, until I have performed a noble deed to your glory."

Lucy gasped. "Oh, my lord, no! You cannot go into battle half-blinded! I forbid you to do so!"

"Nenny, nenny!" He smiled sweetly at her. "I have so sworn, and I shall strive to do you great honour, my love."

She realized for the first time that several other knights were also wearing eye patches, and then heard Sir Guy making the same preposterous vow to Philippa. The ninnyhammers! How could they be so stupid? To handicap themselves in such a manner! Anger choked her throat. Nodcocks – all of them, with their romantically absurd notions of chivalry. All these gallant, valiant young idiots –not to mention the older ones, who should at the least have more sense, eagerly dashing off to face death and maiming with a laugh and a joke and a dream of glory. Surely they had windmills in their attics! More hair than wits! She certainly didn't want Edward to take foolish risks just to do her honour! Had she once truly been so ignorant as to imagine that war was romantic? She turned her face away, to hide her rage and disgust.

It was then that she realized that there had been a witness to this tender exchange, as she caught the white-faced scowl Lionallo cast upon her. She made a small conciliatory gesture, but he turned away and strode off to lend his assistance to the sailors.

A fanfare from his herald announced the arrival of the Regent, accompanied by the Turcopolier, Sir James de Nores, who was to act for him during his absence.

"Methinks His Highness has not the look of a well man," murmured Sir Edward to his fellow knights.

"He does have a yellowish cast to his visage," agreed the Frenchman. "But haste, *mon ami*! It is time for us to leave."

"Indeed!" chuckled the other. "It would be ill fortune to be left behind!"

With one last hasty farewell they hurried away, leaving their friends to wave Godspeed.

"Enough of your tears, *mon enfant*," Philippa's father chided. "Your Knight will return safe and sound, and covered with glory, I assure you! *Allons*! *Allons*!" and he shepherded them away from the docks, to their waiting horses and back to his mansion.

A few days later, they bade farewell to Roberga. She was to accompany Will's master's lady to Nicosia with the rest of the household, and Lucy and Philippa had helped her prepare for the journey. Mostly they had kept an eye on the children, who were wild with the excitement and hurry-scurry of the last few weeks. Now, the little family were ready to join the migration to the capital.

The last chest was thrown aboard the last mule cart, the last reluctant child rounded up, the last tearful farewells uttered, and the cavalcade set off, followed by the cheers of those left behind. Since M'sieur l'Mesurier still had business to discuss with one of his stewards, who was making the journey to the capital, he had decided to ride part of the way with the travellers, and was allowing the girls to do the same. It was fun to trot along beside the wagons, but both Lucy and Philippa were glad that they did not have to ride inside. Roberga and her family travelled in a mule cart with another woman, her children and their baggage. If it should rain, a canvas cover would be erected over them. The ladies were not so lucky. They were packed into long, springless wagons, with gaily patterned canvas covers that totally excluded light and air. To compensate, flaps cut in the top and sides of the material were rolled up and tied with cord so they could easily be let down again in case of inclement weather.

Lucy shuddered at the mere thought of travelling under such conditions. There must have been a dozen women, several of them pregnant, packed into each conveyance. Their pets, which ranged from lap dogs to monkeys, travelled with them. There was even a tame squirrel, and several singing and talking birds in wicker cages. There were no cats, as, in those superstitious times, felines were regarded with arch suspicion as witches' familiars and agents of the devil (strangely enough, nuns were allowed to keep cats but not dogs, which were forbidden the cloisters). The animal noises, combined with high pitched female voices, laughing, chattering, or complaining in half a dozen languages, whining children, and bawling muleteers, were ear-shattering – a regular Babel, thought Lucy.

She turned to Philippa. "However can I thank your Papa for rescuing me from this?" She waved a hand at the trundling train. "I think I should have died or gone mad long before I reached Nicosia!" Philippa, riding beside Lucy, could only chatter mournfully of her separation from Sir Guy. Lucy, however, found that the memory of a certain dark-eyed fisherman, no matter how hard she tried to exclude him, kept nudging her own blond knight out of her mind. She had not seen Lion since he had watched her bidding farewell to Edward, and the Stella Maris was gone from her usual moorings in a secluded part of the Bay of Famagusta.

It was going to be a tiresome journey. After a few miles, when the novelty began to wear off, the children became restless and fretful. Lucy did what she could to help Roberga, taking the youngsters one at a time to ride behind her on Gertrude, her mare. Occasionally, she persuaded their mother to mount while she took her place in the cart, entertaining the little ones with stories and inventing games for their amusement.

It was Roberga who put an abrupt end to Philippa's tearful complaints. "Knights are seldom killed," she snapped. "It's the men on foot who die. Knights just knock one another around a bit, to decide who takes who prisoner. Afterwards, they sit around and carouse until the ransom money arrives. Then they shake hands and go home!"

"Oh Roberga!" laughed Lucy.

"'Tis true. Ask anyone – it's the likes of my Will and his mates who are killed in battle!" Her voice wobbled, as she sniffed and wiped her sleeve across her nose.

That was another thing Lucy had noted. No one had proper handkerchiefs, although among the upper classes it was customary to carry a cloth square called a sweat wiper, which could be called upon to double duty.

The time came for the final parting. Tearfully the two young ladies bade Roberga and her children Godspeed, with promises of meeting again when the fleet returned. Lucy produced from her saddlebag a few small gifts for the children – rag dolls she had sewn for the girls, and little wooden swords she had persuaded a young page to make for the boys. She hoped the toys would help keep the youngsters entertained and give Roberga some respite.

They watched until the long line of wagons and its mounted escort wound its way slowly westward, and then turned back toward Famagusta, and home.

Philippa's father rode with the girls then, and engaged Lucy in quiet conversation. He was interested in the young woman, with her intelligent mind, and enjoyed answering her unusual questions. Though she lacked nothing in femininity, a youngster with a head like hers should have been a boy, he thought! Not that he would change one atom of his own beloved little ewe lamb. Nor, fortunately, did he need to, with two fine, intelligent sons, and a smart son-in-law attending diligently to the family business, at home in Montpellier. It gave him pleasure to explain to the little English mam'selle that the reason for Famagusta's popularity as a port was its geographical situation.

"You must know, my dear, that Cyprus is as far east as European ships care to venture – pirates and Infidels, you understand. On the other hand, the spices and silks and other treasures from Cathay and other oriental lands are always in great demand, and can be turned to a fine profit. So this is where the Occident and the Orient meet. It is the great trading crossroads of the world. It is trade that has built Famagusta. Less than a hundred years ago, the city did not exist. There was only a small, unimportant port called Ammochostos, meaning 'Buried in the Sand'. Then, it was in 1291 I think, the Infidels defeated the Crusaders, and drove them out of Acre. That was when the Venetians and other

European merchants and bankers, trading from ports along the Syrian coast, fled to the only safe and suitable port left to the Christians, and founded Famagusta."

"How exciting!" breathed Lucy, her eyes shining with such genuine interest that the French gentleman was encouraged to continue.

"It was an excellent choice," he informed her. "In a bare score of years, the residents had become the richest people in the world. They still are, I believe. Not long ago a citizen's daughter is reputed to have worn at her betrothal ceremonies a jewelled head-dress that was valued at a worth more than the entire collection of the Queen of France's jewels."

"*Magnifique!*" bubbled Philippa who, until mention of jewellery, had been rather bored with the turn the conversation had taken. She fluttered her eyelashes mischievously at her father. "Shall you dower me with such a coronet at my betrothal, *cher papa*?"

He grinned down at her, teasingly. "That would be an unnecessary waste!" he told her, with mock solemnity. "Your beauty would out-dazzle any jewel yet discovered. A wreath of daisies is all that you will require!"

"Oh Papa!" she pouted. "You are impossible! And you have no tender feeling for me either, Lady Lucy!" she scolded her giggling friend, breaking into laughter herself.

9

Life in the l'Mesurier household proved extremely pleasant. Madame was a lady of cheerful and easygoing temperament, running her establishment with a firm but kindly hand, and Lucy easily dropped into the family routine. The good lady and her benevolent husband reminded her in many ways of her own dearly loved lost parents. Even though the French couple treated her as another daughter, she envied Philippa her good fortune in still enjoying the presence of her own Mama and Papa.

In this house no clothes were hung in the guarderobe, which itself was kept in a more sanitary condition than those of the court. Instead, gowns were hung in cedar lined armoires, or folded into immaculate chests of scented sandalwood. Madame was as dedicated a housekeeper as Mama had been. There were even carpets, gorgeous oriental creations, in the bower and the bedrooms, and the rushes on the floor of the hall were frequently changed and sprinkled lavishly with flea bane, mint and other insect-discouraging herbs. The lady's small lap dog was the only canine not forbidden the indoors. The furniture was well preserved with a beeswax and turpentine polish, and elegant containers of potpourri sweetened the air.

Madame was happy to accept Lucy as a member of the family, and was gratified to discover that the newcomer was more than ready to take on her fair share of household duties, particularly in giving assistance to Madame Henriette, in the still room. She was especially delighted with Lucy's sewing skills. "I have much admired the splendid tabard you made for Sir Edward," she told her. "I would be greatly obliged if you would assist us in our own special project. Come– I will show you."

She led the way to the bower, where several of her ladies of the household were occupied in various activities –spinning and weaving plain materials for making servants' clothes, mending, and, for the more particularly adept, embroidering, dressmaking or working at the tapestry frames.

"Ah, Madame Mathilde!" She beckoned to a middle-aged lady, supervising the younger girls. "I wish to show our guest the cope."

Raising her eyebrows, the woman crossed to an elegantly carved sandalwood chest and lifted out a large piece of cloth. With the assistance of two other women, it was held out for Lucy to view. The English girl gasped. She had never seen anything like this!

Her hostess smiled, pleased with the reaction her project had excited. "We have been working on this for more than a year," she informed Lucy. "But there is still much to be accomplished. It is intended as a cope for our bishop at home, in Montpellier. As you can see, we are working with the 'Opus Anglicanum' stitch. Very time consuming, and hard on the eyes."

"And is this what you want me to help with?" Lucy whispered, awed.

"If you will be so obliging," affirmed Madame. "What I have seen of your work is so impressive that I am sure you will be a great asset to our little undertaking."

"Little!" Lucy was overwhelmed. "But Madame! This is so – so stupendous! I would not dare to lay a finger on it!"

Madame laughed. "Do not under-rate your talents, *ma chère*. As I said, I have seen your work. If you will but give us an hour or so of your time now and then, I shall be forever grateful. See – the design is already laid out upon the cloth, and here are the coloured cartoons from which we work."

Lucy leaned forward to study the detail as the various sections were explained to her. The cope was divided into four. The background was to be red outside the quatrefoils, and green inside. Each quatrefoil was being delineated in gold thread and would contain a picture, carefully embroidered, in exquisite detail. Two of them were already in progress – one depicting the expulsion from the garden of Eden, with Adam and Eve sadly leaving their erstwhile paradise beneath the threat of the Angel's flaming sword, while a gloating serpent lurked in the background. The other showed Saint Christopher carrying the Christ Child across a raging river. The work was exquisite, and Lucy doubted if she were competent to do justice to such a piece of art. But when she voiced her doubts to Madame l'Mesurier, that good lady pooh-poohed her misgivings and arranged a time with Madame Mathilde for her protégé to work on the cope. The latter assured Lucy that she herself would teach her the intricacies of the Opus Anglicanum stitchery.

"*Maman*! You have never allowed me to work on the cope," complained Philippa.

"You, my child, have not yet acquired the patience, nor the skill, required for such labour," retorted her mother, calmly. "But you shall try your hand at practising the stitches with our dear Lucy, when Madame Mathilde instructs her."

Philippa greeted this concession with a little moué of distaste, leading Lucy to believe that her protest had been a mere matter of form, and that her friend was not really enthusiastic about participating in the great task. She found that she herself, however, was becoming quite interested. She was looking forward to her new occupation, and the chance to make some small return for the affectionate hospitality this warm-hearted family was extending to her. Madame Mathilde, when the opportunity arose to instruct her new assistant, was mightily pleased at the speed with which she acquired the competence to take her part in the actual project.

Life settled into a comfortable routine during the warm days of late summer, and Lucy found herself fully accepted as one of the household. She developed the same rapport with Madame Henriette, the keeper of the still room, as she had enjoyed with Dame Agathé, and soon dropped into her old habits of gathering herbs and seaweed for that lady.

Then, too, there were young children in the house, who loved games and stories as much as had Roberga's children. Sometimes they would come to the bower and beg for a tale, encouraged by the other women, grateful to be entertained as they laboured at their tasks. Lucy was extremely careful never to mention "magical" conveyances, such as velocipedes and trains or anything strange or startling from her old life. She confined her recitals to the old fairy stories and the miraculous legends of the saints, and tales of knightly deeds of derring-do, remembered from Morte d'Artur. Occasionally she ventured to translate into court French some of the stories and poetry that her Papa read to her and Mama on winter evenings. "Young Lochinvar" and "The Lady of the Lake", as well as condensed versions of some of the Waverley novels, were romances that particularly delighted the ladies of the household.

It was in the bower that the story-teller herself heard stories, mostly of court intrigues, and illicit romances that were not so secret as the participants liked to believe. The liveliest topic of the moment concerned the Queen's treatment of one of the King's two favourite mistresses.

Pierre de Lusignan had left behind in Famagusta the widowed Joanna l'Aleman, eight months pregnant with his child, Lucy heard. The ladies of the household were deeply concerned for the poor lady's fate, discussing her sufferings for hours as they sat at their work in the bower.

"It is shocking," commented Madame Mathilde. "As soon as the King was gone, Queen Eleanor immediately apprehended her. She did not dare kill her, although unpleasant things have happened to other 'friends' of His Majesty in the past. But she had the poor creature horribly tortured, ordering great weights laid upon her belly, in the hope of causing her to miscarry. But that, by the grace of God, did not happen. So Joanna was sent home to await the child's birth." She paused, to bite off a thread. Another woman took up the tale. "As soon as the poor infant was born, the midwives, on the Queen's command, delivered the babe to her. What happened to the poor little innocent can only be guessed at, as it was never seen again."

Joanna had been sent to the bleak northern fortress of Kyrenia, where she was kept in the dungeon under the rigorous supervision of one of the Queen's own officers, who had orders to make her imprisonment as miserable and uncomfortable as he could.

Lucy was horrified. "Did no one tell the King?" she asked.

"Oh, of course," she was told. "And as it happened, she was only in the dungeon for a few days. As soon as news of her imprisonment reached the Regent's ears, he immediately took steps. He replaced the Kyrenian keeper with Sir Luc d'Antiaume, a man of his own and kinsman to Joanna, with orders to make her sojourn in the fort as pleasant as possible, if he valued his King's goodwill. King Pierre soon heard of the affair, you may be sure, and wrote to Queen Eleanor. It is said that he bade her do her worst before he came home, for if ever, by God's help, he should return safely to Cyprus, he would do so ill with her that many would tremble."

"Those were his very words," asserted Madame Mathilde.

"Was the Queen not afraid?" asked Philippa, who had not heard of the affair in such detail before.

"She would not admit that it was so," said her mother. "But Joanna was removed from the prison and put in the convent of the Saint Clares, in Nicosia. Her Majesty gave out that her leniency was a favour to the d'Antiaumes, who had petitioned her on their kinswoman's behalf."

"Echive de Scandelion fared better," remarked a young niece of Madame Mathilde.

"She had a husband to protect her," snapped her aunt. "I cannot conceive how one woman can treat another so atrociously," she continued. "It is most unchristian."

"Whatever will King Peter do when he returns?" queried someone else. "The Lusignan's do not take such affronts lightly! And there is the talk about Queen Eleanor herself, and Sir John de Morphou!"

"Which will not be repeated in this house," Madame l'Mesurier promptly rebuked her. "The l'Mesuriers shall not be accused of *lèse-majesté*!"

The woman who had spoken bowed her head in embarrassment. It was not pleasant to be the object of Madame's infrequent wrath.

To change the subject, Madame decreed a blackberrying expedition, to be undertaken by Philippa and Lucy.

*   *   *

The two young women were happily gathering the early fruit, and keeping a watchful eye on the small troop of children in their charge, when they met old Matthew in the company of an equally ancient goat herd.

"Did y'hear the news, then?" he asked. And when, in turn, they inquired what news, he was delighted to enlighten them.

"The Regent!" he informed them, swelling with importance. "He's back!"

"But it has been such a short time!" exclaimed Lucy. "Surely the war cannot be over so soon!"

"Are the knights here, too?" demanded Philippa, her face aglow with excitement.

"Nenny, nenny!" The old man raised a quieting palm. "'Tis only the

Prince and en's apothecary. 'Is 'ighness 'as a malady, that laid en low. The army went on without en. A swears a'll join 'em, agin, when a's recovered."

The girls questioned him eagerly, but he could add no more to his report. He knew nothing more than what he had already told them. Naught would satisfy Philippa but that they should return home immediately and seek a more detailed account. Lucy knew that she was harbouring a secret hope that perhaps Sir Guy had also come back, but was sure her friend was doomed to disappointment.

Gathering the protesting children they set off, Philippa in the lead, but Lucy held back, chatting to Matthew. She had neither seen nor heard of Lionallo since the military convoy had left Famagusta. Casually she inquired of the old man as to the Corsican fisherman's whereabouts and was shocked to learn that he had gone to Lammasol on the southern coast.

"Has he gone for good?" She forced the query from her clogged throat.

"Nenny, nenny! Back avore Holy Cross, a zed. Lookin' for a change o' scenery, I reckon, and avisitin' wold friends."

"He has friends in Lammasol?" Surprise sharpened her voice. "I didn't know that."

"Ar. Moves around the coast, he does. Doan like t' bide in one place too long, they Corsicans. Got itchy feet, they has. Stepped on a wanderin' sod, I shoulden be zurprized. Doan know for why en stayed so long here, this year."

Lucy suddenly realized how little she actually knew about the stalwart young man who occupied so much of her thoughts these days – more than the one who should rightly do so, her knightly betrothed. Of course Lion must have a family, and friends. One didn't exist as an isolated being with no connections whatsoever – unless one were Lucy Lightfoot, weirdly wrested from her true life and environment and set down in a world and an era in which she did not belong! She shivered at the recollection, then pulled herself together, as Philippa's voice broke into her consciousness, urging her to hurry.

Holy Cross! He would be back for Holy Cross Day! That would be September 14 – the middle of this month, just a few days away. Suddenly her heart felt lighter than it had for days. She bade farewell to old Matthew, and sped on winged feet to catch up with her companions.

Soon there was more news of the Regent and his hasty return. It was given out that Prince Hugh had every intention of returning to the wars, as soon as his health would permit. After a brief convalescence, His Highness insisted on setting forth once more, determined to support his brother's holy cause.

*   *   *

The whispered gossip concerning the Queen's affair became louder and more explicit, alarming the King's other two brothers, Prince John and Prince James. Feeling that the King should be made aware of their sister-in-law's infidelity, and neither wishing to cast himself in the role of the talebearer, they joined forces to bully John Visconte, Comptroller of the Royal Household, into taking action. They demanded that he send a report to King Peter. Forced to acquaint her Royal spouse with the rumours of Eleanor's alleged infidelity, Sir John insisted that he himself did not believe the scandalmongers, begging Peter to inquire into the matter himself, as he hoped to be proved a liar.

Madame l'Mesurier was very much disturbed. "One cannot conceive of the Queen committing adultery, but the rumours are very prevalent," she commented to her husband in the privacy of their solar. "How will His Majesty react, do you suppose?"

"There will be the devil to pay, and no pitch hot!" asserted her spouse.

"You think he will believe the reports, then?"

"No doubt about it!" He was confident. "I'm sure he is already giving the matter his considered attention. But enough. Such gloomy conversation is bad for the digestion. Let us change the subject."

Life went on calmly, as ever, in the l'Mesurier household. Holy Cross Day dawned with the usual celebrations. After mass, the priest captivated the children with the story of the True Cross from its beginning as the Tree of Life, growing in the Garden of Eden. He told of how Adam and Eve took a sacred bough with them on their wanderings when they were forced to leave Paradise. Noah built this same bough into his ark, and Abraham used it as a tent pole, when unsuspectingly entertaining angelic guests. Although Solomon had used it in constructing his great temple, it was not destroyed when the building was burnt down by

Nebuchadnessar.

It had been thrown into the Pool of Bethesda, where for many years its power worked miracles of healing, until it was hauled out and fashioned into a cross for the Crucifixion of our Lord. Lost after that for nearly three hundred years, it was found by Sainte Helena, mother of Constantine, the first Christian Emperor of Rome. And mother-in-law, Lucy later informed the little company of the bower, of Britain's legendary Old King Cole!

She had then, perforce, to teach the children the old rhyming game, with its appropriate actions, some of the women joining in for sheer amusement.

Father Giorgio allowed each child, as they filed out, to lay a reverent finger on the Cathedral's own sliver of holy wood, before dismissing them to enjoy their freedom for the rest of the holiday. Outside, the youngsters still chattered about the story, repeating other tales of miracles attributed to the wondrous Tree.

With Holy Cross Day behind them, the l'Mesurier household began cheerful preparations for the celebration of Michaelmas. Madame and François had many consultations before choosing the geese that would grace the table for the Feast of Saint Michael and All the Angels.

"And see that you save the wings intact, François," bade his mistress. "They make the best of dusters for corners and crevices."

Lucy remembered that her grandmother had used a goose wing for just the same purpose. A goose pinion also made an excellent hearth brush, she knew.

"Tell us the story of how Saint Michael and the Heavenly Host drove Satan out of heaven," a small boy demanded, climbing on Lucy's knee. "I would rather hear about great battles than tales of nimminy-pimminy saints dropping roses all over the place!"

"Ti-Jean! You are a wicked rascal! What if I were to tell Father Giorgio of your naughtiness?"

"But you will not," he answered serenely, making himself comfortable in her lap.

"Bad boy!" She dropped a kiss on the top of his head. "Well, now," she began. "God's favourite son, Lucifer, had behaved very badly, and his rebellious conduct had made his Father so angry that He called on His oldest son, the Archangel Michael, Commander of the Heavenly

Host, to drive Lucifer and his evil companions out of Heaven. Michael came, bright and shining in his golden armour, carrying his flaming sword, with all the Angelic Warriors streaming behind him, and stood face to face with his erring brother."

"Who was tall, dark and evil-looking," put in Ti-Jean.

"Not at all!" retorted Lucy. "I wonder why the Devil is always pictured as ill-looking, with scowling visage, horns and a tail? Actually, he was very handsome – the most handsome of all the Sons of God. Lucifer – Son of the Morning they called him, and he was radiantly beautiful. Everyone loved him, God most of all. That was his downfall, you see. He was too vain to believe that his Father would really punish him."

"Then he must have become ugly, after his fall." Stated the little boy, positively. "I have seen pictures of him. No one so wicked could stay beautiful! He could never tempt me to wickedness!"

"Oh Ti-Jean, Ti-Jean! That is rash talk. But do you think the Devil would really let himself be seen as ugly, when is hunting for souls? No one would fall for his wiles if he did. No – and his temptations all appear very attractive, too, like Cook's little honey cakes when he sets them out to cool!" she added, slyly, chuckling at the blush that suffused his little round face.

He slid from her lap. "I think I hear Paul-Luc calling me," he mumbled, avoiding her eyes, and ran hastily from the room.

"Lucy," laughed Philippa, "You are unkind! I hope you will not choose to expose my secret little peccadilloes!"

"I cannot believe that you have any, my dear," replied her friend, causing Madame Mathilde to actually snort!

The week before Michaelmas brought a change in the weather. The days grew somewhat cooler, and a succession of unseasonable thunder storms set in. Philippa began to tease her father for new winter clothes. He sighed, hemmed and hawed, and vowed she would make a beggar of him, and then bade her mother, since he must not play favourites, to clothe the whole household.

"I believe it does not get as cold here as it does in England and France," remarked Lucy.

"True," agreed her host. "But winter is winter wherever one dwells, and so the ladies must have their seasonal gowns and their fur-lined cloaks!"

"Not to mention the gentlemen, of course," Lucy teased, with a chuckle, knowing that this gentleman in particular was quite a dandy, with his own fur-lined velvet cloaks and jaunty, flat, feather-trimmed matching caps.

The Feast was superb. François had outdone himself. As well as the geese, there were huge game pies, a suckling pig, and sweets without number. Such of the blackberries that Madame Henriette had not commandeered for her jellies and cordials had been incorporated, with other fruits, into succulent pies. And of course there was a seemingly inexhaustible supply of his wonderful pastries and sweet cakes. He beamed with honest pride when M'sieur l'Mesurier insisted on everyone drinking to his good health.

After the meal there was music and singing for a while, until the younger folk became restless and began games of hide-and-seek and blind man's bluff. Lucy joined cheerfully in all the merrymaking, but the face of the Corsican fisherman was always in the back of her mind. Perhaps he had decided to go back to Corsica and never return to Cyprus. If so, she realized with a shiver, she would never really know for sure if he were alive, or lost in the untrustworthy waters of the Mediterranean Sea.

On the next sunny day, Madame Henriette insisted that they should finish harvesting the blackberries. "They must all be picked before Martinmas, as you well know," she reminded them, "for they are of no use, after the Devil has spat on them!"

Philippa sniggered. She leaned over, to whisper in Lucy's ear. "My brother Jean-Claude told me the real truth about what His Satanic Majesty does on Martinmas Eve! He said that what the Devil really does is not to spit but to piss on the berries!"

"Philippa!" Lucy was reduced to shocked, hysterical giggles. "If your *Maman* heard you say that!"

The French girl shrugged. "Well, I expect it is true. Boys always know more than girls about these things. But of course, you have no brothers to 'educate' you, have you? You are an only child. You do not know what you have missed!"

"Yes. It must be nice to have brothers and sisters," agreed Lucy. "But I was never lonely. I had neighbour children to play with, and Papa took me with him, whenever he could – to the market, and riding the estate, and to hounds, of course! No – I was never a lonely child." But then, that was why she missed her dear Papa so very much. All the splendid times they had spent together. She had never thought that their joyous companionship could ever end. How could she have been so foolish as to take such happiness for granted?

She sighed as she took up her basket and gathered the children for the climb up the cliffs to the sheltered gullies where the berries grew thickest. Today her heart was not in the outing, enthusiastic as she had been on their previous trip. Her eyes kept wandering out to sea, looking for a certain boat, hoping that this would be the day of Lion's return. Old Matthew had said Holy Cross Day – but that was long past. Anything could happen on such a long voyage. In spite of the bright sunlight she felt a distinct chill in the air that was more than the mere harbinger of winter.

By the time that Lucy and Philippa had filled their own baskets, the children were hungrily clamouring for the luncheon they had brought with them. They sat on a rocky outcropping to enjoy their meal.

"Mm'm!" groaned Lucy, as they opened up the food baskets. "Every time I as much as see one of François' wonderful pastries, I fall into the Deadly Sin of Gluttony. He should be forbidden by law, or at least Church Law, to create such irresistible temptations!"

She had not expected to enjoy such tasty dainties in this era, believing honey would be the only sweetener available. It was Philippa's father who told her of the great royal sugar plantations maintained by the Knights Hospitallers in another part of the Island.

"François is a nonpareil among cooks," Philippa assented. "His savoury concoctions are just as admirable. Do have one of his mutton pies!" She handed out the delicacies to the eagerly waiting children, and for a while there was no sound but the munching and lip-smacking of hungry youngsters.

Appetites sated at last, they all lounged on the sparse grass, or leaned against the jutting rocks, telling childish jokes and favourite stories.

"Wouldn't it be exciting if we met The Queen?" remarked one of the older girls.

"That's hardly likely, up here," laughed Lucy. Even if she were in Famagusta, I can't imagine Her Majesty climbing up here with a blackberry basket, Marie!"

"No, no!" cried the girl. "I do not speak of Queen Eleanor – I mean The Queen. The one who lives forever, and travels the whole country over. The Queen who looks after maidens, and mothers. The one the women leave gifts for, in the shrines."

"You mean the Queen of Heaven? The Virgin Mary?" asked Philippa, curiously, but the girl shook her head.

"No. The Queen has been here always, since the beginning of time. Long before the Blessed Virgin. Everyone knows about her, although Father Giorgio does not like us to speak of her. There is a shrine not far from here, if you would like to see it."

The girls of the party all clamoured to go to the shrine. The boys were definitely not interested. So the two oldest lads were left in charge of their brothers, on condition that they would not leave the spot. They were soon organizing a game they called Crusaders and Saracens that, to Lucy, looked to be almost identical to the game of Cavaliers and Roundheads she had often played in her own childhood.

Marie took the girls to a small grotto, now housing a statue of the Madonna, but she assured them that this was originally the place where one might make request of, or leave thank offerings for, The Queen. While the Island was now Christian, the custom of offerings still continued. The statue of Our Lady was a Christian innovation with the Church cunningly incorporating, as it so often did, the rituals of earlier religions. Marie pointed out wax hands, small carvings, scraps of material, and small dolls – all gifts of gratitude from those who had been healed, or had received prayed-for blessings.

Both the English girl and her French friend felt uncomfortable, and soon began to shepherd their charges back to the berry baskets, although they noticed that nearly every one of the Cypriote children left some small offering – a hair ribbon, a bead bracelet or a hastily gathered handful of wildflowers. Obviously, the legend of The Queen was not unknown to them.

The wind had begun to rise, dampening the air, and tumbling grayish clouds across the sky. Fearing rain, and their own baskets being full, Philippa and Lucy turned their efforts to helping the little ones fill theirs. Soon, all were heaped to the brim, and the small entourage started hastily back the way they had come. By now, the sky had assumed a dull leaden hue, and the wind-whipped sea was piling itself into gray-green pyramids. Small fishing boats could be seen, beating slowly shoreward, striving to make harbour before the storm should hit. Was one of them, by any chance, the Stella Maris? Lucy wondered.

The berrying party had scarcely reached the shelter of the l'Mesurier home before the full force of the tempest struck the city. The rain came down in a veritable cloudburst, while lightning jetted across the sky and great cracks of thunder shook the house to its foundations.

"God bless all at sea!" prayed Madame, crossing herself, and Lucy uttered a fervent "Amen!", silently petitioning that one sailor in particular should find a safe harbour, and fighting off the terror that, since that fateful day of the eclipse, now assailed her in violent weather.

The severe storms continued for several days, with thunder, lightning, and sporadic downpours keeping most of the household indoors. Lucy took advantage of every short break in its fury to patrol the shore, watching for the Stella Maris. Once, she found oranges scattered among the flotsam washed up on the littoral and paled at the thought that they might have come from Lionallo's boat. Didn't seamen carry citrus fruits with them, to prevent scurvy? She knew he had a liking for oranges. She chided herself, immediately, for such foolish imaginings. There was no reason to think that they had come from his boat. There could be a hundred reasons for their presence on the shore. Only a fool would jump to such hasty, unsubstantiated conclusions.

One cool November dawn, she quietly slipped out of the castle and, wrapped in her scarlet wool cloak, wandered slowly down to the shore. She was not the only one searching the lowering horizon. Old Matthew was there before her, leaning on his staff with both hands as he stared into the distance.

"Ar! Thee b'st watchin' for en too, then." It was a statement rather than a question and Lucy accepted it as such, merely nodding her head, as she joined him in his vigil.

"The storms have been very severe," she remarked, after a few minutes.

"A's a good seaman, siddee. Knows what en's about."

"And the Stella Maris is a sturdy craft." Lucy raised a hand to her brow. Was that just a cloud, on the horizon? The sky was fast darkening, with only a pale paring of the fading moon fighting the gloom.

With a heavy heart, Lucy gathered her cloak more tightly around her and turned away, matching her pace to her old companion's limping gait.

When he left her, she returned to her harvesting. Another disappointing day. Then, late in the afternoon, straightening up to stretch her back after wrestling a stubborn root of purple dulse from its rocky anchor, she saw the Stella Maris sliding into her accustomed moorings. Forgetting her basket, she gathered the skirts of her green kirtle and flew along the littoral, her unbound hair streaming behind her like a ship's pennant.

Lionallo saw her coming and jumped, barefoot, into the water and onto the sandy beach, awaiting her with a grin that split in two the short, curly beard that now adorned his face and practically threatened his ears!

She stopped dead, a few yards away from him, embarrassment flooding her face with scarlet as she realized her unladylike lack of restraint. Whatever would Mama have thought of her hoydenish behaviour? Or Madame l'Mesurier, as far as that went! She hesitated, staring at him with tear-bright eyes. He opened his arms. With a smothered sob she rushed into his embrace and wept against the rough cloth that covered his broad chest, as he gently rocked her back and forth.

"I was afraid you were never coming back!" she mumbled.

"So you missed me, little one," he murmured, "Are you ready now, to come with me to Corsica?"

She pulled away from him. "Certainly not! You will recollect that I am still betrothed."

"Then these tears are not for me? I thought you wept for joy, at my safe return." His dark eyes twinkled with mischief.

"Of course I am happy that you have come back safely." Lucy tossed a defiant head. "I would be joyful for the return of any friend. I have not so many that I can afford to lose a single one."

"Not even a rough, lowly fisherman?" he chuckled.

Lucy clicked her tongue in exasperation. "Oh, don't be such a sapskull, Lion!" she exclaimed, with an impatient toss of her head.

"Come here!" He beckoned with both hands.

Unthinkingly, she moved toward him, and he reached out to draw her into a fierce embrace that robbed her of breath, as his lips came down on hers in a passionate kiss that she was shocked to find herself returning.

She beat at his chest with both fists, persuading him to ease his grasp a little.

"Let me go. Please!" she entreated. "This is wrong. You know that I am promised to Sir Edward."

"That laggardly Englishman!" Lionallo's voice and face both registered disgust. "How can you chain yourself to such a dreary fool?" He let her go.

"You are not to disparage him!" she flared. "He is a good and noble Christian knight, and he is very dear to me! I care very much for him."

"Dear to you! Care for him! Do you know how feeble your protests sound? Do you 'feel' for him, what you 'feel' for me, when you are in my arms?"

"I feel nothing but anger, that you should use me so!" she retorted, avoiding his searching eyes.

"Liar!" He reached out for her, but she skipped back, beyond his reach. He leaned forward, hands on hips, glaring into her face. "You deny that your heart did not respond to mine – that you did not return my kisses, with as much passion as I gave? Deceive yourself if you will – you will not convince me that you were indifferent."

Lucy bit her lip. "I was taken by surprise. I feel deep friendship for you. That is all," she muttered, uncertainly. She gasped as, with an exasperated groan, he stepped forward and again caught her in his arms, to capture her reluctant lips beneath his own, once more drawing a passionate, if unwilling response. Abruptly, he released her. His shout of laughter startled her.

"Little witling!" he chided softly. "But I am a fool, to have rushed you so. Come. I will not press you -- now. We will be friends, until you understand that you were sent here for me. Not Estur. You are my destiny, as I am your doom!"

He held out his hand. Hesitantly she took it.

"I do not want to be at odds with you, Lion," she murmured, anxiety wrinkling her brow. "You were my first friend in this world, and will always be the dearest."

"Then that must be enough for now." He gave her a hearty hug, and watched with speculative interest as she made her way back to her harvesting. For a moment he hesitated, with half a mind to join her, then shrugged and turned away, scrambling up the cliff, to take a short cut to the town.

*   *   *

M'sieur l'Mesurier entered his solar, to find it deserted except for the presence of his young guest *la petite Anglais*, ensconced in the window embrasure. Lucy jumped up, to greet her host with a sketchy curtsey, a cheerful smile smoothing out the frown lines on her brow.

"Good day, M'sieur," she greeted him.

"And to you, *ma petite*," he returned. "You looked troubled, when I entered. Does something worry you?"

Lucy hesitated. She needed to talk to someone. At home, she would not have delayed to pour out her heart to her dear Papa. Philippa's Papa was almost as kind and understanding. Perhaps she could confide in him.

"M'sieur," she sighed. "I must confess that I am in need of guidance and wise counsel. If I might impose on your good nature ... "

"But of course, *ma chère*. Look upon me as your own Papa – and I will, if it be possible, advise you as I would my little Philippa." He lowered himself onto the wide window seat, facing her.

Lucy twisted a handful of the stuff of her gown, between nervous fingers. "It is about my betrothal to Sir Edward. I no longer feel that I wish to marry him."

Her companion made no answer, merely regarded her with an inquiring smile, as if waiting for her to continue.

"I do like him, very much, and he has been so wonderfully kind to me, but the fact remains that I do not care for him as one should for the man one is to marry and spend the rest of one's life with. What should I do?"

"How do you feel for Sir Edward?"

Lucy hesitated. "I love Edward as I love Ti-Jean, or little Babette, in a protective sort of way. I thought that was how it should be. But now I know I was wrong."

"There is someone else?"

Lucy made her troubled eyes meet his, as she acknowledged his quiet question.

"And the feelings you have for him are those you think you should have for a husband?"

Lucy hesitated. "I think so. I'm not sure. With Lionallo, everything is so mixed up, and different. I feel so alive when I am near him and can't wait to see him again when he leaves. I thought of him all the time when he was away, when I should have been thinking of the man to whom I am betrothed. But I have given Sir Edward my word," she finished, disconsolately.

L'Mesurier frowned. So – it was that young Corsican. Couldn't blame her. Estur was a good Christian soldier, but definitely dull. The quick, inquiring young maid would be wasted on him, leaving her spiritually starved and mentally unfulfilled. But a common fisherman ...

"Papa was very strict about keeping one's promises," Lucy continued. "He was proud that his word was always accepted as his bond. He boasted that all his business deals were made with only a handshake."

The Frenchman grimaced. With an attitude like that, a man would hardly survive in the cutthroat world of international commerce!

"But I do not think he would want me to marry, against my will." Lucy frowned. "He always promised that I should be free to make my own choice."

"Then you will go with this Momellino? Think carefully about this, my dear. Life with a fisherman would be a very different prospect from marriage to an English knight. As Sir Edward Estur's wife you would have comfort, security and social position. You would want for nothing. Whereas married to a fisherman, what kind of life could you hope for, buried in some obscure little Corsican village, where your only companions would be uneducated peasants?" He regarded her, pensively. "Then too, you must take into account that Sir Edward will eventually return to England, where you will be reunited with your own family again."

"There is no one to go back to," murmured Lucy absently.

Hah! So he was right. He had long had a feeling that her parents must have been travelling with her. Having seen them drown, her young mind refused to accept the truth, and had blacked out the memory of their deaths.

"Give me some time to think about this, my child, and you must give it more consideration too." He knew he was procrastinating, but he felt honour bound to do his best for this lost maiden. But he had a duty to Estur, also. What if his own Philippa had been cast up, alone and friendless, on a foreign shore? He would talk to this Momellino, find out what kind of fellow he was. Perhaps he could be made to see the unsuitability of his attentions to a young lady of refinement and gentle breeding.

But Lionallo had brought news. The Crusaders were on their way home. The fleet was heading for Lammasol, and from there the King and his followers would travel to the capital, Nicosia. The French gentleman sighed with relief. Sir Edward would soon be here to take charge of his own affairs.

10

The attack had not been made on Smyrna after all. That rumour had been fostered by King Peter to conceal his real intentions, a strike at Alexandria, the gateway to the East. The Venetians' only interest was in safeguarding their trade routes. They'd sabotaged his earlier Crusade by spreading false tales of its cancellation, so that the armies intending to join him had disbanded and returned to their homes. Remembering this, Peter had taken no chances, even though the Pope, his most enthusiastic supporter, had ordered Venice to assist his Holy Cause.

The l'Mesurier household was as excited as any by the reports, especially as the master decreed that they should journey at once to the capital to take part in the welcome home and the celebrations that were bound to follow. Besides, not all his followers shared the King's idealistic dedication to the Great Quest. Many attended him merely for the opportunity such an expedition offered for pillage and loot. There might be some fine bargains to be picked up.

Mesurier's steward had already rented a fine loggia, and all was ready for the family when they arrived with the rest of the Famagusta contingent, a few days ahead of King Peter and such of his knights who had elected to follow him to Nicosia for the victory celebrations. Great preparations were already being made for these celebrations. M'sieur l'Mesurier recklessly promised all the ladies of his household a new gown apiece, then hid himself in his office to avoid the clamour and frantic activity that immediately erupted.

Lucy refused his offer and sought him in his hideout. "M'sieur, I wish to talk to you. I have decided that, feeling as I do about Lionallo, I cannot marry Sir Edward."

"Then you are going to the fisherman?"

"No. I cannot do that while I am still betrothed to Sir Edward. As soon as he returns I shall ask him to release me."

"And if he should refuse?"

Lucy paled. "In that event, I must honour my commitment." She took a deep breath. "In the meantime, I cannot continue to accept Sir Edward's support. I have no means of my own, as you know, but I do have these." She drew a kerchief from her pocket and unwrapped its contents – a locket, a bracelet, earrings and a ring, all of solid gold, the latter two set with matching pearls, with the half sovereign that her mother insisted she always carry for emergencies. "I was wearing these when I left home. They were all presents from Papa. He wanted to give me emeralds, but Mama said that I was too young for jewels. They would have been useful now." She held them out to him. "I would like you to sell them for me. I hope they will bring enough to pay for the clothes Sir Edward gave me, and for my keep in your home."

"My dear, I have deducted nothing from Sir Edward's funds toward your support. Madame *ma femme* insists that you more than repay her by your industry and services to our household. Keep these until Sir Edward returns and settle your accounts with him personally. Unless," he added, "you wish me to treat with him on your behalf."

"No!" Lucy straightened her shoulders. "I thank you, but I must speak to him myself. Not to do so would be dishonourable and cowardly."

The Frenchman shrugged. She was certainly an unusual young woman. Perhaps she would change her mind when reunited with the English knight, but he doubted it.

*   *   *

There was great excitement when the royal party was sighted. The news ran around the capital like wildfire and the populace rushed out to witness their arrival, Lucy and Philippa among them. Lucy's first glimpse of Pierre de Lusignan, King of Cyprus, startled her. She had been inclined to take the almost idolatrous praises sung of his attractiveness with a grain of salt. But, even allowing for the extra glamour conferred on royalty, she could understand why Pope Urban had named him

Athlete of God. He was exceptionally tall, head and shoulders above most men of his time, whom Lucy found to be several inches shorter than the men of her own era. She herself was considered tall here, although she had been slightly below average height at home.

Towering over his companions, he carried his bascinet, a gift from King Edward III of England, tucked under one arm. His abundant fair hair glowed golden in the pale sunshine, and his brilliant blue eyes sparkled as he beamed on the cheering crowds. He definitely fulfilled anyone's conception of kingliness.

Lucy turned to Philippa, whose anxious eyes were eagerly searching for the face of her lover among the King's train, and belatedly realized that she herself should be watching out for Sir Edward.

"There he is! There is Sir Guy!" Philippa was jumping up and down at her side, wildly waving her silk scarf. "He has returned, safe and sound!"

Philippa caught the French knight's eye and her enthusiasm subsided, blushingly, into modest confusion. His face brightened with a huge grin, then paled as he noticed Lucy standing at her side. He checked his instinctive start in their direction and stood still, his sombre gaze probing the crowd, as if seeking a particular face. When relief relaxed his taut expression, Lucy followed his stare to the portly but elegant figure of M'sieur l'Mesurier. She could not see Edward anywhere, which surprised her, as she had expected the two friends to be keeping close company.

Perhaps Edward had been wounded. Being so certain of his survival, it had never occurred to her before that he might well sustain a wound, even a serious hurt. That would account for Sir Guy's apprehensive expression when he set eyes on her. If so, she fervently hoped his injury was not severe or painful. She did not fear for his life, as she knew that he would eventually recover and return to his Island home.

*   *   *

"No! That cannot be – it is a mistake. Sir Edward did not die!" White faced, Lucy stared incredulously at the other occupants of the solar, all regarding her with pity – Philippa softly sobbing and Madame's eyes bright with sympathetic tears.

"I am afraid that it is so, my dear child," said M'sieur. "You must reconcile yourself to the fact that he will not be coming back. He has gone to his honourable reward."

"No, no! I know that there has been an error. He cannot be dead. I am sure that he is still alive. A search must be made for him!"

"My dear Lady Lucy." It was Sir Guy who answered her, his voice trembling with emotion. "I myself saw him fall. We were fighting together, each guarding the other's blind side. You will recall that he wore a patch on his right eye and I on my left."

"And wasn't that a stupid idea," she thought.

"Then a sudden shift in the battle set His Majesty in imminent danger. His squire called for help and Edward immediately forced his way toward the King. I was held at bay for several minutes by the foe I was engaging and won free just in time to see a Saracen knight attack him from the right."

"His blind side," muttered Lucy.

"Quite so. He struck Edward such a mighty blow on the head with his sabre that it split the bascinet and could not be pulled out until Edward had fallen to the ground. No mortal man could have withstood such a blow. It was impossible for me to reach him, as I was fully occupied with my own antagonist. Afterward," he continued, apologetically, "I was unable to search for his body as I was sick with wound fever (Lucy heard Philippa catch her breath) from some small cuts I had taken, and was put on board ship. But Onfroi and his friends sought most diligently for him, for two days. They could find no trace of either him or Geoffrey. I am sorry, dear Lady. I grieve for your loss. I myself have lost a good friend and companion."

"He is not dead – I know that he will return home," Lucy insisted, doggedly. "You will see!"

Eustache l'Mesurier regarded her with pity. Without doubt it was guilt, knowing that she intended to jilt the man, that prevented the poor child from acknowledging his death. It would take time to reconcile her to the fact that the knight would never return. Well, at least she was well provided for. Estur's chivalrous consideration had taken care of that.

11

To everyone's delight, Pierre de Lusignan's first act on returning home was to bring the Lady Joanna out of the convent. It was unanimously agreed that her beauty had been in no way impaired by her incarceration. The victory celebrations, which were to last for eight days, began with a great parade and a Grand Mass, presided over by Pope Urban's famous legate, Peter Thomas. He had accompanied King Peter on his western tour to seek allies and support for his Crusade, and remained by his side until the hostilities ended.

The entire city, in gala mood, participated wholeheartedly in the festivities. Nicosia seemed suddenly to be the hub of some gigantic fair, with stalls and entertainers appearing as if by magic out of thin air. Tumblers, sword swallowers, knife throwers, and strong men performed at every street corner. Wherever one went there were hurdy gurdy players, singers and story tellers. Already, the Crusade and its participants were immortalized in song and spoken word. Individual feats of heroism, especially those pertaining to royalty, were loudly proclaimed in both prose and verse. The l'Mesuriers, Sir Guy in tow, went everywhere and saw everything. Lucy went with them, as she refused to mourn Edward, maintaining that he was still alive.

There was a royal banquet each day, and M'sieur l'Mesurier, as a Deputy Consul, and his family were included in the royal guest list, attending all the feasts with delight. Madame was diligent in her instructions on correct behaviour, and Lucy was hard put to hide her smiles when the good dame forbade, on pain of unmentionable retributions, that any of her charges should poke their fingers into eggs, polish bones with their teeth, or use their thumbs to butter their bread.

Neither must they use the table cloth to wipe their mouths or their knives, and heaven help any one of them should he or she spit across the table!

Ladies having had ample opportunity to complete their toilettes, and most gentlemen having by that time taken care of their business and other commitments, dinner was served about ten o'clock. That left plenty of time for other activities, sometimes a performance by acrobats and jongleurs, sometimes a cockfight, or bear-baiting, or country style dancing, or even a hunt.

As the diners entered the hall, servants met the most favoured guests with a washbowl and an aquamanile – a grotesque bronze water container from which they poured clean rose-scented water over the personage's hands, providing a linen towel for drying. The less important folk washed their hands in a lavabo just inside the door, and dried their hands on a long communal towel, which was disgustingly black before the late-comers reached it. Lucy could see the need for hand-washing, as most diners shared a platter. Since Philippa was seated next to Sir Guy, who was now officially accepted as her suitor, Lucy was paired with an older lady, a widowed dependent of her hosts. She hoped her companion had washed her hands as thoroughly as she herself had done! Their dishes and cups were of pewter, although Madame Clothilde had brought her own silver goblet. Lower down the table, the dinnerware was made of wood, while at the high table, Royalty dined off the new, very rare earthenware platters, imported from Spain.

M'sieur had offered to purchase some for Madame, but she had pooh-poohed the suggestion.

"My dear Eustache," she had declaimed. "You will not waste your gold on such frippery. Earthenware dishes, indeed! All very well for royalty, who, I am told, have one serving man whose whole duty it is to take care of those platters, but how long do you think they would last in this household? The slightest knock and they will chip, or crack – drop one, and it would shatter into a thousand slivers. They are as fragile as glass. No, no, *mon cher mari*! It is but a passing whim. Such nonsense will never catch on."

Lucy, with a stupendous effort, had kept a straight face and a still tongue.

There were no forks, but by now she was quite adept with her pretty knife; like everyone else, she always carried it with her as it often came in useful during the day for minor chores like trimming finger nails or cutting embroidery thread.

Their trenchers were each lined with a thick slice of bread which, soaked from the meat juices, would later be saved and given to the poor. The food was plentiful and sumptuous, all kinds of meat, fish and birds – even gulls, herons and storks. Most of the meat was seethed or pounded, as it was very stringy and tough, but, well cooked and seasoned with strong spices, it had been made into delicious stews and pies. There was also roast venison and suckling piglets cooked whole. Wine, ale and mead were all available. Lucy, as usual, chose watered wine, flavoured with honey and ginger.

Her companion was more interested in food than in conversation, so Lucy was able to study the company with undisturbed interest. She noted that a great many of the guests, especially the men, had definitely not been tutored in table etiquette by such a particular lady as Madame l'Mesurier. Not only did many of them "polish bones" with their teeth, one man actually cleaned his teeth with the tablecloth!

Each day revealed a new demonstration of the kitchen staff's artistic ingenuity. These culinary masterpieces were borne in by pages on stretcher-like serving trays and presented first in front of the high table, where the King and his most favoured guests were seated, to be admired and applauded by the assembled company.

One day the *pièce de résistance* was a roasted peacock served with its feathers replaced. The next day the place of honour was given to a cockatrice, a strange creation formed from the head of a piglet and the body of some kind of large fowl. Another day produced a large spun-sugar swan with a gilded beak, swimming on a green pastry pond. And the last feast was concluded with the presentation of what Lucy knew as a "subtlety", quite popular as a party dessert in her own time, being a confection of almond paste, sugar and jelly, modelled to represent the fort at Alexandria, with small marchpane figures, representing the King and his knights, standing triumphantly before it.

But Lucy and Philippa both agreed that the most spectacular piece had been presented on the day when a hunt had been arranged for the afternoon. The knights, and those ladies who hunted, had brought their falcons and hawks with them, and each bird perched on the back of its owner's chair. Several pages staggered in, bearing an enormous pie. The cook accompanied them, begging the King to do him the honour of cutting the first piece. His Majesty, obviously involved in the conspiracy, graciously agreed and sliced off the whole top – causing immediate panic, as a flock of small birds erupted from the dish, to fly wildly all over the hall, inducing pandemonium among hawks and diners alike. With wild whoops, the hunters released their own birds, who instantly swept down with enthusiasm upon the easy prey. Ladies shrieked and covered their heads. Men laughed, and swiped those avian intruders that came within reach, and the entire gathering disintegrated into chaos.

It was on the third day of the celebrations that Lucy was presented to King Peter, who spent some time each day moving among and talking to his guests. That she was Edward Estur's betrothed intrigued him, and he immediately offered his condolences on the knight's death, going into some detail as to Sir Edward's gallantry.

"We were indeed in dire straits at that moment, and but for the fearless efforts of our valiant companion, We fear We would not be here today," he told her. "We grieve for your loss, which is also Our own. Edward was a friend of long standing." He eyed her with an interest that she found rather embarrassing, so open was his appreciation of her trim figure and attractive face. "Do not worry, my dear. You shall not be unprotected. We shall soon find you a husband worthy of your charms."

Lucy stifled a gasp. "Your Majesty is indeed considerate," she answered hastily. "But I am sure that will not be necessary. I am convinced that Sir Edward is still alive, and will soon return to us."

"Alas! We could wish that were true," sighed the monarch, sympathetically. "But too many of us saw him fall beneath the Infidel's blade. No, my dear. Do not deceive yourself. Much as we might wish it otherwise, our beloved Edward has gone to his just reward. He has gone as a good Knight would wish to go. But of course, you must have time to mourn him. I shall keep you in my thoughts, and we will speak again." He bent his golden head and kissed her soundly, full on the lips, leaving her astounded, and passed on.

The message she read in his eyes, added to the caressing look he bestowed on her as he moved away, sent a small shiver down her spine.

She hoped he would forget her. She caught the eye of a sophisticated beauty, radiant in green samite, among his attendants and was shocked by the vindictive stare turned upon her.

"Who is that woman in green?" she asked.

Madame Clothilde peered after the royal party. "Who? Oh, that is Echive de Scandelion, the King's mistress."

Lucy was confused. "But I thought the Lady Joanna . . ."

Her companion smirked. "His Majesty is too much man to be satisfied by one woman," she answered. "Joanna and Echive are his favourites, but there are others, and I think you will be offered the opportunity to join their company! Did not the great Pierre de Lusignan promise that he would not forget you! It can easily be seen in which direction that wind blows."

"I do not understand you, Madame," murmured Lucy, a puzzled frown wrinkling her forehead, as she gazed after the departing King.

Vaguely disquieted by the soft whisperings of those onlookers who had noticed the attentions de Lusignan bestowed upon her, Lucy looked around warily. Leaning against a supporting pillar, and regarding her with cynical amusement, she saw the hard-faced man whom Philippa had named L'Amoureux. When he saw her looking at him, he made a sarcastically elaborate bow. For some reason she felt intimidated, and was relieved when, with a glance at the people surrounding them, Madame Clothilde took her arm and led her to a more secluded area.

"You are very fortunate, my dear," she said. "His Majesty has obviously conceived a *tendresse* for you."

"Ridiculous, Madame!" Lucy was shocked. "You must not say such things, even in jest. What if one of the Queen's ladies should overhear? They might believe it to be true."

"And that would be most unfortunate. Eleanor brooks no rivalry."

"I shall give her no cause for jealousy," declared Lucy.

"You may have no choice," warned the older woman. "If he really desires you. Pierre de Lusignan will not be denied. For appearances sake, he will marry you off to one of his more impecunious knights, one who will be content to look the other way in return for a suitable settlement, and that will be that! You will have no say in the matter, either way."

Lucy glared at her companion. "Fustian!" she snapped. "I am not one of his subjects. He cannot command me!" With an indignant toss of her russet curls she stalked away, leaving the other woman to follow or not, as she pleased.

"You think not, my child?" The older woman hurried to keep pace with her. "Consider. Alone and with no dowry to secure you a husband, what are your prospects? An obliging and complaisant husband will be provided for your protection. You will have your position at court, and the King is known to be a most accomplished and generous lover!"

"And the Queen a ferocious and implacable enemy! I have no desire to suffer Joanna l'Aleman's fate!"

"She does well enough, now that the King has returned. Besides, Eleanor needs to step carefully herself these days. They say that His Majesty is seriously investigating the tales of her infidelity with Sir John."

And indeed, Peter was inquiring into the tales told of his queen and Sir John de Morphou. The whole capital rumbled with malicious interest, with a dozen different scandals daily making the rounds.

"They say that de Morphou has bribed Joanna and Echive to accuse poor John Visconte of having concocted the scandal himself out of whole cloth!" Madame Clothilde, who had connections in the palace, informed her eager listeners in the bower one wet afternoon.

"And who are 'they'?" demanded Madame Mathilde, biting off the end of an embroidery thread – a practice she would roundly rebuke, in any of her underlings, as being disastrous for the teeth!

"Henriette had it from an old herb woman – a serf of Sir John's."

"But His Majesty will not be taken in by their lies," Madame l'Mesurier put in, quietly. "Everyone knows Sir John's character is above reproach. Anyway, the King has decided to turn the whole business over to the Haut Cour."

12

L ucy was curious when her host approached her one morning, saying,
"I should like to speak to you *ma chère*, privately, if you will. The
matter is of grave importance." M'sieur Eustache l'Mesurier nodded to
his wife. "And perhaps, *ma chère femme*, you will lend us your presence.
We shall most certainly need your advice."

Lucy and Madame put aside their needlework and followed him into
his office, where he courteously seated them before his desk. He did not
sit down, but picked up a small scroll from his desk, and walked
thoughtfully back and forth a few times, as if preparing for a speech.
Madame sat with quiet hands folded in her lap. Lucy waited, appre-
hensively, manners preventing her from hurrying him. Could it be news
of Edward?

At last he unrolled the scroll, saying, "This was brought by a messen-
ger from the Chancellor, Sir Philippe le Mézières. It is a list of names of
gentlemen whom the King considers a suitable match for you. I . . ."

Lucy jumped to her feet, aghast.

"For me? A match for me! He has windmills in his cockloft! I am
already betrothed, as he well knows, to Sir Edward Estur, who . . ."

"Who is no longer with us, my dear."

"I refuse to believe that he is dead. Indeed, I know he is not! But
even if it were so, I would never marry a man not of my own choosing.
And certainly His Majesty has no right to demand it. He is not my
king. He has no authority over me."

"I am afraid that he thinks otherwise, my child. Sir Edward is his
sworn liege man, and as his promised wife, you are now under King
Peter's wardship."

"We'll see about that!" A thought came to her. She spun around to face him. "Besides, who would want me? As you say, these men marry for gain, for land or fortune, and I have neither," she finished, triumphantly.

"You are wrong in that last. As Sir Philippe well knows, Sir Edward's fortune, left in my care, is considerable and very attractive to an impoverished knight."

"But that is not my money!"

"Before he sailed, your betrothed named you his sole beneficiary, apart from a sum set aside for the Church for masses to be sung for his soul's welfare."

Lucy stared at him, for once speechless. M'sieur took advantage of the moment to offer the parchment. "Here are the names of the men His Majesty suggests you consider."

She gazed blankly at the scroll, but made no move to take it. He sighed, and himself began to read out the names.

"Sir Thomas Farnliegh."

His wife gave a gasp of horror. "Not that villain!" she protested. "Two wives have already died at his hands. He is a vicious, evil, drunken brute who does not deserve to be named human – even his hounds run from him!"

Her husband did not disagree. He returned to the list. "The Compte de Langeville."

"Surely you jest!" Madame was tight-lipped. "The man is in his dotage – and disgustingly filthy in his person and in his habits. A swineherd's widow would refuse him," she raged.

"Gustave L'Amoureux."

Lucy's stomach rolled over. A frisson of fear sent the tiny hairs on her arms aquiver. L'Amoureux! Never! There was something about that man, handsome and courtly though some might think him, that radiated evil. She remembered his sneering smile … Why was Madame's expression so peculiar?

"So-o-o!" breathed that lady, disgust twisting her normally charming features. "Now I understand." She turned pitying, tear-bright eyes on the girl whom she had come to regard as another daughter, rising to enfold her in motherly arms. "Oh, *ma pauvre enfant!*"

"What do you mean, Madame? What is it that you understand?"

Lucy drew away from the good lady, in some alarm. M'sieur was glowering in an anger as fierce as his wife's.

"This means that the King desires you for himself," he said.

"Impossible!" gasped Lucy. "I cannot believe that!"

Her protector regarded her with grave concern. He tapped the parchment with a blunt finger. "I am afraid that it is so," he told her. "These first two names are merely for show. No woman would marry either, of her own free will."

"Nor would any woman in her right mind accept Gustave L'Amoureux," cut in Madame, angrily. "That – that – creature!"

She was too overcome to say more.

Lucy looked from one to the other of her foster parents, in bewilderment. "I don't understand," she muttered.

"Of course you do not." The Frenchwoman's eyes turned to her husband. "How could a young girl have knowledge of such a wretch. Eustache!"

That gentleman's tanned face reddened as he took the girl's hand. Avoiding her eyes, he said, "*Ma chère*, there are some men born into this world who are innately evil. They acquire base, unnatural vices that set them apart from decent human beings. This l'Amoureux is even more monstrous than they. He caters to their loathsome appetites. He provides them with . . ." He looked to his wife, and shrugged. This was embarrassing. "The means to satisfy their brutish cravings." Confound it! The child had no inkling as to his meaning. He cleared his throat, and tried again. "This man is a slave trader. He buys and sells young girls. Very young girls. He condemns them to a life of misery and sin." He removed his spectacles to wipe the perspiration from his brow, then, to gain a few moments, carefully polished the lenses. He was rather proud of his glasses. Spectacles were not easily come by. He had purchased his from an Arab merchant with whom he did a considerable amount of business.

Actually, Eustache knew a great deal more about Gustave l'Amoureux's nefarious transactions than he would dream of revealing to his wife, let alone an innocent young maid. The man's name was anathema to any decent Christian. There were whispers of torture chambers, and even Black Masses. It was believed that there was no corrupt or wicked practice beyond his touch.

Lucy knew about slavery, of course, and she had sometimes heard conversations between her father and his friends, about discussions on the subject in Parliament. As for what M'sieur was hinting at ... She had heard the ladies of the court whispering of such things, but had paid scant attention. Her mind had not really accepted such chilling gossip as more than bizarre slander.

To be bound to such a man! The blood rushed to her heart, leaving her cold and dizzy. Madame's arm encircled her, and guided her back to her chair, into which she sank most gratefully.

"But why?" she asked piteously, staring from one to the other of her friends. "Why would the King wish me to marry such a ... brute? What does he want from him? And if this l'Amoureux creature despises women, why should he consent to the marriage, even to please His Majesty?"

"L'Amoureux is always at *point-non-plus* ... pockets to let," was the answer. "He is an incorrigible gamester. He has gambled away his inheritance and is over his belt in debt. For such a dowry as you would bring him, he would marry the Devil's daughter!"

Lucy shuddered. "But how does that profit King Peter?"

It would be shameful for the King to seduce an innocent young maiden, but a neglected wife ... Gustave wants only your gold, so he would make no objections – nay, he would be delighted were his wife to become His Majesty's leman – Pierre would be under an obligation to him – would owe him favours."

"I fear the King will not be denied," interjected Madame, sadly.

"Then I must leave here, immediately! I must hide from them," Lucy declared.

"At once! And we shall help you, *chère enfant*. Eustache!"

Not so fast, my dear wife!" l'Mesurier held up a warning hand. "My duty to my country demands that I do not offend the King of Cyprus."

"You will not desert this child? She is as one of my own – I will not see her sacrificed!" Angry tears sprang to Celeste's eyes as she tugged at her husband's arm.

"Softly, softly, *ma chère*! He patted her hand. "The situation calls for diplomacy. We have time. Certainly our little Lucy cannot be expected to jump into matrimony before her betrothed is cold in his grave."

"He is not in his grave! I know he still lives," insisted Lucy, but the

Frenchman's kindly face and encouraging tone warmed her frightened heart.

"First, we must leave Nicosia," reflected M'sieur, pacing gravely back and forth the length of his accounting room. "I have it on good authority that not all the ships came back to Lammasol. Some vessels carrying wounded were separated from the main fleet by the terrible storms they encountered on the return voyage, but they have since made port at Famagusta."

He grinned wickedly down at them, as they sat expectantly forward in their seats, intrigued by his air of conspiracy. "I am convinced that my official duties make it imperative that I should return to Famagusta as soon as possible, and, since my own affairs are now in such good order that I may safely leave them in the capable hands of my steward, we shall now go back home, particularly as Madame feels that Nicosian society is becoming too rowdy for gentlewomen to countenance. There, perchance, we may hear news of the good Sir Edward. I would not wish to raise your hopes unduly, child, but I understand that many wounded have been put ashore there, in the care of the good Knights Hospitallers."

Madame was ecstatic. "Yes! Yes! Eustache, you are brilliant! The King and Sir Philippe well know that our little Lucy has not accepted Sir Edward's death. She will come with us, for she is persuaded that she will find her betrothed there." The good lady beamed at Lucy. "Is that not so, my dear?"

Lucy's face brightened. "Of course! That must be where he is … Thank you, Madame, M'sieur. Thank you."

M'sieur grimaced, and his wife took the girl's two slender hands in her warm clasp. "*Ma petite*, you will not allow your hopes to rise too high, *hein*? None of his friends believe that he could have survived such a terrible wound."

"Oh, but I know!" Lucy hugged her foster mother. "I shall find him in Famagusta. Everything will be all right now. May I go and tell Philippa?"

She dropped a sketch curtsey as Eustache, forbearing to mention that Madame's earlier suggestion that removing the girl from the King's vicinity would only temporarily prove true the old adage "Out of sight, out of mind", smiled his assent.

With a Gallic shrug, he sighed. "At least this buys her some time. And there is always the Corsican."

"The Corsican?" Madame pounced on his absent-minded remark, and was soon in possession of all that he knew about Lionallo Momellino.

13

Lucy was in high alt as she kept assuring Philippa, who was not too
enthusiastic about the move until Sir Guy, now released from his
knightly vows, asked for and received permission to accompany them.
Then she flew even higher into the boughs than her English friend.

They could not leave immediately. The festivities were to conclude
with a Grand Tourney, and the Montpellier Representative intended to
be careful to give no cause for offence. He informed Sir Phillipe de
Mézières of his impending departure, and suggested that it would be as
well to allow the little Lightfoot to continue with her search for Estur.
The Chancellor was not an unkind man, and agreed to allow the maid
some latitude. She must eventually realize that Sir Edward would never
return, and bow to His Majesty's orders. Although he made no com-
ment, it was obvious that he found the whole affair distasteful.

He proposed Twelfth Night as a suitable date for the nuptials – a
dramatic conclusion to the Christmas festivities. Assuming that Gustave
L'Amoureux would be the chosen bridegroom, as was the King's intention, the marriage ceremony would be conducted at the Pope's
Cathedral. Lucy made a small moué of distaste when told of the
arrangements, but was not really worried. Long before then she would
have found Edward, begged her release, and married Lion. Everything
was going to work out splendidly. A fig for Pierre de Lusignan and his
machinations!

The l'Mesurier family attended the Tourney with little enthusiasm.
Since Sir Guy's wounded shoulder prevented him from participating,
the field held no interest for Philippa, and her parents had other matters
on their minds. Lucy was hard put to hide her revulsion when Gustave

L'Amoureux mockingly kissed her hand, begging a glove from her to wear on his helmet as a sign of her favour.

She would have liked to refuse but, advised by an almost imperceptible nod from her protector, she coldly acquiesced, remembering, with a pang of sorrow, the blue scarf that Sir Edward had so proudly flaunted on that last morning, before he boarded the ship that was to bear him off to the wars. It would be wise, she realized, to appear submissive to the King's will – best not to allow any suspicion as to her real intentions.

Pierre de Lusignan had a great fondness for tournaments, being an accomplished participant himself. One of his most cherished possessions was the helmet awarded him by King Edward III of England, a fellow monarch and an equal enthusiast of the sport. During the King of Cyprus' visit to England to drum up support for his Crusade, King Edward could not resist the urge to host a tourney to outshine all other tourneys. It was his genuine appreciation of de Lusignan's prowess and gallantry on that occasion that prompted the treasured gift. Peter was wearing it today, an imposing figure in the field.

At last it was over and the move to Famagusta could be made with no objections. Lucy seethed with impatience on the seemingly interminable journey. But at last they were home in the l'Mesurier loggia, and she was free to commence her search for Edward. Wherever she went, accompanied by a serving woman who had some healing skills, she could find no one to give her news of Edward. Diligently, she worked for the Hospitallers, gathering herbs, mixing potions, and pounding comfrey root into powder for poultices to draw out the poison and heal wounds too long neglected. As she worked she continued her questioning among the returnees. No one had seen or heard of Edward since he had fallen beneath that terrible blow to the head.

The last tardy remnants of the fleet struggled, one by one, into the bay, but none of the latecomers brought news of Estur. Secure in her secret knowledge, Lucy refused to accept that he was not still alive. There must be one laggardly vessel, somewhere, limping home. After all, the King himself had been almost shipwrecked and had promised generous gifts to every monastery in Cyprus should he make safe harbour. It was when visiting the St. Clares on his journey home from Lammasol to Nicosia that, in fulfillment of that vow, he had found Joanna and sent her ahead to his palace.

Life in the l'Mesurier household dropped back into its cheerful, familiar routine. In the evenings, as they sat in the solar, Sir Guy entertained the family with his account of the expedition. Ti-Jean and his small partner in mischief, Paul, lay on the floor on their stomachs, propped up on their elbows, chins in grubby hands, fascinated into silence. His tales were tempered to his audience, stories of gallantry, of mighty sword fights, chivalrous conquerors and gentlemanly surrenders, and comical fiascos. But his private talks with his prospective father-in-law were of an entirely different character.

To that gentleman, he revealed the other side of the coin. "It was a massacre," he groaned. "It was Friday, October the 10th. Our contingent landed at Alexandria's Old Harbour. At first the people thought we were traders, and came rushing out to greet us. It took them some time to realize that we were invaders. We were still in the water, when they came to understand what was our real intent and began to fight back. Then there was some rough going, for a while. That was when Peter ran into difficulties. He was always in the forefront of the action. His companions called for aid, and Edward and I forced our way to his side to render assistance. It was then that my dear friend was struck down. He was attacked from his blind side. I could see what was happening, but I could do nothing about it, being under grievous attack myself." He started to his feet, clenching his fists. "Why Edward? There were many there whose loss would be unregretted and of little consequence. It was at that time I myself was wounded. But the Hospitallers managed to debark their horses at the New Harbour. They came up behind our foes, who did not last long after that, poor souls! A few of them made it back inside and closed the gates. "The others ... " The young knight covered his eyes for a moment, as if in prayer.

His host poured him a glass of wine. "Here, my dear young friend," he sympathized, laying a fatherly hand on Guy's shoulder.

The young man took a grateful swallow. "Although they had managed to close the gates, they were too late. We had them surrounded. That was when it all began to go wrong." He stared at his host, with haunted eyes. "His Majesty called a Council of War, and half the men demanded that the city be abandoned. They had enough booty! Can you comprehend that?" He shook his head, unbelievingly. "But the King had his way, and we attacked. The gates were strong, but we found one vulnerable spot overlooked, near the Customs Gate. There was no moat there, and a seaman found a way in through a fresh water conduit. He climbed the ramparts and secured ropes, so that the wall could be scaled. Once our own men were in, they met with small resistance. The people and the garrison all ran out through the gates."

Sir Guy and Edward had been among those of Pierre de Lusignan's followers who truly shared the monarch's high ideals. The majority, while professing that their only interest was in acquiring honour and in serving God's divine will by driving out the Infidels from the Holy Land, revealed their true characters. Their sole desire was to plunder and pillage. Beyond de Lusignan's control, they looted the city for several days. "I shall never forget it. What happened was a disgrace to our Cause."

Guy lifted his head, and glared at his future father-in-law. "Nothing and no one was safe from their evil rampage. They slaughtered men, women and children, old and young alike, and whatever goods they could not carry away, they destroyed. They demolished churches and mosques, warehouses and palaces. Seventy vessels were loaded to sinking point with the spoils. The surplus was wantonly thrown overboard."

Listlessly, Guy sat down at the table, and lowered his head into his hands. "There was worse. Five thousand Jews, Eastern Christians and Moslems were captured and taken to be sold into slavery. The scoundrels would have left without us, if they had dared. And then those damned Genoese ... " He gulped the rest of his wine. M'sieur quietly refilled the goblet. "There were five Genoese ships," Guy snapped, savagely. "With four hundred men aboard. Sent by their Doge, at Pope Urban's specific request, to assist us. Assist us! They just sat there, out in the harbour, watching the battle, until the surrender. Then they came ashore, looting with the worst! I heard that they picked up booty worth eighty thousand florins – God rot their souls!"

He jumped to his feet again and walked over to gaze blindly into the fire. He struck the mantel with a fisted hand. "Those other dastards refused to stay and consolidate our position. No true knights, they. They had their 'wages', and saw no need to linger. Sir Philippe de Mézières and the Pope's Legate, Peter Thomas, stood by the King. But his own two brothers and that cowardly dog Admiral le Sur supported the rebels. The traitors over-ruled His Majesty and insisted on evacuation. There were too few of us to defy them. We left on the sixteenth of October. All that slaughter – for nothing!"

A malicious gleam brightened his eyes. "We were barely out in the open sea before we encountered a terrible tempest. The fleet was driven in all directions. There were those of us who hoped and, I'll wager, some who feared that the Almighty might be about to avenge the atrocities that had been committed in the name of Christianity. But we all survived. Mind you, there were some very hasty prayers sent up, and vows made, before that storm was over." With a grim laugh, he added, "I wonder how many of those pledges will be honoured, apart from His Gracious Majesty's?"

14

Christmas seemed to come upon them with alarming speed. The Court moved to Famagusta for the holiday. In the King's train came Gustave l'Amoureux, who paid casual and sardonic court to his intended bride. Lionallo, restless as ever, and unaware of the King's intentions, had gone off on one of his junkets around the coast. Lucy wished he would come back. She was afraid.

Old Matthew, her usual source of information, for once knew nothing of the Corsican's plans. "Reckon as how en'll just fossick around, 'til ens ready to come back. No tellin' when. Born wanderer, that lad."

Lucy did her best to keep a cheerful demeanour for the sake of her friends but, as Twelfth Night drew ever nearer, she knew that her new family were as concerned as she. She was surprised to discover how many friends she had made, both at court and in the l'Mesurier family. Although they did not express their sympathy at her impending fate in words, the wedding gifts they pressed upon her spoke for them. They gave her dainty shifts and night rails of lace trimmed cotton, elaborately embroidered cushions and cloths, and other small but appreciated trifles.

They all seemed to wish her well, in spite of their disapproval of her appointed bridegroom, and Lucy was touched by their kindly affection. The Lady Timphainé contributed two pieces of hard scented soap, a great luxury, imported from Castile. Madame Henriette and Lucy's old friend from the Palace, Dame Agathé, both bestowed on her packets of herbs, pots of salve, and some of their secret and most prized recipes for potions, drafts and other medications.

But man proposes, and God disposes! On the 6th of January the holy

Peter Thomas, who had long been ailing, died. What would happen now? For the moment the funeral of the great churchman occupied everyone else's thoughts, but there was much speculation among the members of the l'Mesurier family. Surely Lucy's wedding to Gustave l'Amoureux must be postponed while the court was in mourning. Or would the King insist on going ahead with the nuptials as soon as the burial ceremonies were over? At least they now had a brief respite and perhaps Lionallo would return in time to save her. Eustache l'Mesurier was now convinced that life as a fisherman's wife would be vastly superior to that with the dissolute nobleman.

Quietly, he made his plans known to Lucy and his wife. In his considered opinion, the young Corsican was to be trusted and respected. If Lucy wished, everything would be prepared for her to escape with Lionallo when he returned. Pray God it would be in time.

Fortune appeared to be with them. Even when the mourning period was over, Pierre de Lusignan was too preoccupied with other concerns to pay such attention to l'Amoureux's needs, and with the present mood of the King the scoundrel felt it best not to press his case.

"I am afraid that his setbacks and disappointments have sadly affected His Majesty's well-being, both in mind and body," Sir Guy confided to his betrothed's father, as they sat in that gentleman's office sharing a bottle of wine. "His worst frustration is being unable to pursue his Divine calling to free the Holy Land. Then there is this business of the Queen and John de Morphou. The Haute Cour is dragging its feet. The barons are afraid that if they find Eleanor guilty, she and de Morphou must both be executed for treason – and you can imagine how that would go down with Aragon." Aragon was Her Majesty's native country. "It would mean war!"

The older man shook his head. "The tale going around about his persecution of John Giblet and his children – is it true? It seems unbelievable."

The knight blushed, and lowered his head. "I am afraid so. Because the lad would not sell his Turkish greyhounds to young Prince Peter, the King had James Giblet put in irons, and sent to dig ditches, with common labourers. He had the father imprisoned. The daughter … " He looked up at his companion. "Indeed, I fear for my lord's sanity. In his right mind, he could never commit the acts of infamy and cruelty that now sully his name. Giblet's daughter. He tried to marry her off to a man of such low degree, it was disgusting. Quite illegal, of course. She hid in a convent, but he found her, and put her in the hands of Sir John de Neville, to be tortured."

"Saints' tears! Surely Sir John would not!"

Sir Guy grinned. "As head of the Police, he had little choice, but I imagine he was scarcely whole-hearted in the matter. The latest under-cover *on-dit* indicates that his work is very imaginative." He laughed aloud at the older man's frown of displeasure. "The whisperers say that he has married her!"

M'sieur's guffaw echoed around the room.

"But not," continued the other, "until she also had been shackled and sent to dig with her brother."

"No! A woman ... gently bred ... " Eustache was aghast. He thought of his own dear child, and Lucy ... Dear God, Lucy ... She must somehow be protected from this maniac.

"The man is insane. The poor child must have been devastated."

"Not she! The maid has the Giblet spirit. She hitched her skirts to her knees and went to work. When the King came by she let them down, but not for the barons. She told them that she had no need to be modest on their account, they were only women themselves. The King was the only real man at court."

"Valiant maid!" They raised their goblets in silent toast.

Sir Guy took a long drink. "I think her disdain may induce some of them into scheming against de Lusignan."

"Rebellion? Surely not!"

"He has been acting so irresponsibly lately. No one can reason with him. Sometimes his behaviour is extremely cruel. He ignores the deci-sions of the Assizes – a law unto himself, as they say."

"Jesu have mercy!" Eustache crossed himself. "What in the name of heaven has Pierre de Lusignan, Athlete of God, come to?"

*   *   *

Soon it would be Lent.

"If we can stave off l'Amoureux until then, there can be no marriage until Easter," Madame told her husband.

"True!   Lenten marriages are not permitted."   Thoughtfully, he stroked his chin. "Our best hope is Momellino. I have had messages left for him at Lammasol and Paphos and several other ports where I have connections. We can only pray that he comes in time."

Lucy prayed so, too. She went daily to the cathedral to petition for the welfare of both Lion and Edward. L'Amoureux's obnoxious attentions were becoming more pressing. She feared he had some underhanded plot in mind. She no longer took her early morning walks, and went out of the loggia only in company. Even if it were Lent, given his present disregard for law, there was no guarantee that de Lusignan would not decide to proceed with the wedding, legal or not, at any moment.

The King's excesses multiplied. He wanted revenge against Eleanor and de Morphou, at any cost. But the Haute Cour, fearful of a war with Aragon, made a scapegoat of poor old John Visconte, accusing him of having invented the slander himself. He was sent to Kyrenia, that bleak northern fortress where Joanna had been imprisoned. Later, a French Lord, on a pilgrimage to Jerusalem, would petition for Visconte's release. But he was merely removed to Buffavento, another gaol, where he eventually died of starvation.

Sir Guy brought news of a formal protest drafted by the barons, which they had bullied the two youngest de Lusignan brothers to present to King Peter.

"I take it that he did not receive them with an excess of brotherly love," remarked the Montpellier representative.

"You are correct! He insulted them both. The nobles are fuming. They claim that he has violated his oath, leaving them free to absolve themselves of their own. The Princes have thrown in with the Lords, who are threatening to leave Cyprus if the King will not come to a proper arrangement with them."

"Will they, do you think?"

"Who can tell? But I think we should be prepared for trouble."

The axe fell when least expected. L'Amoureux seemed to be easing up in his attentions to her, and Lucy hoped that he was losing interest. M'sieur had word that Lionallo had received one of his messages, and was hurrying back to Famagusta. She went early to Mass, and stayed after the service to give private thanks. Onfroi had not been available that morning, so she was attended by one of the l'Mesurier servants.

As she knelt at the altar rail in the empty church, she heard a door opening and footsteps approaching. The chink of arms warned her that it was not a priest. She opened her eyes to see two hefty men at arms standing over her.

"No fuss, lady," said one, as he pulled to her feet, " and we'll do you no hurt."

As if she'd believe that! She managed one scream, before he clapped a callused hand over her mouth. The serving man started forward. The second soldier struck him a blow to the head that sent the poor man sprawling, senseless, to the floor.

Her own kerchief was stuffed into her mouth, and she was wrapped so tightly in a cloak that she could neither see nor move her arms and legs. She could tell that it was through a side door that they carried her out and lifted her into the arms of a mounted man – and then they were riding off, to where she had no idea.

"Good morning, my charming bride." Gustave l'Amoureux was waiting to greet her, as she struggled out of her wrappings. "I was beginning to fear that you would be late for our wedding."

"You!" snapped Lucy. "I am not your bride, and never will be! You loathsome toad."

"T'ch, t'ch! Such unmaidenly language – you shall not speak so after we are wed, I assure you."

"Since we never shall be, my language must be of no consequence to you, sir!" She spat defiance at him, but inwardly shuddered with terror. Trapped. He held her at his mercy, which she knew was non-existent. She stiffened her body. She would never allow him to see her fear. She would not allow him to force her into this fraudulent parody of a marriage. She would simply refuse to speak the vows.

L'Amoureux jerked his head at one of her abductors. The man opened the door and beckoned. A man in brown priest's robes came in, missal in hand.

"See! All is ready for us, my sweet. Here is our priest, and here", he gestured toward the surly soldiers, "our witnesses."

"Father!" Lucy addressed the cleric. "I do not wish to marry this man. He is holding me against my will."

She might as well have been talking to the wall. The man did not even bother look at her. He said nothing, his face a forbidding mask.

L'Amoureux repeated the vows as instructed, with mock reverence. When Lucy, in her turn, kept her mouth stubbornly closed, her bridegroom calmly announced, "She so promiseth!"

In spite of her protests, the short mockery of a service proceeded. At its conclusion l'Amoureux kissed her roughly, laughing when she scrubbed her lips in disgust.

"This is no true marriage," she snarled at him. "A forced marriage is not legal. You do not have my consent."

"How can you say so, Beloved?" he grinned. "A priest, two witnesses, and a devoted bridegroom – what more could you demand?"

"It will not stand!"

"Oh, but it will, my dear lady. We have Royalty's approval."

"The King will never countenance this."

"You think not? Could I be mistaken, think you? In that case, I shall have to accept you for myself."

"I would die first!"

"Afterward, perhaps." His colourless eyes were daggers of ice as he moved toward her. She backed away as he unhurriedly stalked her, but there was no escape. As he reached out for her she remembered her knife and pulled it from her girdle. She made a wild swipe at him but he was too quick. His stronger hand shot out and wrenched it from her grasp. He tossed it aside, raised his clenched fist, then hesitated. "No. We cannot present His Majesty with damaged goods, can we? He will expect perfection, when we pay him his dues of *droit de seigneur*. We must make sure that he gets it. So my love, it seems that I must hold myself in restraint, until he has had his pleasure – but then – well, we shall see."

He locked the door as he left. Lucy searched the room, but there was no other exit. She had not paid attention to the place when she was brought in, but looked around it now in despair. The walls and floor were bare and the one window was shuttered and barred. There was only a rough table and stool for furniture, with a straw pallet of doubtful character thrown in one corner. She was grateful that she had at least been left a light, a branched candelabra on the wooden table.

Hours passed, it seemed, but no one came near her. Seeing that the candles were burning down, she extinguished all but one, replacing each with another as it melted down to a small stub. She was glad of her forethought. The last candle was sputtering when the door finally opened.

Her captor wasted no time in conversation. Grabbing her arm, he propelled her out into a dank passage, through darkened halls, and up a short flight of stone stairs to a carpeted, well lit area. A complete contrast to the floor they had just left. A young man was sitting on a stool beside a carved door. Lucy recognized him. Gilet de Cornalie was one of the King's ushers. Such a relief! He would surely come to her aid. Before she could speak, he had risen and opened the door without looking at her, and she was summarily thrust inside.

"My dear! What a pleasant surprise." Pierre de Lusignan came forward and took her hand. "I had no idea I was to be honoured tonight." He bowed his head and raised her fingers to his lips, lightly kissing the tips. Lucy was shocked at his appearance. The beautiful blue eyes had a wild, almost feral gleam and the muscles of his handsome face seemed to have slackened, giving him a look of almost childish petulance. She could only curtsey and murmur, "Your Majesty," before he went on in a complaining, almost whining, tone.

"You can have no idea how delightful it is to see a friendly face. And such a charming one! These days, it seems that everyone is in league against me. Even my brothers conspire to thwart me. Always urging me to sign this paper, or that proclamation. My barons defy me, and my wife betrays me."

"Dear Lord," thought Lucy. "Is this the Athlete of God? He really is mad." Would she ever be able to escape from this predicament?

"Sire," she began again. "I am in dire trouble and seek your aid. Sir Gustave l'Amoureux … "

"Ah yes! My good friend Gustave. One of my last true friends – and your husband, is he not?"

"No, not my husband, Sire. Today he abducted me and forced me to go through a wedding ceremony which I am sure is not legal."

"Now, now! Don't worry your pretty head about it. I shall set everything to rights."

"You will?" Relief flooded through her. "Your Majesty is so kind."

"I am still the King, you know. In spite of what some may wish. So Gustave was a little too precipitate, was he? I cannot say, under the circumstances, that I blame him." He smiled meaningfully at her. "But I shall make everything legal, you can rest easy."

"But I don't want … " A knock at the door silenced her, as a woman's voice called, "Pierre! Pierre! Let me in! It is I – Echive!"

Lucy could have laughed aloud at the flustered expression on the King's face.

"Quickly!" he urged, pushing her across the room. He picked up a corner of the rug, and opened a trap door. "Wait down there for a while, my dear. Please!"

A ladder led to a room below. The King thrust her down and Lucy stood looking up as he hurriedly closed the trapdoor. She felt a fit of panic coming on, and took herself sternly to task. She did not want the King's leman to suspect her presence. Too, there might be another way out of this room. Perhaps she could escape from both the King and his good friend Gustave! Didn't the Lord help those who helped themselves?

The voices from above were too low-pitched for her to eavesdrop on the conversation. She began her search for a door. Apparently, the room was a catchall for saddles, discarded weapons and various odds and ends. A loud knocking overhead stayed her search. A man's voice called and the King answered. A moment later the trap door opened and Echive de Scandelion came tumbling through, cloak in hand.

The two women stood facing one another. Lucy was silent.

"What are you doing here?" demanded the newcomer.

"Looking for a way out. Do you know of a door?"

They both looked up, as loud voices were raised upstairs. They heard someone say, "A good day to you, Sire."

"Prince John," Echive told Lucy.

They heard Peter's reply. "Good day to you, my good brother."

John said, "We have worked all night. We have written down our opinion, and have brought it for you to see."

"My princely brother." The King sounded exasperated. "Go outside for a little, for me to dress, and I will look at what you have written."

Echive shrugged. "Well – he'll be some time reading their nonsense. If you really want to get out of here … "

"I most certainly do!"

"Then come … "

The door upstairs burst open again. Loud raucous voices split the silence. They heard the King shout, "Faithless traitors! What are you doing at this hour, in my room, attacking me?" There was the sound of fighting and shouting.

Echive started to cry at the sound of the King's voice. "My Poor Pierre! He is all alone and unarmed, and there are so many of them," wept Echive. Lucy put her arms around her, trying to soothe her. The noise overhead became more furious. There was one last cry from the King of Cyprus. "Help! Mercy! For the love of God!" A moment of hushed silence followed. Then someone else rushed into the room, shouting, "You wished today to cut off my head and I will cut off yours! Your threat shall fall upon your own self!"

Echive shuddered in Lucy's arms. "That is Pierre's steward, Sir John Goram," she sobbed. "Pierre was angry with him at dinner today. The sauce for the asparagus displeased him, so he had him thrown into prison and said he would have him beheaded. I'm sure he didn't mean it. He would have set him free, in a day or so when his temper cooled. And now they have killed him. Pierre!"

"Hush, hush!" warned Lucy. "They will hear you and if they find us here ... "

She had no need to say more. Echive knew as well as she that they could expect short shrift from the rogues upstairs.

Echive pulled herself together. "Over here," she said, leading the way to a dark alcove. "The panel slides."

Together they pushed it aside, to disclose a half dozen steps that led to another door and out into the courtyard. They separated and Lucy sped cautiously to a small postern gate that she had often used when she lived in the palace.

15

Her return to the l'Mesurier loggia was greeted with joy and relief. Since the serving man's story of her abduction, the whole family had been in a state of desperate confusion. Madame and M'sieur had harboured no doubt as to the identity of her captor. Who else than l'Amoureux would dare, or would have reason to do so? But what to do about it had been the problem. Under the circumstances, they could hardly appeal to the King. And now, even that would have been impossible. Pierre de Lusignan was dead. Foully murdered – and Lucy was witness to the dreadful deed. As M'sieur pointed out, she now stood in double jeopardy. L'Amoureux would maintain his claim to her and to Edward's fortune from an even stronger position, with the false marriage ceremony to back his plea. And since her presence in the King's quarters was known to Gilet de Cornalie at least, she was at risk from the murderers as well.

In the privacy of Eustache's office, her foster parents worriedly discussed their joint dilemma with Lucy.

"This will be the first place l'Amoureux or anyone else will seek you," M'sieur said. "We must find a safe hiding place for you until Momellino returns. If he is willing, then he shall take you with him to Corsica."

"Perhaps you could stay with your friends, the armourer and his wife," suggested Madame.

"Oh no! If I were to be found there, it would be disastrous. I could never agree to put them and their children in such peril."

"You have the right of it," admitted her foster mother. "I had not thought of that."

A scratching on the door sent M'sieur to open it. A servant waited outside, with a visitor, who was muffled in a cloak, with the hood pulled over her face. She stepped quickly inside the room, closing the door behind her before she revealed her face. It was Echive de Scandelion.

"I had to come," she said. "It is known that you were in Pierre's apartment when he was killed. Cornalie was keeping watch at the door. He recognized you. They intend that there shall be no witness to their awful crime. I do not think they will bother me. I have powerful connections, but you have none." She gestured apologetically to M'sieur. "Your pardon, M'sieur, but you are a foreigner – and your position – you cannot afford involvement." She began to cry. That horrible Goram! The coward – he did not dare face Pierre when he was alone. He rushed in after they had killed him, and cut off my poor darling's head!"

"There, there, my dear!" At once Madame was all motherly sympathy. She guided the distraught woman to a chair, while M'sieur poured her a goblet of wine.

"I think we all need a restorative." No one spoke until he had provided a drink for each of them.

"Now, my lady. You say the murderers are aware of our *chère* Lucy's knowledge of their crime?"

Echive nodded.

"But I did not see them!" Lucy protested. "I do not know who actually killed His Majesty."

"It was d'Ibelin, de Gaurelle, Arsur and de Giblet who first broke into the room. It was they who stabbed him to death. Goram came in afterward. The others had broken him and de Giblet out of prison to help them. After it was done, that filthy beast Nores, the Turcopolier, heard the clamour and came in and mutilated my poor darling's dead body. His beautiful body." Her sobs renewed. "When he did it he said, 'It was that that cost you your life!' Do you think that Eleanor could have had anything to do with it? She has always been jealous and vindictive."

"Do not even think so, my lady," warned l'Mesurier hastily. "In such a thought lies danger, indeed!"

Lucy knelt beside Echive and took her hand. "I did not take him from you, my Lady," she told the weeping woman. "That vile l'Amoureux carried me off and forced me into marriage before rushing me into His Majesty's rooms. Your Pierre was not expecting me. I was just explaining myself to him when you came, and he was promising to set things right." She felt that Heaven would surely overlook her slight manipulation of the truth, since her intent was to offer a small measure of comfort to Echive, who had truly loved the dead King.

"L'Amoureux married you?" Echive raised her head in surprise. Lucy, thinking to distract her, described her horrid adventure.

"I think l'Amoureux already has a wife," said Echive, thoughtfully. "Not here, of course. But back in France – in the provinces I believe. But the one who married you – describe him."

"There isn't much to describe. He wore a brown habit, with a hood. His complexion was very pale, yellowish, in fact, and he had a huge wen … "

"On the left side of his nose!"

"You know the man?"

"I know of, and have seen him. Nothing good. But you have no need to worry. You are not married. He is not a priest. He is but a monk – and a defrocked one at that. An evil creature. He makes a living in nefarious ways."

"You have greatly relieved me," Lucy said, truthfully. "Now that I know I am definitely not married to that rogue … "

"That is of little consequence, my dear," broke in her guardian. "This man has abducted you once and will not fail to try again. He still desires the Estur fortune and will not easily give up."

"I must go." Echive rose to her feet. "I felt that it was my duty to warn you of your danger. Pierre would have wished it." She drew her cloak close. "I wish you good fortune."

"I shall escort you," said l'Mesurier.

"Not necessary, my friend. A trusted servant accompanies me. But you must find some other refuge for Lady Lucy. Soon." With a brief farewell, she hurried away.

"Madame de Scandelion spoke the truth," said M'sieur. "You are not safe here. We must find a safe haven for you."

Lucy chuckled. "There is only one way out," she said, mischievously. "I must die!"

Madame's small shriek of horror was followed by her husband's frowning rebuke. "Do not speak so, even in jest."

"But don't you see? If they think I am dead, they will stop looking for me."

"Perhaps. But how can we convince them? They will demand to see your corpse. They will not hesitate to open the casket, even if they must dig it up after the burial."

"Ah, but there will be no casket – and no body. I shall drown, and my body will never be found."

Madame's shocked protests were silenced by her husband, as he regarded Lucy with interest.

"What do you have in mind, if I may ask?"

"Suppose my basket and cloak should be found on the shore and a note left for you, saying that, without my dear Sir Edward, I no longer wish to linger here? Here, mind you, not on earth. I do not wish to lie."

"I must admire your piety, my dear." M'sieur commented, with a touch of irony. "But where shall we hide your body? It will still be with us, you know."

"I think I know where I can go. Old Matthew is a friend of Lion's, and he likes me. He lives in a hut in the hills. I am sure he would take me in."

"Impossible!" cried her foster mother. "Not at all suitable. You cannot live with that old man. It would be most improper."

Eustache laid a soothing hand upon her shoulder. "This is not the time for proprieties. Lucy's safety must be our first consideration. No one would dream of seeking her in such a place, and we can have all in readiness for her departure by the time Momellino arrives."

And so it was decided. Matthew was willing, indeed eager, to help. Madame bundled up blankets, clothing and food enough for an army. The letter was written, Lucy insisting on adding to it her "will", leaving her inheritance from Edward to the Estur family. Then Lucy again handed over her gold to her foster father. This time he weighed it and exchanged it for coinage, some gold and some silver, to an amount which he swore was no more than the worth of the jewellery.

"I shall not sell it in Cyprus," he explained. "As you have been seen wearing it, and someone would be sure to recognize it. Questions might be asked."

The move was made in the dead of night, with Philippa the only other person in the household in their confidence.

"I shall be so unhappy to lose you that no one will doubt that I grieve for your death. Whenever I remember that I shall never see you again,

I shall wash away my eyes with tears," she sobbed, as they wept in a farewell embrace.

As it happened, her stay with the old blacksmith was brief. Lionallo made safe harbour two days later. The Montpellier Representative, who had posted a lookout, himself hurried down to meet him before he could hear of Lucy's "sad fate", the primary topic of interest in the gossip of the day.

"So – that is the present situation," summed up l'Mesurier, as he and his two ladies sat, closeted in his office with the Corsican.

"I will kill the black-hearted villain!" Lion leapt to his feet. Cold fire flashed from his eyes. "Such filth cannot be allowed to defile God's earth. That he should lay his obscene hands on her ... "

"Softly, softly, my friend. She came to no real harm, and thanks to the de Scandelion lady we were alerted to her continued peril, and so have taken what steps we were able to protect her. You will do better to take her out of danger than seek revenge. She must not fall into the hands of that fiend again."

"You think he may suspect that she is still alive?"

"He is a devious man, and we have no corpse to show him. He is always a menace."

"Then you must help me persuade her to forget that Crusader she pines for, and fly with me."

Madame intervened. "I think you have no problem there. True, she has a fondness for the Englishman, but that is all. I have it from her own lips that her heart is yours alone."

"Can this be true?" Lionallo's face lit up with joy. "I will go to her, at once!" He rushed toward the door, but was restrained by the older man.

"Not so fast , my friend! Caution rather than enthusiasm is required in this matter. It is common knowledge that you have a *tendresse* for the maid. To dash about with the *joie de vivre* of an eager bridegroom, when the supposed love of your life is but newly dead, would surely give rise to some speculation. A mournful mien, an air of despair ... you understand?"

"Of course." The woe-begotten face he suddenly assumed set Philippa a-giggling. "Will this do?"

"An improvement. And now to business."

Two nights ahead there would be a high tide at midnight and a dark moon. Enough time to provision the fishing boat. Lucy could take none of her own possessions. Some of the ladies would be sure to notice their absence and query their whereabouts, but Madame and Philippa secretly packed a lovely carved oriental chest, a gift from Eustache, with linen and clothes more suitable for the new life ahead of her. Wrapped in stout sailcloth, it was smuggled aboard by Lion, helped by old Matthew, who, on the appointed night, led him to his home, and Lucy.

Lucy, wrapped in a fur-lined cloak of Madame's, was ready and waiting. Did he still want her, after all this time, or had he come to save her, only for pity's sake? She spoke, tentatively, "You have been away so long." He stood silently before her. Now that, at last, he was to have his heart's desire, he was stricken with misgiving. Was it really as her friends had told him? Did she really care for him, or was he just second best? Then he knew it made no difference.

"I have searched for your Englishman round all the coast of Cyprus, and to Alexandria and back again," he told her, truculently. "I found no trace of him, dead or alive. It is enough! There is no more time. You are in dire jeopardy. Come with me, now, before it is too late."

It was too much. All the terror and stress of the past months engulfed her. Sobbing, she ran to the shelter of his ready arms, and laid her head on his shoulder. "Oh, I will. Dearest Lion! I will do whatever you wish. Only never leave me again. I could not bear it."

"Never, my Star, I swear." For a few precious moments they lingered, savouring the sweet relief of their comforting embrace. Then he gently released her, to guide her cautiously down to the cove where the Stella Maris waited, quietly swinging on the turning tide.

16

Shadowy figures came out of the dark, and Lucy drew closer to Lion. "No need for fear, my Star" he reassured her. "Friends."

He was right. Friends indeed. M'sieur L'Mesurier, now that her safe departure was certain, had, with the Corsican's approval, brought Sir Guy and Will into their confidence. The three men had come to bid them Godspeed and a safe voyage, to Lucy's great joy. It had pained her to think that her friends would grieve for her and believe her to be a lost soul, a suicide. She would never forget the debt of gratitude she owed Will and his Roberga, and told him so once more. Sir Guy she loved for his devoted friendship and loyalty to Sir Edward. She insisted that he would eventually hear from his friend again, and begged him to explain her situation to him when he did.

And then there was no more time. The tide would not wait. The men exchanged arm clasps, Guy and Will kissed Lucy good-bye, and her dear M'sieur kissed her and gave her a father's blessings.

Lion swept her up and waded through the rippling waves to heft her into the swaying Stella Maris, quickly clambering after her. As soon as the little boat was free of her restraining anchor, she seemed to gather the small dawn wind into the wings of her anxious sails and hastened out into the eager sea. One more glance back at the dark outlines of Famagusta and they were on their way.

Long before sunrise they were out of sight of the city of Famagusta, speeding southward along the eastern coast. Wrapped in Madame's warm cloak against the chill of the rising breeze, watching Lionallo in the stern of the Stella Maris leaning negligently on the tiller, Lucy could not help wondering what the future now held in store for her. How could she have imagined in her wildest fantasies that she, the pampered darling of well-to-do, adoring parents, was to be cast away in time and space, marooned in a world and an era so primitive, so alien to all that she had ever known? Now she was putting her life in the hands of a stranger, a man of whom she really knew very little. He could not be more different from the country gentlemen among whom she had once expected to find a husband! A cold finger of panic traced a shiver down her spine. Might it not have been wiser to have surrendered to the King's demands? Papa had often quoted, "Better the Devil one knows … " But the King was dead. And no devil could be worse than that monster l'Amoureux. The way he had looked at her! The cruel delight he took in her fear. She looked back at the dark sea almost expecting to see a ship in full pursuit with that hateful villain at the helm. She shook off her forebodings and turned her attentions to her companion.

Lion's dark eyes were fixed warily on the coastline on the starboard horizon. Lucy moved to stand beside him, laying her hand on his shoulder as she too stared at the faintly purple skyline, dotted with a scattering of white buildings.

"T'were wiser, I think, that we do not put in at Lammasol," he remarked thoughtfully. "There may be those there who could recognize either one, or mayhap both, of us." She made no reply, nor was one needed. She had put her life into his hands – why should she question his wisdom now?

"I think, if the water holds out, we shall try to make for Paphos," he went on. "At the worst, we can always run into one of the smaller coves and ask for more."

"Paphos! How exciting! Oh, I shall love to see that place! Is that not where Aphrodite was born?" asked Lucy, eyes asparkle with delight. "My Papa has often read that story to me."

"So it is said." He smiled at her eagerness. He did not doubt that her father had somewhat edited the tale for her youthful ears. "Perhaps I shall throw you overboard when we arrive, and let you amaze the citizens when you drift ashore on an abalone shell, gowned only in sea foam!"

"Evil-minded beast!" She poked him sharply in the ribs, then dodged quickly out of his reach.

"Vixen! You shall pay for your sins, once we are wed!"

"I think that perhaps I do not wish to be wed," Lucy remarked thoughtfully.

Lion snapped to attention. "And what does that mean, pray?"

Her hands plucked at the rough smock she was wearing as more suitable garb for shipboard than a kirtle and bliaut. Avoiding his eyes, she answered, "I have noticed at court that while gentlemen are very attentive and chivalrous toward the ladies they profess to love, once they are married their wives are sadly neglected and often ill-treated – sometimes kept prisoners in their own castles. Therefore it would seem wiser to stay courted, rather than wed!"

"Ah!" Lion hitched a rope to the tiller. "I too, have noticed that often the most charming and compliant of females, be she never so meek and docile, becomes a nagging, shrewish termagant once she has safely ensnared a husband. Perhaps you have the right of it, my love. So ... we are agreed – we shall not marry, then, but merely stay betrothed."

His teeth gleamed white against the weathered brown of his face, as with a devilish grin, he pounced across the small space dividing them and clasped her in an overpowering embrace. "You know, of course, that here in Cyprus, as it is in my country, a betrothal is as legal as a marriage, just easier to escape from. A broken betrothal serves as a divorce, which can rarely be obtained after marriage. That is why few country folk bother with a wedding ceremony until a child is on the way. Often not even then!"

"Lionallo Momellino!" Lucy pounded on his unflinching chest with both fists, attempting to wrench herself out of his arms, but he held her close with one imprisoning arm, deftly securing her two thumbs in his other warm square hand. One foot hooked around her ankles, preventing her from kicking his shins, immobilizing her completely.

"If you think that I shall live in sin with you, you have attics to let, you ... you ... Corsican pagan!" she raged, before he covered her angry mouth with his own.

"Little witling!" he teased as he released her. "What kind of a fool would I be to leave you a chance to renounce me? I insist that we marry at the first opportunity. Until then, I honour my promise to your good foster mother. I shall not seek to anticipate our wedding."

"You promised Madame?" Lucy was astonished.

"Had I not, she would have sent old Matthew with us as a chaperone,

I do not doubt," he returned with a rueful grin. "She is a good Christian lady, and has a great fondness for you. Although I cannot agree with her on certain points of conduct, I made her many promises with regard to both your spiritual and physical welfare!" He sighed and asked plaintively, "Do you think that, since such vows were given under duress, they must all be kept?"

Lucy's gray eyes raked his wickedly dancing black ones with rising suspicion.

"For instance, must I never beat you? Even when you drive me to madness with your willful obstinacy?"

"Hah!" With an indignant toss of her russet locks, Lucy strove to intimidate him with her most imperious stare. "Any man who raised a hand to me would not grow much older ere he came to regret it!"

He threw back his head with a great guffaw and enveloped her in an exuberant hug. "That I do not for one moment doubt, my Star! I shall keep my distance whenever I may chance to raise your ire!"

"It shall go better with you that you do not raise it!" she retorted, ready for more argument. But he merely went off, chuckling, to trim the sail.

"I've been thinking that perhaps we should avoid Paphos also," he said later. "A small town might be safer."

"I will leave that for you to decide," Lucy told him, pertly. "That is one area, at least, in which you are more knowledgeable than I."

The Corsican fisherman was well known in the tiny seaside village he chose, as was the Stella Maris. When she sailed into the little harbour of Paria, several small boats rowed out to meet them, and people on the shore could be seen, waving enthusiastically. Visitors were always welcome there. A new face, or a visit from an old friend, was excuse enough for a celebration. When Lionallo disclosed that he had brought his betrothed and intended to be married there, excitement ran higher than usual, especially among the women, who descended on Lucy *en masse* and carried her off to the home of one of Lion's closer friends, leaving him in exclusively male company.

Lucy was glad that her gift for languages, and the natural gregariousness that had often brought her into contact with the natives of Cyprus, had enabled her to pick up the local patois, so that she was able to communicate fairly well with her new acquaintances. She told them of her betrothed's intention that they should be quietly wed that same day. The hoots of derisive laughter that greeted her news bewildered her. What had she said to cause such merriment? Taking pity on her confusion, Maria, the matron in whose home they were gathered, explained.

"Maids around the entire coast of Cyprus, to Corsica, and all ports in between, have been trailing their bait for our wily Lion for years! We have waited too long for our handsome fisherman to be caught in love's seine! A quiet wedding, he thinks? Hah! We shall not let him off so easily. No, my dear, you shall have as fine a wedding as any other maid. There is a tradition to these things, and we women shall not be cheated of our fun. Your wedding day comes only once in a lifetime, please Our Lady, and it shall be one to remember!"

In spite of the bridegroom's protestations, Maria had her way. Lucy had never seen Lion so discomfited. Her hostess overrode his arguments with cheerful disdain. This was women's business and he could just take himself off – fishing, hunting or to the taverna, whichever he pleased, so long as he stayed from underfoot. Surely he had enough patience to wait for two days.

"Hell roast it!" he roared. "Two more days! I've already waited for two years!"

"Then two days shall be but the blink of an eye for you," Maria laughed.

In spite of his objections, Lucy suspected that in truth he was not displeased at the affectionate care she was receiving. He dabbed a kiss on her cheek and mumbled something to the effect that she probably did need time to recover from the voyage, but two days was the limit he was prepared to wait. Glowering fiercely at Maria, which troubled that lady not one whit, he announced they would be leaving immediately after the ceremony.

Lucy had not given thought, until now, that she would be marrying among strangers with no one of her own to support her and wish her happiness. Her mother would not be there to help her dress and whisper words of love and encouragement. Nor would she walk up the aisle to meet her bridegroom on her father's loving, dependable arm. There was no one living in her world who cared a jot for her save Lionallo.

She was soon jolted out of her self pity. Maria had taken her to her heart as one of her own.

"Only boys, the Good Lord has seen fit to send me," she told Lucy. "I shouldn't complain. They're all decent, healthy lads, with no more of the devil in them than is seemly. But it has been hard to stand by and watch my sisters marry off their daughters. You and your wedding are a gift to me from heaven!" Her sincerity was so obvious that Lucy truly believed her, and, both touched and enchanted, was prepared to go along with what ever local custom required.

Lionallo had brought her chest from the boat and she and Maria rummaged together through its contents. The older woman shook out and held up a beautiful samite gown that Lucy had never seen before.

"I did not pack that!" she disclaimed. "I had no notion that my dear foster mother had included such a magnificent gift!"

Maria stroked the silken folds with appreciative touch. "It is beautiful! It must be worth a fortune. I have never seen its like."

Lucy stared at the gown. It was a nonpareil among gowns, her favourite daffodil yellow over pale leaf green. She would look well in it. Her foster mother had chosen it with great love and care.

With a beaming smile, Maria carefully hung the garment on a clothing pole before she again delved into the chest. The dear woman was enjoying herself immensely, Lucy realized.

"What is this?" Maria was holding up a soft, kidskin bag.

"I don't know." Lucy frowned. "It is nothing of mine. She took the small pouch from her new friend's outstretched hand and loosened the draw string. A probing finger brought forth a small scrap of parchment.

"A wedding gift from your loving family," she read.

She tipped the contents out on the bed, and revealed the little array of jewellery that she had left with Eustache l'Mesurier. Tears filled her eyes. How could she have been so selfishly miserable? There were people who cared about her, very dear people, her real family in this world. She was lucky beyond permission to have fallen into the hands of such wonderful friends, when almost any imaginable horror might have been her fate. Remember l'Amoureux!

"My father gave them to me," she told a curious Maria. Both my dear fathers, she told herself, wordlessly, as she held the trinkets to her heart. "I will wear them on my wedding day, also."

Maria, returning to the chest, had found something else.

"Do you mean to tell me that ladies of the court parade around in such shameful garments?" she demanded, holding up an exquisitely embroidered night rail, of sheerest cotton, a gift from Philippa. "It is almost transparent. It would reveal all!"

Lucy collapsed into an almost hysterical fit of the giggles. "Oh, Maria!" she gurgled. "One does not wear such a thing in public – it is for wearing to bed ... a night robe."

Maria stared at the wispy gown in puzzlement "Why in heaven's name would you wear clothes in bed?" she asked. In summer one needs nothing and in winter who bothers to undress at all? This," she shook out the shift, regarding it with contempt, "would be of no protection against the cold."

"In winter, it is exchanged for one of heavier wool," murmured Lucy.

"Ridiculous," was Maria's verdict. "Although it is pretty. A shame that all this fine work should be wasted on such useless frippery." She was equally contemptuous of the shifts which were to be worn beneath the everyday dresses. But that did not surprise Lucy, as many of the court ladies did not wear underwear.

Once all of her possessions had been examined and admired, and the dainty slippers to match the wedding dress had been unearthed, Lucy was whisked off to meet with the other women of the community, who were enthusiastically engaged in making her marriage bed. She gathered that this was a tradition, the origin of which was now, as it would have been phrased in her own time, "lost in the mists of antiquity".

She and Maria were greeted with cheerful animation as the women eagerly displayed their work. Several of the matrons were making a large stout linen bag, about six feet by four feet, Lucy estimated. Now and then one of the young girls was permitted to sew a few stitches but, for the most part, the maidens were engaged in gathering wild flowers and herbs to mix with the straw which was to stuff the pallet. As they worked, the women made sly little jokes, which made the intended bride blush and the young girls giggle and whisper to one another, behind their hands.

With so many willing hands available, the bed was soon completed. Lemonade and little honey cakes made a small feast for the participants as they lounged on the grass and reminisced about their own weddings.

Lucy gathered that the festivities were likely to last for a week or more, everyone seizing on such an event as an irrefutable excuse for a prolonged celebration to break the monotony of their isolated lives. She wondered if Lion would wish to stay away so long, anxious as he was to remove her from Cyprus – and l'Amoureux's vicinity.

The short interlude over, the women rose to their feet. Several of them picked up the bed and began to dance around with it held high above their heads, everyone singing to a sweet, high, keening tune. The words were quite unintelligible to Lucy, but she had the feeling that a blessing was being sought on her behalf from some pagan deity. She wondered if it might be The Queen. Gratitude toward her new friends, and the haunting charm of the melody, touched her heart with nostalgic melancholy, and bitter-sweet tears sprang unbidden to her eyes. Then, suddenly, all was cheerfulness and fun again. Someone caught up a small boy, watching, thumb in mouth from the sidelines, and hoisted him up onto the pallet, where half a dozen women tossed him mirthfully into the air, laughing at his shrieks of half fearful joy, and wishing the bride many such lads of her own.

The next day was spent in an orgy of cooking, each housewife determined to out-do her friends in culinary achievement. Children ran about from house to house, begging or slyly thieving small tastes of anything left unattended. The men took themselves off to the taverna, performing only the most necessary of chores. Lion and a couple of friends went on an early morning fishing trip, adding their catch of red mullet to the rapidly accumulating supplies of party food. He and his companions were definitely foxed, in spite of their overdone courtesy, and Lucy guessed they had taken more than solid sustenance on their piscatorial expedition. Lion, though, seemed no more than slightly fizzed, so she had no scruples about joining him for a private ramble when he complained to Maria, loudly and vociferously, about being deprived of his bride's company.

"Will you be so anxious a twelvemonth from now?" she teased.

"A century – five centuries from now," he claimed airily, with a wink at Lucy.

"Where are we going?" she questioned, taking a little skip to keep in step with him.

"To visit a tomb." His hollow voice sent a cold little frisson sliding down her backbone.

Lion laughed at her startled expression. He slowed down and caught her hand in a warm clasp, swinging their arms back and forth as they wandered through the grassy fields. The cool sunshine cast a glistening sheen along their path, and Lucy basked in a comforting serenity she had not experienced for years.

"Here we are. This is the resting place of Umm Haram."

"And he is ... ?"

"Not he, she. The Holy Woman of Islam. Some say she was the mother of Mahomet. They say that he would sleep with his head in her lap and dream of the future, and from thence came his prophecies."

Lucy was fascinated. "Do you know any of the Prophecies?"

"He is supposed to have dreamed of the sea, and that Umm Haram would be the first to cross it. That was in Syria, of course."

"Then how came she to be buried here, on Cyprus?"

"Because, my insatiable little almost wife, the prophecy came true."

"Tell me! Tell me!"

"T'ch t'ch! Such impatience. If you must know, about seven hundred years ago the Governor of Syria raised a tremendous fleet to attack Cyprus. One of his allies was the Governor of Palestine, Umbada, who happened to be the husband of Umm Haram. She was treated with all honour, of course, and when they came ashore she was given a white mule to ride. But somewhere around here, they were attacked by the traitorous Genoese and she fell from her mule and broke her neck."

"Oh how tragic! I don't like stories with unhappy endings."

"Much as I love you, my Star, I cannot rearrange the past to suit you." He slipped his arm around her waist. "We are here."

Three hanging stones, similar to those she had once seen on a visit to Stone Henge, formed a colossal arch over the grave. A small party of women knelt around the tomb, their heads covered with gauzy white veils. On the grave a pile of offerings, wax hands and pieces of children's clothing, reminded Lucy of The Queen's shrine she had seen near Famagusta.

"But surely these women must be Christians," she whispered. "Why would they come to pray to a Moslem saint? Is that not heresy?"

"Men make war in the name of religion," shrugged the Corsican. "Women will seek help wherever it can be found – and for a woman's sorrows, well, who better than another woman could understand? Umm Haram, The Queen, Mary, Mother of God – the name makes scant difference to these women. Umm Haram was a holy woman. That is all that matters to them."

The supplicants were rising from their knees now, laughing and joking among themselves. Some of them recognized Lucy and came toward her, asking in friendly fashion if she had come to ask a blessing on her marriage, teasingly advising her that she must ask for many strong sons to support her and her lover in their old age.

They told her of their own successful pleas and went on to relate some of the many legends surrounding the tomb.

"The three great stones," one old lady related, "walked of themselves, over land and sea, all the way from Jerusalem. At first there was only one, hanging in the air over her body, but folk were afraid to pray there lest it should fall upon them and crush them to death. So the other two came to prop it up."

Another told how she made a practice of visiting the tomb every year.

"Tomb!" An ancient shepherd, lounging beneath a nearby tree, spat derisively in the grass. "That is not a tomb. 'Tis one of The Queen's palaces. She has them all over the country."

"Doesn't look like much of a palace," grinned Lion.

"That is because you cannot truly see it," was the old man's sharp rebuke. "There is a glamour cast upon it to shield it from mortal eyes."

"Has anyone ever seen her?" Lucy asked.

"Some have. But she is guarded by peculiar animals, such as no one sees alive now. My father talked of her often. I do not think he ever saw her himself, but my grandfather may have. Yes, I think he probably did, but that was a long time ago."

One of the women spoke up, excitedly. "One of my neighbour's sons dug up just such an animal made of stone," she claimed. "I was but a tiny girl, but I remember it well. It had a woman's head, a lion's body and wings!" She looked triumphantly around the group.

A sphinx, thought Lucy. It must have been a sphinx. Then the women were gone, in a quick flurry of skirts. She stood by the tomb, hand in hand with her bridegroom. A prayer never hurt anyone and a blessing was a blessing, no matter from whence it came. She closed her eyes and stood silently for a moment.

*   *   *

Their wedding day brought clear blue skies and brilliant golden sunshine, which was as it should be, Maria pointed out with a self-satisfaction that made Lucy hide a grin, certain that if the weather had dared to be otherwise the redoubtable matron would promptly have taken it to task.

Her bath in Maria's wooden wash tub could scarcely compare with the luxurious soaks she had enjoyed at Famagusta. But the water was scented with roses and lavender, and her hair was rinsed with lemon juice, endowing it with sparkling highlights that drew sighs of admiration as it was brushed dry in front of the fire with her own horsehair brush.

Willing hands helped to clothe the bride in her dainty samite gown. Her gold locket was fastened around her slender neck and the bracelet clasped to her wrist. With the ring on her right hand and the pearl earrings gleaming in their gold setting, Lucy was turned round to face Maria's treasured polished metal mirror.

The vision confronting her seemed like a fairy tale princess. As she gazed, bemused, at her reflection, two of the young girls, probably about 13 or 14 years old, Lucy guessed, set a crown of colourful wild flowers atop her burnished curls. An admiring hum of approval trilled through the small assemblage, and Maria was not the only woman whose eyes filled with sentimental tears.

It appeared that it was the custom for marriage vows to be made outside the church door, so it was there that Lucy was led by her temporary "mother". The unwed village girls followed, charming in their picturesque dresses, their long hair unbound and garlanded with flowers, a dancing singing cavalcade of artless joy. As they wound their way through the village, noisy, cheeky little boys and demure little girls pelted the wedding parade indiscriminately with wild flowers, and it seemed as if every dog in the universe was tearing back and forth howling and barking to high heaven!

Surely she was floating, inches above the ground. She could not feel the dirt lane beneath her feet. This had to be a dream, Lucy was sure, as they slowly neared the church where she could see the men gathered. Her eyes settled at once on Lionallo. How pale he looked. Was it only because his face had been so cleanly shaved of its seagoing beard? His usual grin had disappeared, replaced by a solemn frown, an expression she had never before seen on his face. His unruly black curls were now combed severely back, constrained by a black bow. His crimson holiday tunic, mid-thigh length over indigo hose, embroidered at sleeve-edge neck and hem in a gold Greek key pattern, drew sleek attention to his muscular frame.

There was nothing familiar about the man waiting for her. She shuddered and drew back for an instant. Then he smiled. More a grin of relief, actually, she thought, but the brightening of his face brought all her feelings for him flooding back, washing away her fear as she advanced to confront him.

Listening to the priest as she stood beside her bridegroom, she still seemed to hover in that weightless limbo. The world around her appeared and disappeared in misty vignettes. The thin ascetic face of Father Damien, his lips uttering words that did not register in her mind, although she heard them with her ears. The muted colours of her attendants' finery as they hovered silently around her. The faint cries of boys playing club ball, and the thwack of the club striking the leather ball. For a moment she wondered if her worlds were about to shift again and send her hurtling forward to 1831 or – terrifying notion! – to some other unknown era and place.

The thought shocked her into awareness, bringing her senses immediately to the alert. She was standing on firm ground, about to make her marriage vows to this very solid man standing, trembling, at her side. Trembling? Lionallo trembling? Now profoundly conscious of his presence, she realized that standing stiffly at attention beside her, the indomitable, imperturbable Corsican was shaking like a leaf. Who would have thought that he, of all people, would be a nervous groom? Inwardly smiling, she reached for his hand. It was a closed fist, but when she insistently poked into it, it opened then closed convulsively over her own, completely engulfing it. The trembling ceased and he shrugged off his tenseness and his voice, when he was called upon to make his vows, was firm and confident.

Lucy heard herself repeating those same words and the priest pronouncing them "man and wife". When they should have followed him into the small church for the celebration of nuptial mass, Lion first surprised her by placing his hands over both of hers, as if in prayer, as he gazed into her eyes and made his personal vow to her.

"Blood of my blood, bone of my bone,
 I give you my body to prove we are one,
 I give you my soul till my life's race is run."

The swelling in her throat kept her silent, but she bent her head to kiss the back of his hand before they moved inside.

She had been christened, confirmed and brought up in the Church of England, but her father, although punctilious in his religious and charitable duties, had been very broad minded. Indeed, he had been an outspoken supporter of the controversial Catholic Emancipation Bill in his time. He had often remarked, in his young daughter's hearing, that if all roads led to Rome, then surely all religions led to heaven, and God was scarcely likely to discriminate among his children should they call him Father, Pater, Jehova, Allah, or even Papa! The Vicar, Mr. Worsley, had not cared for that one bit, and Mama always shushed him when he fell to talking that way.

It had made for an easy conscience for his daughter in her new life. She had no qualms about attending the Roman Mass in Famagusta, nor in being wed in a Roman Catholic ceremony. After all, the Church of England did not, as yet, exist.

So it was with a carefree conscience that she knelt at the altar, by her new husband's side, the first of the throng to receive the Holy Eucharist. The Mass concluded, all solemnity was thrown to the four winds as the entire population of the village hastened to the site of the feast.

By tradition, Lucy was told, no one else could eat until the bridal couple had gone through the ritual of feeding one another. So she was prepared when Lion, with wickedly twinkling eyes and his usual teasing grin, selected a savoury morsel from the trencher Maria presented and held it to her lips. But she hesitated a moment, knowing his propensity for practical jokes and caught his wrist to pull his offering within sight. She half expected, from his mischievous expression, that he might be tricking her into accepting some tid-bit, which, while it might be considered a great delicacy by her new friends, could be utterly revolting to her. A sheep's eye, perhaps? However, it proved to be nothing more repulsive than one of the delicious spicy little balls of chopped mutton, wrapped in vine leaves, that Maria called "dolmades".

As if he could read her thoughts, the rogue threw his head back with a hearty roar of laughter. In turn she proffered him a similar dainty, pulling back with a little shriek of indignation, as he not only accepted it but nipped her finger and held it, for a moment, between his teeth, causing her to blush and the company to burst into laughter and teasing jests. Then everyone was free to set to and soon the thick slices of heavy dark bread that served as trenchers were piled high.

There was mutton, carved from a whole sheep, roasting on a spit over a huge outdoor fire, goat stew, and a dozen other treats. Children chewed happily on meaty bones and the ever present dogs squirmed from diner to diner, gobbling up orts, begging for handouts, and occasionally making off with some unwary child's portion. The fish, which the groom and his friends had so plentifully provided, sizzled on iron griddles set on charcoal embers. There was ale aplenty, watered wine, and citrus juice for the young and the temperate. Great bowls of yoghurt elbowed baskets filled with fruit, artichokes and other vegetables, and a whole table full of sweets testified to the kitchen expertise of the village housewives. Lucy worried about the expense, which she thought must be enormous and wondered how they would pay for it. She did not know much about Lion's financial affairs, but she feared that the cost might leave him with pockets to let! She doubted if his pride would allow him to use some of her gold. When she confided her fears to Maria, that lady stared at her in astonishment.

"Lion has provided the ale," she said. "And he has contributed more than his share of the feast in fish. So why should he pay for the rest of the food? We are the ones who are eating the meal, so why should we not provide it? Is it not the way in your country that all join together on such joyous occasions? We are only too happy to celebrate whenever an opportunity arises. Maria ha' mercy – those clumsy fools! Men!" She hurried away to supervise the removal of a huge iron kettle of stew from the fire, leaving Lucy with no time to ponder on her explanation before she was overwhelmed by the younger girls, each seeking a bloom from the wedding garlands to put under her pillow, in hopes of dreaming that night of a lover of her own.

"After all, you won't need them!" teased one bright-eyed maid, bringing more blushes to Lucy's radiant face. Really, this was embarrassing beyond all permission!

The sun was well past high noon before all those gargantuan appetites were sated. The more mature participants lounged beside the fires, gossiping or snoozing, while the singers among them entertained with ballads, love songs, or comic ditties. That had been the first time Lucy heard Lionallo sing his silly, boastful little song.

The younger ones were more energetic. Keyed up by the excitement generated by the festivities, they preferred more physical activities. Lucy watched a ring of girls playing Blind Man's Bluff, with a great deal of hair tossing and sly, over-the- shoulder glances, while ostensibly ignoring the loud comments and impudent compliments of young men sitting or leaning on a low wall nearby.

Some of the children were playing Hide and Seek, and a pair of old men were engaged in a ferocious game of Tables, which Lucy thought might be a form of the Backgammon she had played with Papa and some of her erstwhile friends. She sighed in perplexity. Everything was so mixed up. She still sometimes wondered if this was all just a wild dream.

Lion's hand, gently coming to rest on the nape of her neck, brought her head round to see the loving sympathy in his dark expressive eyes, and she knew that he had guessed at her thoughts. Her misgiving dissolved like spring frost in the morning sunshine as she gave him a dazzling smile. No matter what else might befall she had his love and his protection to hold her safe and sound. She leaned against his shoulder, wriggling herself comfortably into the shelter of his sturdy arm – but not for long.

The robust music of the shepherd's pipe brought Maria's husband, Andrios, to his feet. Grabbing Lion, he dragged him over to a clear space where, each with his hand upon the other's shoulder, they began to step to the rhythm of the insistent melody. Others joined them and soon there was a circle of dancers, all male, arms linked in brotherly comradeship, solemnly pacing intricate patterns as if performing an age-old ritual, its origin long forgotten. The music quickened and the tempo of the dance increased to match the beat. Faster and faster piped the piper, faster and faster whirled the dancers until, at last, unable to keep up with the rampaging musicians, the circle fell apart with shouts of laughter and the dancers tumbled back to their seats or to the welcoming turf.

Then it was the women's turn, but they did not join arms, as had the men. Instead, each dancer held a corner of a kerchief, linking her with her partner. Lucy watched, charmed by their grace as they stepped lightly to and fro, now closing the space between them, now pulling apart to the limits of the scarves, spinning beneath their upraised arms, gliding back to back, then twirling to face their partners again, as delightful as the ballet she had once seen on a visit to Brighton.

The merriment gained momentum as the evening progressed. For the bride, now tired and bemused, viewing the revelry by the ruddy, flickering glow of the bonfires, the scene acquired the dream-like ambience of a wild pagan festival. Still a little overcome, she allowed Lion, his silencing finger pressed lightly against her lips, to draw her quietly away, while their companions were distracted by the comic antics of a trio of acrobatic lads. Once outside the light of the fires, he clasped her hand and whispered, "Run!"

Unquestioning, she sped silently beside him until he stopped at a small hut. Once inside, he barred the door and leaned against the wall in an explosion of hearty laughter. Ah! How she loved that wicked laugh. It always brought a smile to her lips, no matter how his teasing might exasperate her.

Puzzled, Lucy looked around. On a wooden shelf, its cloth wick floating in olive oil, a flickering stone lamp revealed a single room, bare except for the marriage bed in one corner of the floor.

"Why are we here?" she panted, struggling to regain her breath. "This is not where we were to stay."

Lionallo laughed again. "You surely have the right of that!" he agreed. "I stole the bed, as soon as the women left the other hut this morning, and brought it here. I worked very stealthily, I assure you. I am sorry I was not able to bring the flowers they had scattered on it, my love."

"But why?"

"Ah, my Star! What the customs of your own folk may be I do not know, but here a man's friends can become a bit too jocund on his wedding night and I have no wish to enjoy the benefit of my comrades' attention on ours."

"Oh no!" Clapping her hands to her burning face, she recalled whispered tales the giggling servant girls at home had told of country wedding shivarees, and bawdy practical jokes played on embarrassed newlyweds by rambunctious "well-wishers", and agreed most sincerely with her bridegroom.

"I doubt they'll find us here, my love," he reassured her with his familiar mischievous grin.

"Aah!" Lucy stretched out tired arms and yawned. "That bed looks so inviting, I vow I could sleep for a week."

"Could you now? Come here!" He beckoned with the old intimate gesture, both hands shoulder high and took both of her hands in his as she came to him, drawing them against his heart. He rubbed his face in her hair. "My Stella Maris. When a man has waited as long as I have for his wedding night, he would be a fool to waste it in sleep, don't you think?"

Scarlet faced, Lucy hid her face against the hard wall of his chest. Yes she did indeed think!

17

Two days later they resumed their journey, accompanied by the lamentations and good wishes of their friends. Lion was anxious to be free of Cyprus as soon as possible lest, by an evil chance, they were recognized by someone from the past they were fleeing. The Stella Maris was once again well supplied with water and provisioned for a lengthy voyage, so he hoped to avoid going ashore at Paphos or any other large port.

Fascinated by everything on board the sturdy craft, Lucy anticipated high adventure, in spite of her bridegroom's warning that she was more likely to find boredom than excitement on their Odyssey. Certainly it was nothing like the pleasure trips to Bournemouth and Brighton on the excursion boat Island Princess that she had enjoyed with her Papa and Mama.

Their wedding bed was rolled up in canvas and stored in a corner of the partially covered stern during the day. There was no cabin. No tables or chairs either – no furniture at all. So odd! But then this was an Adventure! There was a small charcoal burning brazier on which, weather permitting, they could heat drinks and cook some food – a fresh-caught mullet, or a slice of salt pork. Using an iron disc that reminded her of her mother's griddle, Lion taught her how to make a flat kind of bread that was both filling and palatable. He had also stored a good supply of citrus fruits on board.

Since even her plainest gowns were not suitable for the primitive sea-going life, she wore, as on the first leg of her voyage, one of her husband's seaman's smocks over a pair of his chausses – a loose trouser-like garment, bound about her legs with leather thongs. She rather enjoyed the freedom her unconventional garb permitted, enabling her to scramble around the tiny vessel with ease.

When daydreaming of her Crusader, Lucy had often traced imaginary voyages from England to the Holy Land on her father's big globe. At first she would have her phantom vessels leave from England, travelling past Spain, past Portugal, past Gibraltar, to follow the North African coast, or sometimes Europe's southern shoreline. Then Papa had suggested that it was more likely that an army would travel overland, whenever possible, to some Mediterranean port, say Marseilles, gathering recruits on the way, before taking ship to the east. As the coast of Cyprus faded into the distance, she asked her husband which route he would follow.

"I shall try to avoid the mainland, as far as I can," he told her. "For Turkistan and Egypt are in the hands of the Moslems. I prefer to sail from island to island – the small ones, too insignificant for the navies to bother about. Our first stop will probably be Saria, or Karpathos. I wish to stay away from Crete and from Rhodos. There are plenty of safe little harbours in the Cyclades where we can take on fresh water. We have enough supplies to last until we reach home, and there is always fish!"

"Well, they say fish is good for the brain," joked Lucy. "From the amount we are consuming, I shall probably be a genius by the time we arrive. Even you may have acquired some wit!" She darted quickly out of reach of his menacing grab.

Lion was right. After a few days the novelty of her surroundings wore off and she began to question him, often at the least auspicious moments, about the navigation of the ship, about his home, his past – a dozen indiscriminate subjects. He explained his use of the stars in navigating, and pointed out a few of the more familiar constellations.

"Ursa Major – the Great Bear. Yes, I know that one, of course. We have half a dozen different names for it. The wagon, the Plough, Charles's Wain – although heaven alone knows who Charles was. And that is Orion? How huge the stars seem out here. What happens when it rains and you cannot see them? How do you know which direction to steer?" Her questions came fast and furious.

Lion grinned. "I have a little magic box. It came from far Cathay where they know a million secrets. Maybe all the secrets of the Universe, men say."

"Let me see it! Oh do show it to me!" Lucy begged. He bound the tiller and brought a small wooden box with a glass lid from his sea chest, holding it carefully on the palm of his hand. See!"

Watching her face, in anticipation of her wonder, he held it out for her inspection. She looked. "Oh, a compass!" she remarked carelessly.

"You have seen one before?"

"Of course! all seamen carry them, now-a-days. I mean they will, in time."

Lion swallowed his disappointment. He had hoped to amaze her. "Is it not a marvel how the little needle always points to the south?"

"To the north. It points north."

To the south, my Star. To the south, as the Arab trader who sold it to me promised it would always point."

"No. You are wrong. It points north."

"South!" His chin, already sprouting a growth of silky black beard long enough to curl, took on a stubborn tilt.

Lucy stamped her foot. "Don't be such a sapskull! Every half-witted village idiot knows that a compass points north," she snapped, then gasped, as a grip of iron on her wrist spun her around to face his angry glare.

"No one calls me thus! Were you a man..." His snarl startled her. She stiffened, determinedly stifling a tremor of fear that sent a chill running through her veins.

"If I were a man you would not hold me so!" She threw back her head, meeting his smouldering eyes with hot defiance.

He cast her from him with what she was sure was a rude word, and turned his back to her, giving all his attention to the tiller. She stood there, for a long moment, aghast at what had happened. Less than a week married and already they had quarrelled! How angry Lion had looked. She had never before seen him thus, but then how well did she really know him? He might very well be a violent man – even a wife beater, in spite of the promises he had made to Madame l'Mesurier. Didn't Mama always say, "Still waters run deep"?

For the rest of the day they spoke with extreme politeness and only when absolutely necessary, and when bedtime came she was left lying beside his stiffly uncompromising back. Constantly replaying their spat over and over in her mind, Lucy found herself at fault. Lion had thought he was showing her a thing of wonder – of magic, and she had not only doused his pleasure with cold water, she had called him an idiot. It was all her fault and now he would hate her forever.

Miserably, when she was sure he was asleep, she cuddled to his back and carefully slipped her arm around his middle before dropping off into a fitful doze. When the first fingers of dawn pried her eyelids awake, they had both changed positions. She had rolled on to her other side and he was the one with his arm around her, his chin tucked into her shoulder. She dared not stir, lest he wake and turn away from her. So she lay perfectly still, tears running down her cheeks.

Almost immediately, he did awake and pulled her round to face him.

"Tears, my love? What a brute I am to grieve you so." He kissed her eyelids and held her to his heart. "If you never speak to me again it is no more than I deserve."

"No, no! It was all my fault. I am the one to blame. I insulted you beyond forgiveness. I must be the one to ask pardon."

"Are we going to argue again?" he laughed. "A truce! Shall we agree to forgive one another? I will not hold you to blame if you will pardon me."

Lucy sighed with relief and snuggled closer. A burden had been lifted from her spirit but she still felt mightily chastened. In future she would take care to guard her tongue. Never again would she speak harshly to her dear husband – she hoped!

Later, as she perched on the water barrel watching Lion at the tiller, he remarked, "You said that these magic needles – you named it a compass, did you not? – are well known in your time."

"Yes. But they are used on land as well. They are invaluable when a traveller explores unknown territory."

"Why did you insist that it points north? If one considers it rationally, it points in both directions. The mark shows which end to follow."

"You could say that if you did not know how it is made."

"And you do? You know the magic?" His grin was affectionate, if slightly derisive.

She slipped off the keg and crossed to his side. "Shall I show you?"

He nodded toward the chest. "Bring it."

Lucy fetched the small box and opened the lid. "You do know that lodestone attracts iron?""

"Everyone knows that magic."

"Well. Someone found out that if you rub one end of a needle on a magnet, a lodestone, then hang the needle from a string or float it in water, the treated end will always swing to the north. I think it has something to do with what the scientists call the Magnetic Pole, which is somewhere near the North Pole, and that attracts it. I expect they know a lot more than that, of course, but that is all that I understand."

"H'mm. Interesting." Lionallo stared at the compass with marked curiosity. "I'd like to find out more about such things. However, enough for now that this works. North or south, it is a blessing to all men of the sea. Next time I lay my hands on a lodestone I shall try that trick for myself."

As they journeyed on, Lion helped to pass the time by teaching her the language of his own country. True Corsican, he told her, not the tongue of the Genoese and Pisan intruders who now occupied his homeland, fighting one another for supremacy, and tearing apart his beloved Corse in the process. Her linguistic aptitude made the lessons a pleasurable pastime for both of them. She could soon name every article on board ship as well as the trees and buildings seen on the distant coastline. By the time they were out in the open Mediterranean, with Cyprus far behind them, she was learning short sentences.

"Excellent, my Star," her husband praised, after one successful session. "Just one more sentence and that will be enough for today."

Carefully, he enunciated a short string of words, then took her through them a word at a time then, finally, the whole sentence. He made her repeat it until every tiny inflection was perfect.

"Splendid!" he enthused. "We'll make a Corse of you in no time."

"Yes, but you have not yet told me what it means," Lucy pointed out.

"Ah, you are right! I haven't, have I?" with a wicked grin, he translated.

She gasped in indignation. "Lionallo Momellino! How dare you! How could I ever say such a thing to anyone?"

"You can say it to me," he leered. "Whenever you wish."

"It would serve you right, if I were to say it to every man I meet. You villain!"

"It might make for some interesting encounters," he chuckled, unrepentant.

"Oh you coxcomb! Fribble! Nodcock!" She hammered on his unyielding chest with both clenched fists, then subsided into helpless giggles, as his arms clamped around her in an irresistible hug.

"You really are the outside of enough," she told him, when she had recovered her equilibrium. "And do not try to turn me up sweet. How can I ever trust you again?"

"You never can," he intoned in hollow accents, but with a smugness of mien that drew from her a small hiss of exasperation.

"You are an impossible brute! Beyond redemption."

Fortune blessed them with fair weather, favourable winds and starry nights. As Lion had planned, they sailed through the tiny islands of the Aegean Sea, resting for a day or so on one of them, glad of the opportunity to walk on dry land once more. Lucy was surprised and amused to find that, at first, the solid ground seemed to heave beneath her feet, as if she were still on the Stella Maris's rocking deck.

As the days passed she began to lose her fear of l'Amoureux. They had encountered nothing untoward on their travels and there had been no sign of anyone who might have had dealings in Famagusta. All the same, Lionallo decided to bypass Malta in favour of a tiny secluded hamlet in Sicily for their next stop. And after that it seemed no time at all until they were beating up the coast of Sardinia, where Lion directed his bride's attention to the various points of interest as they passed.

The weather in the Tyrrhenian Sea remained kind to the voyagers, hastening them on to the Strait of Bonifaccio.

"Corse!" sighed the Corsican, flashing a proud grin at Lucy. "Home!"

"Is this where we go ashore?" she queried, staring up the towering cliff face to the fortifications above.

"Oh no! Definitely not!" His smile vanished. "The filthy Genoese infest Bonifaccio. Between them and the scurvy Pisan dogs, Corse is being torn apart!"

"I collect you have no liking for the Genoese." She remembered his hatred of Genoa.

"Nor the Pisans. Cursed invaders, both. But the Genoese are the most evil – both treacherous and brutal."

"How came they to hold the land?"

"Our people applied to the Church for protection from seafaring marauders. A grave mistake! The Pope sent the Archbishop of Pisa to take charge. Under him the country was divided up into Sees, under Pisan Bishops and their forces. But the Genoese kept pushing for a share of the loot and eventually invaded us by way of Bonifaccio."

"Good Heavens!" Lucy stared upwards at the sheer precipice. "However did they manage to climb that?"

"They chose the first Sunday of the year, in 1217 – every Corse has that date engraved on his heart. Everyone was in church – weaponless and unsuspecting. No one ever considered danger from the sea. They had no chance. The foul beasts planted their first colony on this cliff and have been warring with the Pisan jackals ever since. Pope Honourius II tried partition. That never works, and Corse has been caught 'twixt the grindstones ever since."

"What absolute arrogance on that Pope's part!" Lucy was truly incensed. "Disgraceful beyond forgiveness! How dare he give away someone else's country. Put a whole nation in bondage. He ought to have ordered the Pisans out!"

Her husband laughed at her indignation, as he assured her, "Neither will be here forever, I can promise you!"

"Tell me more of your country's past," she urged. "I should not like to be ignorant of my husband's home."

"Our country. Our home," he corrected, smiling, his brow clear again.

"Ours," she concurred, agreeably.

"We are an ancient race of survivors, in spite of the many invaders who have harried our shores over the centuries."

"The fate of all islands, I'll wager. It was always so for my country, for hundreds of years. But those we could not repulse, we absorbed," Lucy chuckled.

"In that then, we are of like races." He stretched, relieving his muscular limbs, and yawned mightily. "First we had the Greeks coming and going, all through our early days. But always we met them with all the resistance we could muster. They built a city they called Alalia. We owe them some debt of gratitude for our olive orchards and our vineyards. It was they who brought those good gifts to our land. Even so, we did not suffer their presence with indifference!"

"Knowing my own particular Corsican, I can be sure of that!" Lucy grinned. "I assume that you are a fair representative of your countrymen?"

He knuckled her chin affectionately. "Then the Romans came. They drove out the Greeks and destroyed Alalia. They replaced it with their own city – Aleria."

"The Romans were everywhere. Even on my own little Isle of Wight. They named it Vectis. Truthfully, that was the only part of Britain that Julius Caesar set foot on, although he boasted that 'he came, he saw, he conquered' Britain. It was not as easy as all that for all his vaunted Legions. The Old Tribes fought and harried them for years. Some of them fled to the west, to the mountains of Wales, and never did surrender."

"Our people, too, resisted them for more than a hundred years. They were vicious conquerors. Many of our men took to the maquis, living off the land and harrying the enemy camps whenever they could."

"The maquis – what is that?"

"The scrub land, the wild country between the cultivated farms in the lowlands along the coast and the mountains that run through the centre of Corse. Soon, when we can run a little closer to the shore, you shall be able to smell it – the maquis, the breath of Corsica! No foreigner can penetrate the maquis – only a native can survive in that wilderness. The time will come when both Genoa and Pisa will be driven from our shores and Corsica shall be home only to the Corse, once more."

"We," he added, self-righteously, "have never sought to take another's patrimony from him – and never will."

A knowing chuckle brought his suspicious eyes to her smiling face. In answer to his unspoken query, she murmured, all innocence, "As a matter of fact, when I was born, we were campaigning against an ambitious Corsican who sought to take over half the world!"

"Do you tell me so?" Lion's face was bright with interest. "A Corse, you say? I would hear more of this tale!"

"It is a story that will be long in the telling, but for now ... He was a small man, but with great ambition – a man whom other men followed with loyalty and pride. But his own egotism caused him to outreach himself and, though he was Emperor of France and conquered half of Europe, in the end he was defeated and exiled to St. Helena. Another island. A small English one in the Atlantic ocean, I recollect. My Papa said he was a great man, although he was our enemy, destroyed by his own avarice. The more he gained, the more he wanted. His name was Napoleon Bonaparte. Papa had copies of his essays. He read some parts of them to me. Now that I come to think of it, there was a part that Papa made me translate and copy out, to improve my French and my penmanship." She wrinkled her brow and gazed shoreward, remembering.

"As far as I can recall, it went like this: 'How absurd to declare that Divine Law forbids us to shake off a usurper's yoke . . .' I forget the next bit, but it went on, 'With how much better right, then, can a people drive out a usurping prince! Does this not speak for Corsicans? Thus we can shake off the yoke of France, just as we shook off the yoke of Genoa. Amen.'"

"Amen indeed! Then we will free ourselves from these Genoese tyrants!"

"To be taken over by France. How sad that Bonaparte was not content just to free Corsica. His too-arrogant ambition lost him everything he gained. Even Corsica. Corsica. Such a pretty name. How came it to be called so?"

Lion laughed. "There are those who say that after the fall of Troy, Corso, a defeated Trojan leader, escaped to Carthage and was given refuge there. He rewarded his hosts by seducing the Queen's niece Sica and eloping with her to the Island of Beauty, as it was called then. Its new name was a combination of both of theirs. So, my Star, we are not the first lovers to fly from Royal Wrath to the Isle of Beauty."

"How romantic!" sighed Lucy.

"Perhaps history will repeat itself and rename the island in our honour."

She smiled at the thought. "Lioluce? Lucinallo? Neither really has the right ring to it. Perhaps we should permit our home to retain its present name. At least for the time being!"

"Agreed!"

They sailed on in comfortable silence until Lucy's unquenchable curiosity surfaced again. She turned eager eyes shoreward. "The land is lower here," she said.

"Yes. We have an excellent view of our homeland now."

The land was indeed lower, but in the distance could be seen the tops of towering blue mountains. A tantalizing odour was wafting across the water, mingling with the salty tang of the sea air. She filled her lungs with its astringent sweetness, closing her eyes for deeper enjoyment. "What is that fragrance, Lion? I feel that I should know it, but I cannot give it a name."

"That, my Star, is the scent of the maquis, the breath of Corse!"

"Really?" Lucy turned a puzzled face in his direction. "It seems so familiar. I could have sworn I had smelled it before."

The Corsican smiled knowingly, "Perhaps you have, my love."

A small promontory drifted into view, and the feeling of déjà vu intensified. The deck seemed to melt beneath her bare feet. Her bare feet! Suddenly she knew exactly what hid behind that jutting cliff – exactly what she would see when they rounded the point! "Lionallo Momellino! You sapskulled gudgeon!" She made a dash for her canvas covered chest, dragging off the covering and throwing the lid wide open.

She quickly pulled off her smock and untangled the cords from her chausses. Lionallo watched her, leaning on the tiller, enjoying the view from his perspective. He remained quietly appreciative as she donned a dark green kirtle, then obligingly drew up and tied the back laces on her demand. She pulled an apple green silk bliaut over it and turned, slippers and hairbrush in hand, to confront his slightly bemused grin.

"I admire a woman who can dress as quickly as she can undress," he murmured.

Apart from a haughty frown, she did not pay him the compliment of an answer but applied the horsehair brush vigorously to her riotous curls. "This is the only fashionable gown I have," she sighed. "Madame thought I should leave my trousseau behind. Then no awkward questions would be asked if my possessions were examined. Everyone could assume that I had cast myself into the sea rather than marry against my will. She has given me several gowns more suited to my new life."

"I thought you looked well enough as you were. What need to change?"

"To go ashore and meet all of Terra Vecchia in those rags?" She was scandalized.

"Terra Vecchia?" he asked, in pure astonishment. "How did you know?"

She returned his amazed look with a shocked gasp. "Am I right?"

He nodded. "Just a few more minutes." They travelled on, not speaking, with only the sound of the waves slapping against the ship, the high thin wail of a sea bird and the rasp of the brush as she continued, absent-mindedly, to draw it through her hair.

She had never seen Terra Vecchia before, had never been on Corsica, yet the little town, set behind the sandy littoral with tall chestnut trees for a backdrop, seemed as familiar to her as the coastal towns of her own English home.

"It is so strange," She slipped her hand tentatively into Lionallo's. He gave it a reassuring squeeze. "It's like reading a story you've read before and forgotten. You don't know how the plot will unfold, yet each page is remembered as it is reread."

"I know the feeling," he said. "It has been with me since the day I found you on the shore. A feeling, a conviction, that you were for me!" He brushed his lips over her shining hair. "Ah! We have been sighted." He gestured landward where several tiny figures could be seen scurrying down to the docks. "Our ship has been recognized in spite of her change of name."

As they came abreast of the moorings, willing hands reached out to catch the ropes and fasten them to the posts. Hoarse male voices shouted welcomes, hailing Lion by name.

Lucy found herself the centre of interested, appraising, masculine scrutiny and, blushing demurely, sought shelter behind her husband's protective bulk, until he grasped her hand and pulled her forward, proudly claiming her as his wife.

18

Lucy adored her new home. It was like keeping house in the play-house her father had built for her in the garden at home, when she was a little girl. She scrubbed the flagged floor with such vigorous enthusiasm that Lion swore she would wear it away in a six-month! She attacked the unvarnished tables and chairs with silver sand from the seashore, scouring them to a dazzling whiteness. She refilled their marriage bed with fresh straw and sweet scented herbs from the maquis and plumped it on the wooden frame criss-crossed with stout hemp rope that Lion built, and spread it with linen sheets and a warm wool covering that her kindly foster mother had packed in her chest. She chivvied her complaining, but secretly delighted, husband into carving wooden trenchers, spoons and goblets, and then into building shelves on which to display them.

Iron kettles and clay pitchers came from the local blacksmith and potters, paid for by barter with Lion's fish or his services. It seemed that very little cash was in circulation, everyday needs being supplied by the exchange of goods or work hours.

She found her new friends and neighbours congenial and helpful. They taught her how to make polenta and pasta from the indigenous chestnut flour, which they truthfully claimed was far superior to that made from any grain. As a gentleman farmer's daughter, she was not completely unacquainted with dairy work and, at her urging, Lionallo procured a small goat family for her. From his observance of upper class ladies he expected her to tire of the work involved once the novelty had worn off. He was pleasantly surprised when, far from waning, her interest increased. She was soon providing their table not only with milk but with cheese and later, learning other skills from her new friends, with the yoghurt so much enjoyed by his countrymen.

She was glad she had learned to spin while living with her French foster family, and grateful that Madame, ever thoughtful, had included a spindle among her gracious gifts. Perhaps she might be able to barter her own services for wool, perhaps by sewing or taking care of children for some busy family who owned sheep. Too, she had acquired a goodly store of herbal knowledge and lore from her French mentors and Mesdames Agathé and Henriette. That would come in useful, also. Not that she intended to go behind Lion's back, but she would not mention her plans to him until they were fait accompli, in case he should object. He sometimes had such silly feelings of guilt for having taken her from a life of luxury to what he considered an inferior existence as a fisherman's wife. Such fustian! Even if her safety had not been in jeopardy in Cyprus, she would still have been more than willing to elope with the darling ninny! Apart from Papa, which was different of course, she had never met another man who could even begin to compare with her Corsican. Not dear sweet Edward, for all his charm and chivalry, and definitely not George Brewster and his bucolic friends!

She still had her jewellery and her precious store of gold. When she had offered it to Lion as a dowry, he had been typically pig-headed about making her keep it, refusing to allow her to spend any of it on their home. But she had plans – oh yes indeed, she had plans.

She planted her herb garden with herbs gathered from the maquis in the company of Magdalena, the wife of one of Lion's cousins. The two young women became fast friends and Magdalena took pleasure in helping Lucy settle into her new life. Lionallo had no immediate family, which possibly explained his roving life. He came home one day with a boisterous half-grown pup that looked as if it might achieve bear-sized growth. It promptly began to wreak havoc in the tidy cottage.

"I did not know you had such a great longing for a pet," Lucy gasped, out of breath, as she finally mastered the animal by clinging to its neck and sitting firmly on the floor.

"It is not for myself, wife, but for you."

"For me? Now why would I want such a ruffian around the house?" she demanded, adding, quite untruthfully, for Lion had a seaman's fetish for neatness, "Do I not have enough work to do, tidying up after you?"

"I would not have you wandering around in the maquis unprotected. These are dangerous times, and the hound will also serve to guard you when I must be away overnight."

"It is not at all necessary," she objected. "The last thing I need is an untrained pony galloping about the house. Surely there is nothing to worry about here? I do not go into the maquis alone. I am always with Magdalena and her friends. This is not Cyprus. The people here are all kind and friendly. I cannot imagine any of them behaving badly."

"Huh! There are bad apples in every barrel – but it is not Corsicans we need fear. Do not forget we are an occupied country and enemy soldiers, far away from their own homes, are not always the most chivalrous of men."

"I have not seen any here."

"That is not to say you may never. To please me, my Star?" He clasped his hands in pious supplication with such a ridiculous expression of mock humility on his far-from-humble face that she burst out laughing.

"Sapskull!" she scolded, but understood that his drollery masked his determination that, willy nilly, she should have the dog. He was merely saving her pride by not making it a direct order.

"Well, if you have your heart set on the creature, I suppose you must have your way," she conceded. "What shall we call him?"

"He is your dog. You choose his name."

Lucy stroked the golden brown head, now lying peacefully in her lap. "Dandy, I think, after my poor dear horse. I wonder what happened to him? I left him tied to the church railings. I do hope he came to no harm." Her gray eyes glistened with remorseful tears. Lion slid down to the floor beside her, encompassing her with a comforting arm, while the newly named Dandy contrived to lick both their faces at once.

"Tomorrow is going to be a fine day," Lion prophesied, pulling Lucy to her feet. "I think you should sail with me." He gave her his most devastating grin, quite prepared for the enthusiastic reaction his invitation would generate. Sometimes, when the weather was clement, he would take her fishing with him. He knew how much she enjoyed those trips, so was not taken unawares to be "climbed like a main mast", as he complained when Lucy threw herself at him.

Having been an excellent sailor all her life, she always declared it was well worth crawling out of their warm bed into a still dark world, the only sounds those of the constant sighing of the waves breaking on the shore and the mysterious whispering of shivering leaves as the dawn wind searched eerily through shadowed branches. Lucy, clothed in Lion's smock and chausses, loved the pushing out from shore and the swelling of the sails of the Stella Maris as she crept out of the shelter of the bay to the open water and on to the fishing grounds.

That particular morning, however, Lucy found the usual rhythmic progress of the fishing boat seemed less comfortable than usual. She felt slightly giddy and then, suddenly, she needed to rush to the side of the boat.

"I am never seasick!" she denied, indignantly, as her husband secured the tiller and hastened to her side.

"I never said you were," he replied, taking her comfortingly in his arms, a peculiar smile lighting his face.

"It must be something I ate, but what I can't imagine. I have the digestion of an ostrich."

"Oh, I doubt that it was that," he said, still wearing the same knowing smile. "I have been expecting this. Did you never learn to keep tally, my love?"

She stared at him in bewilderment.

"You do not think, perhaps, that you are breeding?"

"Breeding? You mean that I might ... I am ... I don't ... I never thought ... !"

"I did! But, of course, I am accustomed to mark the waxing and waning of the moon. It has been long since you had to deny me pleasure, my Star."

Lucy felt suddenly weak and clung to him for support. He carried her over to the water keg and sat her down.

"Do you wish to go home?" he asked gently.

"And lose a day's fishing? Certainly not! We shall need all the fish we can catch with another mouth to feed!"

Lionallo threw back his head and roared. "That's my little wife – the soul of economy. Though I doubt if our young Angelo will starve for lack of one catch. Are you sure you feel well enough to stay?"

"Oh I feel splendid now. I think little Angela is going to be a fine sailor. Do you think I really am increasing? Do you mind?"

"I am sure of it. And why should I mind? I am delighted. Every man surely wishes for at least one son to follow him. This is the second happiest day of my life. The third will be when I see you holding our babe safely in your arms."

"Will you be very disappointed if it should be a girl?" Her gray eyes searched his tanned visage intently. In turn, his dark ones rested somberly on her anxious, upturned face. "A female? I suppose I could cope with the aggravation, even if Providence should saddle me with a duplicate of you," he sighed, tragically, then ducked and caught her wrist as she sprang to attack him.

A brief tussle and a prolonged kiss brought them back to a sentimental discussion of her condition and the little one who would be the tangible symbol of their love.

"If it is a boy, we shall name him for your father," Lionallo decided.

"Oh no!" Lucy disagreed. "He shall be called Lionallo, so that I will always be reminded of my folly – falling in love with a barbarous Corsican!"

The barbarous Corsican laughed. "Then, should she be a girl, she must be another Lucia, to remind me of my folly."

"I should, of all things, like to have a large family. I never had brothers or sisters. Not that I was ever lonely, or unhappy. Mama and Papa were the dearest of companions, and I did have good friends."

"You must know that it is my most sincere desire to fulfill your every wish." A wicked sounding chuckle brought her eyes quickly to his face, now adorned with an equally evil grin. "And this is one dream that will give me the greatest of pleasure to help you achieve!"

"Gudgeon! Look to your nets, or our children will all starve!" she scolded him.

The boundless energy Lucy had always possessed did not desert her during the ensuing months. Her housekeeping in the small cottage took but little of her time, in spite of the frolicsome Dandy, who never left her side, so she was able to devote herself to her garden, putting to practical use all she had learned from those two knowledgeable ladies, Madame Henriette and her court counterpart, Dame Agathé. Armed with their receipts, she carefully selected her herbs, often absorbed for hours at a time deciding which plants would be most useful in her new life, and choosing the best spot to plant them. Of course she must have all the common kitchen standbys, and then there were those needed for medicines, cleaners and dyes.

"I must certainly have aloe," she told Lionallo, as she sat cross-legged on the floor, sorting through her scraps of parchment. "It is useful in so many ways – for burns, constipation, insect bites and worms ... "

"You are planning to breed worms, my Star?" he asked with feigned innocence.

"Ninny hammer! You know I'm not! But little children do get them, you know. From playing out of doors, or from pets, I think," she surmised vaguely. Magdalena's mother will know. She knows everything about children."

"Ah! You plan well ahead. It is good to be prepared," he teased, and laughed as she showed him the length of her tongue. "I hope you will teach the child to pay his father more respect than does my wife," he added with feigned aggrievement.

"It is her father who lacks respect for her mother," with a saucy toss of her russet curls.

Lion laughed, and beckoned her toward him. "Come and give me your opinion of my carpentry."

She crossed the flagstone floor to admire for the umpteenth time the end boards of the cradle he was fashioning. In some ways, she reflected, men never stopped being little boys, never outgrew their need for appreciation and reassurance. Still, the cradle really was going to be impressive. She ran her fingertips over the silken surfaces of the chestnut slabs, exploring the carved depths of the frolicking dolphin ornamentation. Truly, he deserved all the praise she could bestow upon his handiwork.

"This will last forever! A hundred babies could not wear it out."

"I trust you do not aspire to prove that, my heart! I doubt there are enough fish in the sea to support a family of such size."

His "heart" looked him up and down, then, nose in air, taunted, "You flatter yourself, my dear husband!"

"Indeed?" He spoke softly, but the look in his dark eyes sent her scuttling to the door. Too late. Ah well! There would be time enough tomorrow to show him her herb garden.

But tomorrow brought a wonderful surprise. Lionallo had gone down to the docks to work on his boat and nets. Lucy did not expect him back until noon, so she was curious when at midmorning he stuck his head in at the door and announced, "Visitors!"

Assuming that it was his cousin Antonio and Magdalena she retorted, "Well, don't stand there blocking the door. Let them in."

His crooked grin broadened as he threw the door wide and tooted a fanfare before announcing, herald style, "Sir Guy Bouvier and his most gracious lady!"

Lucy stared open-mouthed. There stood Philippa, with Sir Guy grinning as widely as Lion right behind her.

With shrieks of joy the two girls ran into one another's arms, tears running down their cheeks. Lion and Guy exchanged mutual shrugs, easing past them to move into the house.

Lucy pulled herself together. After all, she was the hostess. She made her guests comfortable while Lionallo brought forth some of his home made wine to go with the bread and fresh goat cheese, both of her own making, that she set before their guests. Then she felt justified in demanding of Philippa all the news of her foster family that could be supplied.

"How do you come to be here?" she asked. "And with Sir Guy. Are you ... "

"Yes! We are married and going home to Montpellier."

"Are your Mama and Papa with you? Lucy queried hopefully.

"No. There are just the two of us."

Sir Guy took up the tale. "When de Lusignan died, the crusade was abandoned. The Pope was anxious for it to go ahead, but there was no one left to lead. The army disbanded. Most knights are leaving Cyprus and seeking other allegiances." He sipped his wine and added, diffidently, "Our friend l'Amoureux is reputed to have gone to Genoa, to offer his services to the Doge."

"A master to whom he is eminently suitable," growled his host. "If there is anyone more detestable than a Genoan, it can only be l'Amoureux."

Lucy shuddered. "Please. Don't even mention that barbarian's name. I never want to hear of him, or think of him again."

"There is war in France. Shall you campaign against Britain's Black Prince and his allies?" Lion wanted to know.

"Against my lost friend's countrymen? No. I know not the rights and wrongs of that quarrel and I have seen enough of bloodshed – enough of war. I shall hang up my shield and live a country life."

"Guy's *grand-mère* has a small estate not far from my oldest brother's holdings," Philippa interjected. "She has asked him to go home and manage her affairs now that she is old and infirm. She has promised to make him her heir."

"My honoured father-in-law has been most generous in the matter of Philippa's settlement," added her husband. "It will make us quite comfortable."

Lucy laughed. "Then he did not restrict you to a wreath of daisies, my sweet," she teased the bride.

"I am so glad to see you wed," Lucy told them. "We often speak of you both and wish you every happiness. And we will never forget the kindness and generosity of Madame and M'sieur."

"How is it that you are here now?" Lionallo asked. "This is not a usual port of call for ships sailing from Cyprus to France."

"Ah, but this is Papa's ship!" Philippa spoke up. "*Maman* was so anxious to have news of you that she persuaded Papa to order a special stop here. Not that he needed much coaxing. He was as eager to have news of you as she and I. Of course, he made a big to-do, and insisted that if he must ask the Master to deviate from his course he must give good reason. So Mama had to pack a chest to be delivered to you."

A loud knocking on the door proved to be Onfroi, who was made as welcome as his master. Onfroi carried with him a large packing case, which he brought into the house. After opening it for them, Lion left the two women to unpack and examine the contents unhindered, and took Guy and his squire off to the taverna for more masculine enjoyments.

There was no question of the visitors staying for more than a couple of hours, as the ship must leave on the evening tide. Lucy regretfully watched her friend sail away, then returned for another examination of her new treasures. Tucked away in a small corner she discovered two pieces of scented hard Castile soap.

19

Lucy took a deep breath, raising her arms to the sky. "Ah ... at last!" She exhaled luxuriously. "I thought the rain would never end."

"Oh, it wasn't so bad," Magdalena soothed. "You would not have noticed it so much if Lion had not confined you to the house. It is really quite amusing," she chuckled, "how he clucks over you like a hen with one chick! As if no woman in the world had ever born a babe before you!"

"Disgusting, is it not?" groaned the mother-to-be. "And I do not even show yet! I am sure every woman in the village is laughing at us."

"If they are, it is gentle laughter." Magdalena, also pregnant, took her hand. "They remember how their own men, at least most of them, carried on the first time they were breeding. My Antonio growls at me from morn 'til night. 'Don't do this. Don't lift that.' It's a positive relief when he goes to sea."

"I hate it when Lion goes out, unless he takes me with him. But he won't do that now." Lucy swept a hand across the panoramic view spread out before them. "This is all so beautiful."

With the sea and the sandy littoral behind them, they gazed upon what could have been a miniature continent. One hundred and fourteen miles of snow-capped alpine backbone, sparkling in the spring sunshine, reared up nine thousand feet into the new-washed cerulean sky from a dark jungle of giant larico pine. There were chestnut trees too, the beauty of whose blossoms would only be exceeded by the glory of the harvest, the glossy, deep coloured nuts which yielded the rich flour the inhabitants used as one of their main staples.

Below were the cork trees, the vineyards and the citrus and olive groves, the ubiquitous maquis and the pasture land that supported the hardy native sheep.

Crystal torrents cascaded down the steep hillsides to the sea. The fragrant odour of the maquis permeated the cool clear morning, filling Lucy with an exuberance both spiritual and physical.

"Come!" She caught Magdalena's hand, urging her forward. "Let's hurry!"

"Why?" demanded the other young woman, reasonably. "We have all morning!"

Lucy laughed. "Oh my dear! You are so matter of fact. Does not this wonderful morning make you want to run and dance and positively gobble it all up?" She whirled around, arms spread, face lifted to the sky, again deeply inhaling the spicy air before beginning the gentle climb through the fields, with Dandy frolicking around them.

She had devised a game for the big pup, which he found hugely entertaining. While he chased off in pursuit of a far flung stick, she would quickly hide among the shrubs. His unrestrained delight when he managed to find her was highly diverting. Once he started he did not want to stop, pestering her to continue until she regretted she had ever started the sport.

Several more women, bent on the same errand of herb gathering, joined them at different points on their climb.

"I should love to have a farm," Lucy remarked, as they made their way through the pastures and groves.

"Lion could never settle to such a life," grinned her companion. "He is true Corse. A mountain man – all the energy in the world, when it pleases him. Courageous to a fault. But nothing on earth will stir him to any action against his will." Her mouth twisted in a small rueful moué. "That describes them all – my Antonio is as bad as any. Honour above all, and to the devil with compromise. Honour! The main cause of Vendetta. Why must these men make such a fetish of honour when common sense would serve the world far better?" she ended bitterly.

"Has your family ever lost someone to the Vendetta?" Lucy was curious.

"Not in my time. But it was touch and go, two years ago. One of the Sampieri men fell in love with my sister. Our family did not approve of this as some of his kin are banditti, although Isabella liked him well enough. Coming out of church one day, he pulled off her head scarf. It would have been enough if he had just touched her. Everyone started yelling and screaming, '*Dishonorata,*' so it had to be either Attacar or Vendetta. Fortunately my mother liked Giacomo and persuaded our men to settle for Attacar."

"Attacar. That's immediate marriage, is it not? I remember Lion telling me about it." He must have had his cousin's fate in mind, she realized. "You mean she actually had to marry him, just because he pulled off her scarf? That's unbelievable!"

"That's how it is. Is it not the same in your country?"

"Not really. If one were caught hugging and kissing, marriage is expected or one risks creating a scandal," Lucy answered. But to be forced to marry a stranger, perhaps someone truly objectionable, because he behaved unmannerly was incredible! Terrifying! "Were your parents not horrified?"

"Yes. My father was furious at first, as he had hoped to marry her to a widowed farmer – a 'good' match, from his point of view. But Isabella was not very happy about it. Fortunately, everything has turned out well, especially since little Luciano's arrival. They named him for my father, who thinks the sun rises and sets in his little belly button. Sometimes, though, I suspect that my sister conspired with Giacomo, as she knew of our father's intentions for her and dreaded the very thought of it. I wouldn't even have put it past Mama and Nona to have encouraged her."

Lucy laughed, but sudden tears stung her eyes. She realized that her own father would never even know of his grandchild's existence.

Other women chimed in with stories, some personal, some second hand, that ranged from hilariously comic to tragic. The tale that horrified Lucy most was of a young girl, stabbed and left to die a lingering death in the street because the villagers were too scared of her killer to go to her assistance until after dark. By then, all they could do was bury her. Her offence? She had fed a man fleeing from her murderer's wrath.

For a while Lucy was silent, but when they began to dig up the herbs they had come to gather, her natural high spirits returned as she cheerfully discussed with Magdalena the stocking of her garden.

After a while, a loose cane in the handle of her basket began to chafe her hand. She set it down on the ground and straightened her back.

The sun was at mid-point now, and the day was growing warmer. She pulled off her kerchief and wiped her face and hands, then wrapped the cloth round the basket handle to cover the break.

Dandy came bounding up, stick in mouth, jumping around her, wanting to play. While she rested, the others, Magdalena among them, began to work their way gradually down the hill. Magdalena looked back and waved her on.

"Just one last time," Lucy told the hound and threw the stick with all her might.

Stepping behind one of the larger shrubs to hide from Dandy she came face to face with a man in soldier's clothing. Smiling, she would have apologized but the words froze on her lips as she recognized the older of the two men who had abducted her back in Cypress – l'Amoureux's henchman. Several small dead animals hung from his belt.

He stared in astonishment. Before she could flee, his hand shot out and grabbed her wrist in a punishing grip.

"So!" he grated, an evil sneer twisting his mouth. "We have a ghost, have we? A lively, unadorned ghost, at that. My lord will be uncommonly glad to see you, woman."

Lucy screamed. Magdalena and her companions turned toward them puzzled, for a frozen moment, before horror distorted their faces. Lucy called for Dandy. He came lolloping up, eager to participate in this new game. As he pranced, yapping, around captor and captive, the man aimed a shattering kick at the pup's head, sending his body flying. The dog landed several feet away and lay still.

"You brute! Pig! Monster! You've killed him," Lucy sobbed. She scratched and kicked at him, and bit his wrist. He slapped her face with his free hand and slung her over his shoulder. "Hold, bitch," he snarled, "or I'll break your arm!"

She had the presence of mind to shout at Magdalena, who was staring in horrified stupefaction with the other women. "L'Amoureux! Tell Lion it was l'Amoureux."

Her captor travelled parallel to the hill for some minutes. Lucy, mindful of this threat, stopped struggling. Already her poor Dandy was dead. She must not incite the man to violence, lest her baby come to harm. She must bide her time, hoping for a chance to escape. Now she was being carried downward. The smell and sound of the sea told her that they were approaching the shore, and then she was roughly dumped on the ground.

Two men lazing around a camp fire jumped to their feet and greeted their companion with shouts, crowding him and his captive.

"Ha! Supper and entertainment! Henri, you are the nonpareil of foragers." One of the men stretched out a hand to catch Lucy's hair. Henri swiped the hand away.

"This is meat for your betters, *cochon!*'

"May we not have a taste first?" leered a second ruffian.

"Half an hour with you swine and there would be nothing left worth selling. Make do with this." He unhitched the game from his belt and tossed it on the ground. He dragged his captive to a small boat at water's edge, and rowed out to a ship swaying at anchor a little way off shore. Roughly, he pushed her up a rope ladder, and another lout pulled her aboard.

"What's this, then?"

"Never you mind."

Henri propelled her toward the stern, opened a hatch, and pulled her down a few steps. Looking up from the papers spread on his small desk, l'Amoureux's mouth dropped open. Then an evil grin spread over his saturnine features. He rose to his feet, to greet her with a mocking bow. "So, you are still with us my dear. What a pleasant surprise. You can have no idea how I have grieved for your demise. It gladdens my heart to see my dear wife alive and well."

"I am not your wife," she spat. "That was no legal marriage, and you know it."

The look he gave her chilled her to the bone.

"Henri, you may leave us. I am in your debt." His dour henchman nodded and climbed back on deck, closing the hatch behind him.

"Come into the light and let me see you clearly." L'Amoureux picked up the lantern from his desk and beckoned. She backed away.

"Nothing to fear, my dear. I do not intend to ravish you. Your charming body does not hold the least attraction for me, I do assure you."

"Then why am I here? What have you to gain by keeping me? I am of no value to you. I have no fortune."

"I am well aware of that. But you cheated me of Estur's gold. You must make amends, as far as possible. You will not bring as much profit as you might have done, at first, but there will still be a market for your considerable temptations." He regarded her appraisingly. "I am afraid you have neglected yourself, my dear. Too much sun, I believe, and surely you are a little heavier?" Lucy prayed desperately that he would not guess her secret. "Never mind. A few weeks in confinement should take care of both problems." His smile was ugly. "We must make sure that the merchandise is in prime condition before we go to market."

"What do you mean, market? Where are you taking me?"

"I shall find a market. There will always be a buyer for such as you." He regarded her thoughtfully. "I must say, your attire leaves much to be desired. Your taste has sadly deteriorated, my dear. As to your destination – why, we sail on the ebb tide to Bonifaccio. As liege-man to the Doge of Genoa, I go to join his forces there – his envoy, with special powers. Very special powers," he finished smugly.

Lucy made no reply. To plead or argue with him would avail her nothing. It would merely add to his warped pleasure. She had to think. There was no way she could evade or overpower the brute to reach the ladder, and the trapdoor that was the only way out of the cabin. She would just have to possess her soul in patience, and be prepared to take any chance opportunity of escape that might arise. Her hopes of Lionallo finding her dimmed. She did not doubt that he was already in pursuit of her abductor, but how could he guess that she would be on a boat? Her spirits sank even lower. No. There was no one to help her. She had only her own wits to rely on. Only she could rescue herself and her unborn child.

*   *   *

Lionallo sped up the slope to where Magdalena had last seen Lucy, closely followed by his cousin Antonio. It was late afternoon before he had been told of Lucy's abduction. He had delayed only long enough to arm himself with cudgel and dagger, his heart filled with cold, black terror.

"There!" he shouted. "Her basket!" The gay green and yellow kerchief he bought her so long ago, in Famagusta, to replace the red one he had stolen, fluttered like a banner in the breeze. As he stooped to lift it, a low whimper drew his eyes to a clump of sage where Dandy was stretched limply on the ground. The dog pulled himself to his feet and staggered to greet him.

"So, boy, you are not dead, after all." Magdalena had been sure the poor creature had been done for. Perhaps his recovery was an omen. The dog responded to Lionallo's distracted fondling with a brisk shake, stretched himself and licked the soothing hand.

"Where is she, Dandy?" The whispered question was as much for himself as for the dog. "Where to go from here?"

"I see no tracks," Antonio had been scouting around. "Where do we start?"

His cousin stood up, idly running the kerchief through his fingers. He looked down at the dog leaning heavily against his leg. "Poor old fellow. You want to find her too, don't you?" At the words "find her", Dandy began to bark and leap about him. Lion's face brightened. Of course! The hide and seek game! Could the dog track her for a distance? It was a feeble hope, but their only one.

He held the scarf to the animal's nose. "Find her, boy. Find her." He held his breath, waiting for a reaction. Dandy wagged his tail and looked up, enquiringly. "Find her!" The order forced its way through clenched teeth. "Find her." He again offered the kerchief. This time the dog responded. Yapping joyfully, he sniffed at the gaudy piece of cloth and began casting around. The two men held their breath, then pounded after him as he suddenly shot off into the maquis.

It was slow going. At first Dandy charged enthusiastically through the brush. But after a while he slowed down, repeatedly turning puzzled looks at his followers.

"The poor beast is tiring," said Antonio. "No wonder, after the savage blow he took."

"But we can't stop now," argued Lion fiercely. "God knows what is happening to her!"

"Give the poor brute a moment. We don't even know if he is leading us aright."

His kinsman paled. "He has to be right! I must find her, Tonio, and soon! She will be so afraid." But he knew that the dog needed, and deserved, a rest. He dropped down beside the animal, caressing the sleek back and seeking out clinging burrs.

He clung to his patience as long as he was able, then again offered the scarf. "Find her, Dandy."

Dandy, refreshed by his brief rest, rose and trotted off, turning slightly now to the south and downhill. They could only trust him as dusk was fast thickening into dark and the moon had not yet risen.

"We are going seaward," Lion noted, then softly called Dandy to his side. The dog hesitated. He clearly did not want to stop. He returned, whimpering complaint, only when Lion called again. "The scent must be fresher, here. The dog wants to go on. We go watchfully."

Lion tied the kerchief around the dog's neck, restraining him and bidding him be silent as they made their way warily shorewards. The glow of a fire brought them to a halt.

"Two," muttered Tonio.

"And a vessel not far off shore," added Lion. "Is that where she is?"

"We do not know that she is here, at all," warned the other.

"She is here. I know it." His voice and manner radiated confidence. His teeth gleamed whitely in the near darkness, a grimace of satisfaction, and intent.

They plotted their strategy with care, but also with a lightheaded recklessness prompted by the adrenaline pumping through their veins, that reminded them of some of the wilder escapades of their youth. They had been inseparable then, and thought themselves invincible, until one of their foolhardy exploits against the tyrant Genoese had brought wicked and diabolical retaliation upon guiltless victims. That was when Lionallo had begun his odysseys.

Should they dispose of the two men cooking at the campfire first? Or board the boat, hoping to avoid notice? Surely the men on shore must first be immobilized one way or another. There was no knowing how many there were on the vessel and those two would be a hazard if a hasty retreat proved necessary.

They would take them unawares, then bind and gag them. They would approach from either side and take out a man apiece. An excellent stratagem, but they had reckoned without Dandy. As the two conspirators made ready to leap into action, he spotted the discarded offal of the game that had comprised the men's supper and pounced upon it, causing them to start up, knives in hand. The fight was brief.

Lion dug his blade into the sand to clean it. Antonio followed suit.

They exchanged grim stares, then turned toward the sea. There was no boat upon the shore, but they could see in the moonlight a dinghy tied to the bigger ship. They removed their boots and tunics and set Dandy to guard them. They made sure of their weapons, tucking their clubs securely into their belts beside their daggers. Then they waded into the water and swam silently out to the ship.

On deck they quietly oriented themselves. In the stern, a shadowy figure stood leaning against the taffrail. They crept to the man's side, where Tonio cracked his club on his head. Lion caught him and lowered him silently to the deck. The light shining between the planking of the deck drew them to the hatch. About to enter, they spun around at the sound of heavy footfalls to face a tall man at arms, his dagger unsheathed. The newcomer asked no questions but lunged first at Antonio, slashing his arm, causing him to drop his weapon. But before his foe could follow up, Lion was upon him, in a fierce but silent battle he was determined not to lose.

Before he killed him, Lion saw the face of his assailant clearly. From Lucy's description he recognized the criss-cross scar on the man's forehead – it was l'Amoureux's henchman, her first abductor. Quickly he turned his attention to his cousin, who was already binding his wound with a strip cut from their earlier victim's clothing.

"Just a scratch. Nothing to slow me down."

Lion nodded. "Right. Watch my back, cousin. I'm going down."

*   *   *

Someone knocked on the hatch door. Lucy looked up, apathetically. L'Amoureux called permission to enter and the door flipped open. Bare feet, followed by soaked chausses, backed down the steps. Lucy closed her eyes. She must be hallucinating. What she thought she saw could not possibly be true.

"What is it?" barked l'Amoureux angrily. He sprang up as the stranger turned to face him. "Who the devil are you? Who let you in? What is your business?"

"I am Lionallo Momellino. I let myself in. My business? I have come for my wife." He paused then, as an afterthought, added, "And to kill you."

After a moment of blatant disbelief l'Amoureux threw back his head in a shout of delighted laughter. "Your wife! Wonderful! After I kill you, my revenge on this dear lady will be complete." He bowed to Lucy. "You shall watch me widow you, my dear. It will be a sweet memory to carry with you into your new life in a Bonifaccio bordello!"

Lucy's stomach clenched with fear. She felt the blood drain from her face, and an indescribable weakness attack her body. She could not answer. Terror for her love closed her throat. How could Lion possibly defeat a man trained for war from birth? Oh, why had he been so foolish as to follow her?

The fisherman drew his dagger, but when l'Amoureux would have reached for his sword hanging on the wall he barred the way.

"Knives!" One succinct word.

The knight raised his eyebrows. "One way or another. Do you wish to kiss your bride good-bye?"

"No need."

Simultaneously, as if at some unheard command, they began to circle, eyes wary, muscles taut. Lucy could only stare, her eyes held irresistibly on the two opponents. To her fearful mind, the conflict seemed to go on forever, like some ritual *danse macabre*. The knight fought as he had been trained, elegantly and efficiently, almost disdainfully. At one point he drew blood from Lion's slashed knuckles and smiled mockingly. But the fisherman's grim face showed no change of expression. The Frenchman might have been trained by a weapons master, but he was not without experience himself. Knocking around the rough quarters of Mediterranean ports did not exactly emasculate a fellow. He had not survived without learning a thing or two. Suddenly it was over. The knight, executing a showy manoeuvre, exposed his left side. Lionallo did not miss the opportunity. His knife struck between the vulnerable ribs and sliced violently upwards. Gustave l'Amoureux stared at him in open-mouthed surprise, then slid to the floor. He writhed for a moment, blood trickling from his mouth, then he was still.

Lucy could hardly believe her nightmare was over. She staggered into her husband's embrace and sobbed on his shoulder while he murmured endearments and reassurances into her hair.

The hatch swung open and Lion, instantly alert, thrust her behind him and readied his weapon.

"Easy, cousin," called Tonio. "If you've finished here we should be on our way."

"You too, Antonio?" said Lucy. "How could Magdalena permit you to be so reckless? You might have been killed!"

"Permit me?" Tonio scowled. "No woman dictates to Antonio Salvatore! I am my own man – I take orders from no one."

Lion guffawed. "Give over, Tonio. We have no time to waste. There may be others about. Let us be on our way."

Lucy shyly touched her cousin-in-law's arm. "I am sorry, Antonio," she apologized. "I was upset to think you might have come to harm on my account. Magdalena would never have forgiven me. I did not mean to insult you."

His sunny smile returned. "See that you do not," he warned teasingly, and led the way up to the deck.

"Henri!" Lucy murmured, as they skirted the body by the hatch.

"He was the one?" Lion growled.

"Yes."

"Good riddance!"

"Doesn't seem to be anyone else around," commented Antonio. "What shall we do with the debris?"

Lion considered. "Bring the other two aboard and sink the ship."

"What a waste! Could we not dump the bodies overboard and keep her? She's a tidy vessel. Give her a coat of paint, change the colour of her sails…"

"No. If she were ever recognized you know what that would mean for the whole village."

"You have the right of it, of course." Tonio kicked the unconscious sailor they had clubbed. "What about this one? Do we kill him too?"

"In cold blood? I don't think I could."

"Nor me. He's just a boy. I suppose we must just dump him on the shore. He'll come to no harm.

Lucy settled herself on deck while they went to retrieve the bodies from the shore. Never would she go back to that cabin downstairs, even if l'Amoureux's body weren't lying there. Dandy's arrival with the funereal craft was a complete surprise.

"But for him and the silly game you taught him we would never have found you," Lion said, explaining Dandy's achievement to her as they made for deeper water. Far enough out, they tumbled the other three bodies into the cabin and reluctantly hacked holes in the ship's sides until she began to take on water.

They rowed off in the dinghy, and watched from a distance as l'Amoureux's craft slowly sank from sight.

"Home!" said Lion. "And it is our good fortune that we have a clear night and a calm sea."

They did not pull right into the docks, even though it was night. They landed in a secluded spot and Antonio, unwilling to surrender this treasure too, took the dinghy out and sank it, where he swore he would be able to find it again and claim it as salvage – a windfall from the capricious sea. One dinghy looks much like another.

20

See my love," Lucy explained to Lion, a few days later. "I have all my kitchen and still-room herbs. Rosemary and dill, tarragon and cilantro; and here are garlic, comfrey and chamomile for medicines and the treating of wounds. This is horehound, and those are violets for soothing syrup for coughs."

"What an accomplished housewife I have acquired for myself," teased Lion. "Should I perhaps set you up as an apothecary? Then I need never work again. You can support me, while I take my ease in the taverna all day!"

"Nodcock! But come, see here. Bergamot and marigold, and woad – and there are dozens of other plants growing wild, in the meadows and the copses. I shall be able to dye yarn to make you tunics of any colour you choose. Is that not splendid?"

"Splendid indeed, my little one, but how much time do you expect to have once our young Lion arrives? Not much, I'd wager, if he has as much energy as his mother."

"Little Lucia will be the best behaved baby on Corse! I shall have unlimited leisure!"

"We shall see! Now come and sit on this bench and spend some of that leisure time, while it is still available, on your poor neglected husband. I doubt you'll have much to waste on me, after this infant finally makes his bow."

"How can you speak such nonsense! You know that you will always be first in my heart, and in my life, should we have a hundred babes!" She threw herself into his arms.

He feathered kisses on her brow and cheeks. "Are you still insisting that I father such a brood?" he groaned and dodged back as she shot a reprimanding elbow into his ribs.

By the end of her pregnancy, Lucy had collected the basis of a small farmyard: a gray goose and a gander, a broody hen with a sitting of eggs, and new companions for her four goats – two nannies, one with an about-to-be-weaned she-kid, and a voracious billy with an appetite for clean washing.

The baby was born two weeks into the greater October-November wet season. There had been practically no rain at all since March, but the land had not suffered from drought, as the many small snow-fed torrents that tumbled down from the mountains kept the valleys green and fertile. On the day that Lucy took to her bed, however, it had been raining steadily for two days.

The birthing was normal, quick and easy for a first delivery. Lionallo had been on one of the "trading trips" he occasionally made, ostensibly carrying cork or olive oil to Sardinia, although Lucy suspected that while now, as a family man, he no longer took an active part in harassing the intruders, it was not beyond the realms of possibility that he might carry a supercargo, a fugitive escaping from the heavy hand of the occupational forces.

He returned to a kitchen full of women, with the local midwife firmly in charge. All eyes turned to him, with accusation, he felt. Dandy leapt from his whining vigil at the bedroom door, and hurled himself slobbering upon his master. Lion's heart jumped to his throat and once again he tasted cold fear. He stood paralyzed until a small hand tugged at his arm.

"It is all right, Lionallo," Magdalena sought to assure him. "All is going well. The babe will soon be here."

Gratefully he held her to his chest, as his heart resumed its normal rhythm and the colour returned to his face. Doggedly resisting all the midwife's commands to leave the house he took a seat beside the door with the Dandy's head between his knees, and she returned in high dudgeon to the bedroom. Almost immediately, a healthy squalling brought him to his feet and half way to the inner door before Magdalena could halt him.

"You cannot dash in like that, Lion!" she chided. "You must wait a few minutes until Lucy is fit to receive you."

"But what if she's … " He could not say the words.

"Everything will be fine," she soothed. I assure you. See! Here is the midwife's daughter, with your babe!"

A young woman came from the bedroom, her face wreathed in smiles. She held out a blanket-wrapped bundle to Lionallo.

"Here is your son, my friend. As fine and healthy a young rascal as any father could wish for!"

The new father ignored her burden. "Lucy! My wife!" he demanded. "Is she … ?"

"Everything is as it should be. In just a few moments she will be ready to see you." Again, she proffered her bundle.

This time he gingerly accepted the child, as she tucked it into the crook of his arm. Magdalena pulled back the wrapper to reveal a black-haired, red-skinned infant angrily forcing its tiny fist into its mouth.

"How precious!" she breathed. "How beautiful!"

The new father looked at her in disbelief. This? This blotchy, red faced, misshapen lump of humanity was beautiful? Poor little Star. What a shock she must have had when they showed her this tiny caricature of humanity! He must go to her and give her comfort, instantly. He would have thrust his burden into Magdalena's arms, but he was suddenly surrounded by cooing, grinning women, murmuring words of praise and delight. Saint's tears! Were they all blind, or stricken with insanity? Or were they deliberately pretending that all was well? A great force of love and pity welled up into his consciousness. His arm tightened around his son. Never mind little man, he assured him soundlessly. Papa will always protect you. No one shall ever cause you hurt without answering to me!

The midwife was calling him, her face now all beaming approval. "You can come in now. She is anxious to see you."

Of course she would be, poor little love. He handed the infant to his cousin and hurried to Lucy, dropping to his knees beside her bed.

"It is all right, little one," he muttered. "All is well."

"Oh, yes! It is, isn't it?" She leaned over and put her arms round his neck. "Have you seen him?"

"I have. And you must not fret, dear love. You must not let disappointment grieve you."

"Disappointment?" For a moment she was puzzled, then burst out laughing. "Oh I am not the least bit disappointed. I know that I said that I wanted a girl, but that was just to tease you. I really wanted a boy who would grow up to be exactly like you. And that is precisely what I have. Is our son not the epitome of beauty? Am I not the luckiest woman in the world?"

Maria ha' mercy! She truly meant what she was saying! Could mother love really be so blind? Before he could think of an answer, the midwife came bustling back and laid the baby in his mother's arms.

"I shall be back as soon as I have drunk a cup of wine." She waggled a pudgy finger at them. "And then out you go, Lionallo Momellino. We need our rest."

As the door close behind her Lucy caught her hand over her mouth, stifling a giggle. "We need our rest!" Her eyes sparkled with wicked glee. She gazed adoringly at their child. Lion looked too. In a second viewing it did not look so repulsive. If it were not for that peculiarly shaped head and that blood shot eye …

"Uh Lucy. His eye … "

"Oh, were you worried about his eye? You need not be troubled. It is only temporary. He was rather squeezed on his way out. The midwife assures me that it often happens so, but it will not be permanent. By the time his head straightens itself out, it will be perfectly normal."

"His head … ?" Lion swallowed the lump in his throat.

"Yes. Didn't you notice that it's rather squashed out of shape? How is it that men are so unobservant? I thought that would be the first thing you noticed. It looks like that because there wasn't enough room for it to come out otherwise. He's big headed, like his Papa! Probably just as pig-headed too!"

Relief flooded through him, body and soul. There was nothing wrong with their babe! Except having an ignoramus for a father. He looked more closely at the tiny creature. Such perfect little hands, with tiny fingers, complete with minuscule nails. He touched a miniature thumb with his own huge clumsy forefinger, with only the lightest pressure. To his surprise, the small hand turned and caught it with an amazingly firm grip. He caught his breath and looked at Lucy.

"He's holding my finger!"

"Why not?" she returned with a smug grin. "He's a wise child – he knows his own father!"

Lionallo felt again the swift flow of emotion he had known before, but this time it was accompanied by unalloyed joy.

"I suppose he'll do, for a first attempt. A few more experiments and we should be able to perfect the product." He tried for indifference, hiding his true feelings with a teasing grin, laughing when Lucy unblushingly called him an extremely vulgar and unladylike name – in Corse.

His mood changed and he regarded his wife with quiet concern. She looked at him inquiringly. "What is it, my love? You have something on your mind, I can tell." He rose and took the baby from her. He laid it in the cradle then sat down close beside her. "I have news," he told her, "but whether you will name it good or bad, I cannot conceive."

She sat up straight, anxious eyes on his. The very worst she could imagine had not happened – he, her own Lion, was here within touch. She could face anything else that vicious fate could throw at her.

Lion kept sombre eyes on hers. When she heard what he had to tell her, would she still want to stay with him, living and working like a peasant? Would she still wish to stay in this small cottage where she had given him joy and contentment he had never expected to experience, had never known was possible? This required of him more courage than battling any storm at sea, or dodging any Genoese ship with a fugitive countryman hidden in his cargo.

He cleared his throat. "In Sardinia I met an old acquaintance. A seaman, like myself. He had recently come from Rhodos, where he spent some time, fishing for the Knights Hospitallers." His black eyes sought his wife's gray ones. She didn't speak, but nodded, encouragingly. "The pith of it is that among the wounded they were nursing, there was an English knight who had been sorely hurt in the head. He had recovered his bodily health, but his memory had been damaged. He could not recall any part of the battle, or indeed anything of his life, or anyone he had met since he left Famagusta."

Lucy's eyes lit up and she hugged herself with delight. "It was Sir Edward, was it not? That is what you are telling me. How wonderful! This is the most felicitous news I have ever received. Oh I am so happy that the dear man is alive and well. You did say that he was well, did you not?" she asked anxiously.

"Only his memory is impaired," Lionallo replied, his voice as expressionless as his stony face.

"Then he will be going home! And the beauty of it all is that he will not remember me! I have caused him no pain or embarrassment!"

The man beside her drew a cautious breath. "You mean that you still wish to stay here with me?"

She stared at him, uncomprehending for a moment, then leaned toward him, hands outstretched. "Lionallo Momellino! Of all the dunderheads I have ever come across, you are without doubt the clown of them all!"

His hands crushed her with punishing ferocity. "You intend to stay?"

"Of course I am staying – unless – this is a ploy on your part to rid yourself of a plaguey wife. And you are breaking my fingers!"

He loosened his grip, at once, and brought the bruised tips to his lips. "I just wanted to be sure that you are here by your own choice. I would not keep you against your will. Estur is a chivalrous man and, knowing you or not, once he was apprised of your earlier relationship, he would take you to England and provide for you in a manner I cannot. I feel in honour bound to offer you that chance."

"Honour? Oh, Lion! You ... You ... Corse!" She grabbed his ears and pulled his head down to hers, capturing his lips with her eager mouth. Willingly co-operating, it seemed as if the weight of the world rolled from his shoulders. He pulled off his boots and lay down on the bed, angling his arm lightly across her waist, nuzzling into the softness behind her ear. When the midwife returned to chase him out she found them both sound asleep. One look at their blissful young faces sent her smiling back to the kitchen and another cup of warm spiced wine.

Three days later, Lucy was quite surprised when, after examining her and the baby, and making sure he was feeding properly, the midwife took her leave, with a cheerful, "All's well with the two of you. You can get back to your kitchen and feed that hungry man of yours whenever you wish. The sooner the better. He's prowling around the place like a lost soul! I'll see you again. Same time next year, I suppose."

In her time, Mama's friends had always kept to their beds for a full two weeks (could that be why it was called "confinement"?) and were considered semi-invalids for at least another month after that. However, she was eager to be up and around. After months in a hideous sack, she could not wait to put on a pretty dress again. The green gown she took from her chest fitted rather snugly, and her hair needed to be washed, but she gave it a thorough brushing and scrubbed her face with cold water.

The baby was sound asleep in his cradle, well wrapped in soft old linen cloths. Planting a zephyr-light kiss on his cheek, she slipped quietly out of the room.

She found no lack of food in the kitchen. Obviously friends and neighbours had left generous offerings. Fresh baked bread, half a roasted kid and a pot of savoury soup covered the well-scrubbed pine table. Gratitude filled her heart. How lucky she was to have such friends. Of course, she knew that it was as much for Lion's sake as for hers. But she also knew that they held her in approval as well, and had done their best to make her feel at home in their country. Truly she was blessed beyond all permission. And now that she knew that Sir Edward was safe and sound and on his way home to his charming island estate, she could enjoy her happiness with no sense of guilt. The only shadow on her joy was the memory of her dear Mama and Papa. If she could only share her felicity with them.

"What on earth do you think you are doing?" Striding through the open door, Lion swept her up and deposited her on the bench beside the hearth. "Why are you out of your bed?"

"Nona Barbieri said I could," she answered, defensively. "Really, she did. She said I should get up and feed you! She seemed to think you were starving," she added, slyly peeking up at him through fluttering lashes.

"Woman's a fool," he growled. "As if any seaman worth his salt couldn't look after himself and his woman too! Not," he assured her hastily, "that I am not glad to see you on your feet, but is it not too soon after your ordeal?"

"Ordeal!" She laughed merrily, catching his hand in hers. "It was no ordeal. I must admit that I was just the tiniest bit scared, at first. But it was so exciting, and over too soon for me to be really frightened. Oh, Lion! I feel so sorry that you can never know just how wonderful it was!"

"Thank you! But I do not begrudge you your 'wonderful' experience one iota!" he assured her, dryly. "I had enough excitement on my own account, wondering what was happening in there." He jerked a broad thumb toward the bedroom door.

He lowered his lithe length to the bench and laid his arm across her shoulders, his lips seeking the warmth of her throat. "My Star! How could I possibly live without you?"

"Well, you won't need to, will you?" she countered, deliberately quashing the niggling little inner voice that kept suggesting that it was far more likely that Lion might be the one, through some disaster of storm or sea, or other evil happenstance, to leave her bereft. "I have shown that I am fit and able to bear as many babies as we wish, so your fears are groundless. Why, Nona Barbieri even said, as she left, that she would see me this time next year! "

"Next year?" Her meaning sank in. "Another babe? Never! I shall never put you through such a tribulation again. I have heard from other men of the terrible things that can happen to a woman in childbed." (Lucy hid her amusement. Did men then also indulge in idle gossip, capping one another's horror stories with their own exaggerations? How intriguing!) "What kind of monster do you take me for?"

"No monster at all, you silly ninny," she soothed him affectionately. "But there is nothing to fear. I shall have half a dozen little ones and be right as rain, believe me."

"We'll see," he muttered. But the worry lines eased somewhat from his brow.

Four weeks later, on an especially warm and dry late November day, baby Lion and his new little cousin Julie were carried to the village church for their Baptismal service. The four proud parents listened dutifully to the homily to which Father Ambrose subjected them, then returned to the Momellino home to celebrate the occasion with their relatives and friends. Once there, the two young mothers were shooed outside, to sit in the sunshine with the little guests of honour, while the other women took charge of the festivities.

"Julie is such a pretty name," remarked Lucy. "Is that why you chose it, or does it have some significance in your family?"

"Oh, it's a fairly common name among the Corse," her friend replied. "Most families have a Julie. After all, St. Julie is one of our two national saints."

"There's a Saint Julie? I did not know that. Lion has never mentioned it, although he did tell me about St. Devoté." Lucy shuddered, involuntarily. "Horrible!"

"Saint Julie was a martyr, too, you know. If Saint Devoté's story upset you, perhaps I should not tell you of Saint Julie's sufferings."

"It will be better if you do. Otherwise I might disgrace myself if someone should speak of it and take me by surprise. At least if I know I shall be prepared."

"Very well." Magdalena shifted her baby from one arm to the other. "Look at those ridiculous men! How they do love to show off, to be sure, like little boys. No matter what their size they never do grow up, do they?"

"Particularly if there are a few pretty girls around," Lucy agreed, nodding her head toward the well outside the house door, where two girls in their early teens were lazily drawing water.

They were momentarily diverted, watching the masculine coterie who had been entertaining themselves with various manifestations of horseplay. The older men were playing boccia, while the young and in some cases not so young were endeavouring to outdo one another in feats of strength and agility.

The particular enterprise which had attracted their attention was a competition to see who could climb up one side and down the other of an unsupported ladder. Several had already failed in the attempt and now, to Lucy's apprehension, Lion was taking his turn. She watched, holding her breath, as he successfully negotiated the ascent and the precarious changeover. Then she uttered a small scream as he lost balance and leapt free. He landed safely, but the falling ladder caught him a glancing blow on the forehead and sent him staggering.

"Sapskull!" Lucy thrust her baby into Magdalena's free arm and dashed to her husband's side. "What have you done to yourself, now?" she snapped, terror sharpening her voice.

"Let me see!" She reached to smooth back his hair, to reveal a large lump already swelling and turning colour.

"'Tis nothing! A mere flea bite!" he insisted, irritably brushing her aside. "Do not fuss – I am not made of pastry. Next time I shall succeed."

"Next time! You shall not repeat such an addlepated trick. I forbid you. You could kill yourself!"

"Forbid? " His voice was soft and though his smile seemed conciliatory it did not reach his eyes. There was that shining in their dark depths that warned her against further argument. With a shrug she flounced back to her seat, relieving Magdalena of young Lion, but not before her own eyes let her husband know that she was far from capitulating. Pride and dignity would not permit a public squabble, staving off an immediate confrontation, but there would certainly be a private reckoning in the near future!

"Lucia! You should never have spoken so to Lion, in front of the other men." Magdalena's pretty face revealed her concern for her friend. "He will surely beat you for that!"

The English girl turned to her, mouth agape. "Beat me! Beat me! He would never dare!" She stared at her friend with grim curiosity. "Does Antonio beat you?"

Magdalena shook her head in vigorous denial. "No! But then, I would on no account choose to berate him in such a manner, even at home with no one to hear."

"Well, you need have no fear for me. Lion will not hurt me – he has given his word. Now – let us speak of other things. You were about to tell me of Saint Julie."

"Oh, yes. Well there isn't a lot to tell. She was said to have been born in Byzantium, and grew into a beautiful golden-haired young woman. Then, when she was about 20 years old, she was captured by Vandal raiders who sold her into slavery, in Syria. A few years later she was brought here and sold again to someone on Cape Corse. When she refused to renounce Christianity, she was put to the torture and killed. It is believed that one of the things they did to her, among others too ghastly to mention, was to cut off her breasts with red hot pincers. The legend has it that they then threw them over the cliff and they were miraculously turned into twin fountains."

"And you have named your baby for such an unfortunate woman!"

The Corsican girl looked at her in surprise. "You said yourself it is a pretty name. And the little one must have one holy name or she will go through life without a Name Day. Have you not given your own son the second name of James? And was not Saint James, too, a martyr?"

"Yes, but ... oh, never mind." Lucy shook her head, in frustration. True, when advised that their son should also be given a saint's name, Lionallo had left the choice to Lucy. Feeling that it might not be tactful to mention St. Olaf, from whose church she had been spirited away, she had settled for St. James, since, as she told her husband, it was in the town square outside his church that the Gypsy had told her fatal fortune, on his fete day July 25th. "Two loves, one fair and a warrior, one dark and a man of the sea." It was times like this when she felt worlds apart from this place and time and even the nicest of these people.

A raucous cheer drew her attention back to the masculine horseplay. Her husband, holding the ladder with one hand, with a triumphant grin on his tanned face, was being heartily thumped on the back by his friends.

"I was not watching," she remarked to Magdalena, with grim sarcasm, "but I gather my dear spouse has succeeded in his valiant endeavour."

"And are you not proud of him, Lucia? None of the others has been successful. Surely you know that their antics are as much to attract our admiration as to out-do one another. See how young Telesphore peeks sideways at little Ursula and Barbara, wondering if they have noticed how much taller and broader he is than last year, and if they saw him best his cousin Rudolpho at arm wrestling." She gestured toward the two maidens still lingering by the well.

"Of course I know that," admitted Lucy. "But I was so scared when that ladder hit Lion that my fear just burst out in anger."

Magdalena and her husband were the last to leave, Antonio offering, with a sly smirk, to stay a while longer if Lionallo thought he needed support, then departed laughing as his cousin sped him on his way with a vicious glare.

There was silence in the cottage for a long moment. The baby slept in his cradle by the fire, unaware of the tension holding his parents rigidly apart. Lionallo, thumbs tucked characteristically in his belt, lips compressed into unrelenting thinness, rocked slowly back and forth on his heels, staring coldly down his nose at Lucy who, hands clasped behind her back, returned his black gaze with matching frigidity, her chin raised high in defiance. She knew that he would never strike her. But she had done nothing wrong, so she was certainly not going to submit. She kept silence. Let him be the first to speak. She would not be intimidated.

He broke the impasse, all the more incensed that his unspoken anger failed to cow her. "So Madame! I hope you derived much satisfaction in humiliating me in front of my friends today."

"Humiliating you! Humiliating you! Since when has concern for the safety of one's husband's life and limb been charged as an insult?" Now her hands were clamped to her hip bones, as she spat out her words, gray eyes blazing with fury.

"Concern is acceptable, but to forbid is beyond all things unforgivable! Every man present heard my wife forbidding me to do as I please. It will be the talk of the taverna. I shall be named a lily-livered craven, knotted to your apron strings – led around like a hog with a nose ring!"

Lucy was confounded. He actually believed what he was saying, that he would be despised because she had berated him in front of his friends. Truly Magdalena had the right of it when she claimed that men were just oversized little boys. There was a turn to his lip at this moment that reminded her of Ti-Jean in a huff. This was silly – certainly nothing to fight about and maybe sulk for days. She would be the one to surrender and it would be fun to make up. She would not be miserly about her apology either. She would engage every scrap of acting talent she possessed.

She relaxed, allowing her shoulders to drop in discouragement and her lower lip to tremble. With a noticeable gulp she squeezed her eyelids tightly so that she might raise tear bright eyes to his smoldering frown.

"I am so sorry," she whispered. "I did not mean to anger you, but I was so frightened! If anything happened to you I don't know what I'd do. I hardly knew what I was saying. Not for the world would I willingly shame you." She was beginning to enjoy herself now, and threw herself into her submissive role with enthusiasm. Should she dare go down on her knees? That would be fun. No, she told herself, keep it believable. "I will do anything to make it right! You can tell them you beat me. And I will walk behind you to church with my head down looking penitent."

She regarded him hopefully, through thick lowered lashes. Surely he was looking a little less grim? She held out her hands to him with a pretty gesture and a beseeching smile.

Lionallo bit furiously on his inner lip, his face twisted in a wry grimace. The little witch! Did she think she was deceiving him? Hah! He knew his Stella Maris better than she thought. He had past experience of her crafty schemes. Should he let her hang in the wind for a while or call the bluff? Keeping his expression blankly sombre, he turned on his heel and made for the door.

"Lion!" Frightened, Lucy dropped all pretense and sped after him. He spun around and caught her under the arms, lifting her to face him and shook her like a puppy.

"Liar! You meant not one word of that taradiddle!"

Lucy blushed and hung her head, and his great roar of laughter echoed throughout the house. He let her slide to the floor, then enveloped her in a bear-like embrace. "Oh my Star, my Stella Maris! What am I going to do with you?"

"Don't you know?" she asked, all innocence, sending him into another rib-shaking spasm of laughter as he tightened his hold.

21

With the Christmas festivities well behind them, and the early Corsican spring advancing upon them, Lucy's yearning for a farm again beset her. She pleaded with Lionallo, but he was adamant.

"But we have enough gold to pay for it," she urged.

"Your dowry. Your gold, not mine."

"Ours. All you have is at my disposal, is it not?"

"Correct. But that is a different story. A man provides for his wife and family. It is his duty and his pleasure."

"Oh, fustian! You are as stubborn as a mule!"

"Consider the speaker," the "mule" grinned. "But seriously, my star, I could never settle to a life on the land. The sea is my life. I can never give it up."

"But don't you see, my love," she pulled eagerly at his arm. "Your life need not change at all. The house and the babe take so little of my time, and I have all the energy in the world. The farm would be my responsibility."

For once his guffaw annoyed her. "Don't laugh at me, Lionallo Momellino! I am quite capable, and I need something to occupy my time when you are at sea."

"No." He was adamant. "Forget those farouche ideas, my love. You will have enough to occupy you, looking after our young ones." He laughed again at her bewilderment. "Oh, my Star. Will you never learn to study the moon?"

"One moon-gazer in the family is enough," she snapped. "What does your Artemis tell you now?"

He silenced her with a leisurely kiss before answering. "She tells me that soon you will be too busy to worry about farms. Your time will be taken up by little Lion's brother or sister."

"What!" She gaped inelegantly, then hurriedly calculated on her fingers. A broad smile beamed across her face. "You are right – you and your Moon Goddess! How wonderful! Another baby!" She squeezed herself closer into his embrace. "I am so happy! I never wanted my child to be an only one. Perhaps we shall make your hundred yet," she finished, wickedly.

"Jesu forbid!" he mumbled piously into her hair.

*   *   *

Five years and three more children later, Lucy was again sitting on her porch with three-week-old Gianna propped on her chest, one hand supporting the tiny linen-padded bottom and the other pressing the damp curly head to her throat. Basking in the April sunshine, she savoured the pleasure of again holding a tiny scrap of humanity to her heart. Next to feeling herself warmly clasped in her husband's arms, it must surely be the sweetest sensation in the world.

Watching small Philippa and her brother Raphael playing with a rag ball – young Lionallo was down on the shore helping his father check the fishing nets – she pondered on that morning's argument with Lion. She was trying to persuade him to buy a citrus farm, one just having come upon the market. His blunt refusal was still based on the same contentions. He was a seafarer, first, last and always. She had her hands full with the children. A man should be the sole provider for his family. In vain she had tried to convince him that house and children notwithstanding she had as much if not more energy as she had ever possessed. He had merely favoured her with that infuriating stubborn grin of his – his children had inherited it too and used it just as divertingly – and planted a robust kiss on her protesting lips. She watched him striding off to the shore with his eldest son right behind him, manfully imitating his father's sturdy gait, and she strengthened her resolve. Never mind, Lionallo Momellino! She would have her farm, sooner or later, so there. Just wait and see.

*   *   *

Nona Momellino stirred in the seat outside her door, where she had been firmly installed by her daughter, Gianna. That one always had been a bit of a dictator, even as a child. The occasion for the family gathering was the citrus harvest, which over the years had become a family celebration. Everyone came home for the occasion – from "Young" Lion, now a grandfather in his own right, to the latest newborn babe. The sun was comfortably warm and the sound of the children's voices, high and thin on the orange blossom scented air, mingled with the raucous laughter of the younger men. As usual, they were attempting to outdo each other in feats of physical strength and endurance. Pleasant memories of other times and other gatherings came flooding back. There was that time when Lion had climbed the ladder ...

But that had been at the old house, down by the shore, before they had moved to the farm. A good move that had been, in spite of dear old Lion's opposition. It had been six years and four children after their marriage. She had waited until he had gone to sea, carrying a cargo of wine and olive oil for Sardinia, and forged ahead with her plans, enlisting the unenthusiastic aid of Father Ambrose, on one of the visits he regularly made to every member of his parish ...

"My dear child," he had queried, when she tentatively requested his aid in her purchase on the grounds that it was more seemly that business be conducted by a man. It was especially so since the seller would not be so likely to overcharge a man of the cloth, particularly one to whom he must make his confessions. "My dear child, does Lionallo know of your intention?"

"We have discussed it on numerous occasions," she murmured avoiding the priest's eyes.

"And he approves? I would not have thought a Momellino would so easily give up the sea."

"Oh, but he will not need to do so, Father. I shall manage the farm myself. He will never need to do a hand's turn on the land."

"Then he is not in accord?" The priest bent a perceptive eye upon her. "He is unaware of your intent?"

"Not exactly, Father." Lucy squirmed uncomfortably. "He certainly knows of my intent. I have told him, often enough, that I intend to buy a farm, and this one is so opportunely available."

"Opportune, because your husband is not here to oppose you. Is that your idea of wifely submission?"

"It is your own idea, Father." Lucy folded her hands before her, in prim satisfaction. "I am merely trying to follow your advice. Did you not admonish us but two weeks ago in your Sunday sermon, that those of us who aspired to be perfect wives should take our model from the Book of Proverbs, Chapter 31, verses 10 to 31?"

"I believe so," he agreed, cautiously.

"Then you will remember that verse 16 says: 'She considereth a field and buyeth it. With the fruit of her hands, she planteth a vineyard.'" She stared at him, expectantly. He shook his head with a patient sigh.

"And you intend to substitute an orange grove. With what will you pay? Your husband's hard earned silver?"

"Oh no, Father!" Lucy was shocked. "I would never betray Lion so! I have gold of my own." She knelt and rummaged in the chest that Lion had carved for her so many years earlier in Cyprus. She drew out the small kidskin bag and emptied out the gold pieces given her by her beloved friends the l'Mesuriers. "This was a gift from my dear foster parents. Lionallo has always refused to accept it as my dowry. He insists that it is mine, to do with as I please. And this is what I please."

"Yes. I see!" Father Ambrose stroked his greying beard thoughtfully. Mommelino's wife never failed to amaze him.

"It will be all right, once I have accomplished my aim, Father, I assure you. Lion will be angry at first. But he never holds a grudge for long, and our children can only benefit from this. A bigger house and an income that will be put away for their futures, as I do not intend to use one penny of the profits. Lionallo will amply support us as he has always done, and will do so as long as God spares him. But suppose He calls him before our children are grown? Will it not be a comfort to know that his family will not be left destitute! Besides," she grinned, "will the work needed to keep up a farm not serve to prevent me from falling into mischief?"

"There is that, I agree!"

"Then you will help me, dear Father?"

"I suppose I must, or you will go ahead on your own and perhaps be badly cheated."

"Oh, I do most sincerely appreciate your help. And if this gold should not be sufficient, I have jewellery that my own blessed parents gave me."

"They are not alive then, your true parents?"

"Not at this time." A peculiarly worded reply, the priest thought, but the odd turn of phrase was probably due to her foreign birth, even though she had assimilated most admirably. She was indeed, the old priest reflected, a woman of extremely independent character, although, to be absolutely truthful, there were in his parish several women just as strong minded, but less obviously so, and generally widows or single women of more advanced years.

"You must be prepared to face Momellino's grave displeasure when he returns," he warned. "I can only hope that he will not call me to account for this."

"No, no, Father! That will not be so. Lion knows me too well to blame you for my sins! Rest assured, he will not hold you at fault."

"Do you wish me to be present when you inform him of your purchase?"

"Mercy no, Father! It will be no meeting for your holy ears! Rude words will fly, you can believe me!"

"I shall forbid him to take a stick to you, no matter how thoroughly you deserve it." A merry laugh answered his concern.

"My husband would never strike me, no matter how deadly my sins," she replied confidently. "He might, perhaps, take me out to sea and throw me overboard, but I shall not be beaten. He has promised."

"Then God go with you, child. When the business is concluded I shall bring you the deeds."

The Stella Maris was pushing steadily toward the harbour. Lucy gathered up her brood and herded them over to Magdalena's home, keeping only the baby.

Lionallo burst into the house with his usual exuberance, swept his wife into an ursine embrace, swung her around in a wild fandango, set her on her feet, soundly kissed her and went to kneel beside the carved cradle. He drew a gentle finger along the plump curve of baby Celeste's downy cheek. She smiled in sleep and smacked her lips.

"Where are the others, my Star? Did you not see me coming? I expected to find you on the dock."

"They are with Magdalena," his wife answered. She crossed to the hearth to stir the coals beneath a kettle, simmering, if his nose did not deceive him, with his favourite lamb stew.

"I will go for them." He started for the door.

"Yes, do," she concurred. "They shall eat and go to bed early." The grin forming on his face fled, as she added, "Then you can help me pack without them underfoot."

"Pack? For what reason?" he growled, staring suspiciously at Lucy.

Meticulously avoiding his eyes, she cast a few cumin seeds into the kettle. "To facilitate our moving," she told him, with what she considered commendable calm.

"Our moving? We are not moving. This is our home. Where on earth would we go? And why?"

"To a roomier house, where the children can have their own rooms. A farm house." She cast a guarded look in his direction.

For a moment a puzzled silence held him. Then comprehension flooded his understanding. "A farm house? You plan to move to a farm house! The Iaccobelli farm house, I assume? I cannot believe that you have gone behind my back and purchased his citrus grove. You know that I will never approve such a purchase. Never would I consent to be tied to the dirt."

"Of course not, Lion. I would never demand such a sacrifice from you. There will be no need at all for you to ever work the farm. I know you could never survive, were you land bound. The groves will be my responsibility entirely. Your life shall not change by one iota!"

"You are right there!" he snapped. "My life certainly will not change, and neither shall yours. You may forget this ridiculous notion of yours and resign yourself to suffice with whatever I can provide, scant though that may be."

"But that is not at all the idea," she protested. "You already provide all and more than any woman could desire. The groves would be an occupation for me when you are away."

"You have occupation enough, surely, with our children," he growled. "Enough of this nonsense! I will not have it! The deal shall be cancelled, at once!"

"It is not nonsense!" Anger began to rise in Lucy's breast. Why did he have to be such a … a … male! "It is perfectly feasible, and anyway, you cannot cancel the arrangement. All has been concluded, the gold has been paid, and I have the deeds!" She glared at him triumphantly.

"The gold has been paid? By whom? And with whose gold?"

"Not yours!" she retorted sharply. "My own. Do you take me for a thief?"

"A thief indeed," he rebuked her bitterly. "You have stolen my honour and my pride – my reputation. You had far better have stolen my money . That would not cause me such pain and shame."

"Lion!" She reached out to him but he stepped back. "I, Lionallo Momellino, who have never failed to pay a debt, or return a favour twofold, cannot support my own family, to my wife's satisfaction. I shall be a laughing stock – a half man, kept by a woman!"

"That is not true and you know it! I ... "

"Do not fear," he interrupted, black-visaged. "I shall move you. Send for me when you are ready. I shall be at the taverna."

She had not expected such a speedy capitulation. She had foreseen hours, perhaps even days of wrangling, before he finally accepted and forgave her actions. She laid a graceful hand on his sleeve.

"Thank you, dear Lion," she murmured. "I am sure we will be very happy there."

"You perhaps, not we." His voice was winter ice, as he roughly shook her hand from his arm. "This is my home. Here I shall stay." He stalked out of the house, ignoring her beseeching call, slamming the door with such force that the whole house trembled, causing little Celeste to whimper in her sleep, although she did not awaken.

Father Ambrose stood on the steps of his church, watching those of his parishioners who were making their way into the taverna. At last he saw the man he was expecting, striding toward the door, rage evident in every aspect of his face and bearing. Old Nona Barbieri, shuffling by, was shocked by the definitely impish grin that illuminated the priest's usually mild features, then decided that she must have been mistaken when he raised his hand in blessing, his mien calm and devout as always. He had been watching the door of the taverna, she recollected as she tottered off, and he began to walk steadfastly in that direction. Good! He was about to roast the ears off some of those lazy ne'er-do-wells. She hoped her grandson, young Nicholas, would be one of those to benefit from the good man's attentions–he deserved it. What young folk were coming to, only Heaven knew–or maybe the Devil! In her day ...

"Good day, Giorgios," Ambrose saluted the taverna's host. "I will take a glass of your best vintage. Today I feel deserving of a reward. It seems that all of my words do not fall on deaf ears." He hitched up his robe, and took a place on the bench at the same table, where Momellino sat, morosely nursing a tankard of ale. Giorgios wondered what irked the fisherman. Although but a moderate drinker, he was normally a convivial soul, with a quick wit, and a pleasant disposition, ready to join in a song, or oblige an elder with a game of Tables. Today he spoke to no one, and his forbidding brow was as dark as a thundercloud. Probably at outs with that pretty wife he had brought home from foreign parts. Ah, well. 'Twas more likely just a passing cloud. They would soon make up, and there would be another little Momellino for the Father to christen this time next year.

He served the priest his wine and was thanked before the Father gazed at it approvingly, then took first a sip, and then a generous swallow.

"Ah! Very good," he conceded. "Truly your best. But I feel that I merit it. It is a comfort to a man of God to know that at least one of his flock heeds his advice." He took a more moderate sip from his cup and held it up to the light again, admiring its colour. Quite a few pairs of nervous eyes fixed themselves on the priest. His public homilies, while naming no names, were designed to cause considerable discomfort to at least one of his hearers, often several. Giorgios grinned and wondered who was in for it this time.

"You will remember the story I have often told you, of the servants who were given in trust of their masters' gold, and how one wrapped it in a napkin and hid it away in a carved chest, where it did no good at all."

"I thought, Father," ventured one brave soul, "that you said he buried it."

"Buried the gold, or hid it in a carved chest," there was an emphasis on those two words that filtered through Lionallo's gloom to catch his attention. He stared morosely at the speaker. "The result was the same. Hidden, the gold was useless. Not that it should be spent recklessly, without regard to the future, as the foolish virgins spent their oil. But it should be made to work for the good of the owner and of the community.

Knowing looks were exchanged among his audience. The good

Father was throwing out a gentle hint that the parish coffers were in need of replenishment – that some of the coins circulating in the taverna should be diverted to that purpose.

The priest was quite content to let them think so. It might benefit the church, but it would also obscure the parable's connection to his next tale.

"Yes," he continued. "One of my charges – not, I regret, one of the rams, but even a ewe lamb is not to be overlooked, one has taken my words to heart. One heeded my advice, listened to those words from the Bible that describe a perfect wife and did her best to emulate them. I will repeat them for your benefit, then some of you may realize what treasures grace your homes. His sonorous tones held them silent as he recited: "Who shall find a virtuous woman? Her price is far above rubies ... "

He continued, reaching verse 16: "She considereth a field and buyeth it. With the fruit of her hands, she planteth a vineyard." Through half-closed eyes he noted the blood come and go in Lionallo's face and saw the square hand tighten on the tankard it held. So – enough. He continued his conversation, remarking on certain small peccadilloes he had noticed, drawing blushes from some, and sly rib elbowings from others, who thought they could identify the trespassers being reproached. No one but Father Ambrose noticed when Lionallo Momellino unobtrusively took his leave.

It was late when Lion finally returned home, and Lucy could read nothing from his impassive mien. As was his custom, he made his round of the sleeping children, quietly blessing each one, made his own brief prayer then bade her a brusque goodnight as he settled, his back turned to her, into their bed. She relaxed, her own fervent prayer one of relief. She waited until she thought he might be sleeping and cautiously slipped her arm across his middle. The involuntary tautening of his muscles told her she was mistaken, but he did not speak or move from her light embrace. She smothered a sigh of relief. In the morning all would be well.

*   *   *

And so it had been, remembered old Nona Lucina. This house, set among the fragrant citrus trees, had become their true haven, a happy fruitful home in every way. What a brood they had raised! And good fortune had allowed them to raise them all. The family luck had held true, even when the plague of '70 had taken so many lives, including the great Corsican hero Sambuccoci. That was before they had moved up the valley. There the homestead was watered by its own fresh clean spring, which had proved a great protection from the periodic outbursts of typhoid, brought on by bad water and poor sanitation. Their friends had teased her when she insisted the household midden, and the privy, must be located at what they considered an unnecessary distance from the house, but she did not believe as they did that her family's seeming immunity to most of the hot weather maladies were coincidental ... and that dreadful year when babies were dying from diarrhea, she was sure that it was the charcoal with which she dosed baby Gianna and Magdalena's Anthony that saved those two tiny lives.

True to her word, she'd managed the business entirely without Lion's assistance, enlisting the children and occasional workers as necessary, but she had used none of the profits for the support of their family.

Dear old Lion had provided for them magnificently. He was one who could turn his hand to practically anything, be it mend a shoe, fix a broken chair or repair a leaking kettle. His ship loaded with trade goods, he sailed to Sardinia and to the European coast, adding to his income. He bartered his fish and his time for other men's goods and services, and when the time came he was able to build another boat, with the help of work time owed to him by the local carpenter, blacksmith and others, not to mention the strong backs of his older sons, for those of their boys who wished to follow his trade. Happily he had not been so stubborn as to prevent her earnings from providing dowries for their daughters and opportunities for those of their sons who chose other ways of life than his own. Actually she felt that he was secretly quite proud of her, although he would never have admitted it. Ah, yes! They'd had a wonderful life ...

They'd had their ups and downs, of course – and some fine battles on the way! "What could one expect," dear old Father Ambrose, long since gone to his rest, had scolded, "when two such stubborn mules were yoked to one wagon?" Their reconciliations were always the same, their quarrels never intruding into the second day. Every morning gave them a fresh start.

For a while, they had received occasional letters from and news of Philippa and Guy, but gradually the messages dwindled away and the final lingering memories of Cyprus faded into the past. Lucy felt she was Corse now, to the marrow of her bones.

The children had been normal, healthy youngsters, presenting the kind of problems any family must cope with, squabbling among themselves, but presenting a solid front to offending outsiders. Their father's common sense kept even the most adventurous of them from taking to the maquis, for, as he pointed out, to support either Pisa or Genoa was to support the foreign invader. Far better to be loyal to the family and their own kind and let dog eat dog. Not that he ever hesitated to set off at a moment's notice, with an emergency cargo for Sardinia or the mainland, and a secret supercargo stowed among the barrels and crates, if the necessity arose. But for his own family he was determined to avoid both outlawry and Vendetta.

There had been that troublesome, though rather ridiculous, occasion when young Eustache had been smitten by the idea of communistic life and stated his intention to join a commune he had heard of. But her own scandalized scolding, his father's authority, the scorn and roughhousing of his brothers and the stern lectures of Father Ambrose eventually forced him to change his mind. Not, however, without a great deal of complaining and muttering and a brief period of sulking. Fortunately a new interest soon caught his fancy and his recovery was speedy and thorough.

It had been far more frightening a few years earlier, when 16-year-old Lionallo had announced that he planned to aid his best friend in defending his "honour" from some real or fancied unforgivable insult. She shuddered, even now, at the memory of that day. She had watched the confrontation of her first born and his father with terror in her soul, but silently avoided participation. It had been their long-standing agreement that neither should interfere with the other's disciplining of their children, but give their unqualified support to each other's decisions.

Two identical profiles, nose to nose, black eyes blazing, each sturdy body slightly bent forward from the hips, hands tightened into hardened fists, they stared tight-lipped into one another's enraged faces.

"I forbid such foolhardy idiocy," declared the father.

"My honour and my duty to my friend demand that I aid him. I am not afraid to die!" retorted the youngster, proudly.

"Your honour and your duty are first to your family," he was chided. "So you are not afraid to die! But what right have the two of you, for some boy's nonsense that a grown man would properly ignore as beneath his dignity to notice, to lay both your families open to death and destruction? For the sake of your so-called honour, you would bring down Vendetta on your brothers and sisters, on your mothers? That your fathers must take up the knife, and die in their turn to avenge your deaths, may be of little consequence to you. But can you with a clear conscience cause those innocents to be slaughtered?"

He gestured toward the cradle where a toddler happily played with the newest babe, then shook his fist angrily under his son's nose.

"Pah!" He threw up his hands. "God forbid that I should ever strike a child of my own flesh and blood!" He turned away and strode out of the house in disgust.

Young Lionallo stared after him for a silent moment. Then his bravado collapsed, his face crumpled and, with a broken cry of "Papa!", he rushed out of the door in his father's wake. Lucy sank weakly onto a stool, burying her face in her arms on the table, weeping tears of relief. It was all right. Love had won out.

It was supper time before the two returned, the father's arm fondly draped around his son's shoulders. They were accompanied by the chastened and sheepish looking friend. Nicholas's father had been of the same mind as Lion, but had expressed his disapproval with rather less restraint, as the discoloured left eye his son sported bore witness. He had also given his gallant offspring to understand that it might be as well if he kept out of his father's sight for a day or two, hence his visit to the Momellino home.

22

Oh, yes! Life had been very good to them. The hardest blow had been the death of her dear Lion, but even then, when he knew he was slipping away, he had words to comfort her, reminding her that there would one day be a reunion. As she knelt beside his bed, holding his hand to her cheek, she heard his last whispered utterance.

"Flesh of my flesh, bone of my bone,
  I give you my soul till my life's course is run
  ...and through eternity."

She closed her eyes over the weak, sentimental tears that the memory triggered.

"Nona! Nona Lucina. Are you awake?" Lion's voice and Lion's face! But no – it was one of her many grandchildren standing over her. No, again. One of her great-grandchildren. There were so many of her children's children and her children's children's children to keep count of! It seemed that all their offspring were as prolific as she and Lion had been. This one was another Lionallo, grandson of her own first born. He was holding a tiny swaddled bundle against his broad young shoulder as he looked down at her, with a perfect simulation of his great-grandfather's grin illuminating his tanned face.

"Ah!" she smiled. "Lion. This is your first?"

"That she is, Nona. Nono Lion complains bitterly that I have made him a great-grandfather in the prime of his life! But you should hear him boasting at the taverna. No family ever produced such a marvel of beauty and intelligence, as our adorable Lucina. Her future can only be dreamed of." His throaty chuckle was so like that of the first Lionallo that it sent a small thrill shivering down her bent old back.

"So you are calling her Lucina."

"Great-grandaunt Gianna's orders! But Sophia and I had already chosen your name for her, before she was born. Had the good Lord sent us a boy, he would have been Lionallo."

"This family is not at all imaginative, when it comes to name giving," his twice-great-grandmother pointed out.

"Ah! But this child is very, very special, Aunt Gianna says." He stepped aside, to allow his father to set down the still-sturdy old cradle he was carrying. Others crowded around as young Sophia, the baby's mother, took the child from her husband and laid it in Lucy's arms. Automatically, she held it upright to her breast, and tucked the tiny head with its downy crown of damp curls under her chin.

"All babies are special," she reproved Gianna, who was directing the other women to serve each adult member of the family with a cup of the very best family vintage. The clamouring children were given citrus juice, and the older ones watered wine, causing Lucy to raise her eyebrows.

"Of course," Gianna answered her mother. "But this one is the most special of all. Mama dear, you are about to lay in the family cradle the one hundredth of your and Papa's offspring!"

The one hundredth baby! Lucy stared down at the tiny mortal, so warm against her heart. Memory whirled her back to the time of the carving of the cradle, when she had teased her dear old Lion about making it strong enough to shelter a hundred little ones. It had been only a joke, in those happy young days, but now, here she was, holding Baby One Hundred cuddled in her own withered arms.

With her son's steadying arm supporting her, she rose to her feet, then bent to lay the infant girl in the old cradle, to a rousing cheer and enthusiastic response from her family. Back in her chair, she sipped at her wine, as a multitude of voices murmured a toast to the little scrap of humanity, blissfully sleeping through her introduction to the family and its history. The voices seemed to mingle with those from long ago. Edward and her dear l'Mesuriers, Pierre de Lusignan, Sir Phillipe de Mézières, Roberga and Will, her own dear Mama and Papa ... Mama and Papa. How she wished they could have known of this. The one shadow on her life had been her inability to share her happiness with them. She sat for a quiet moment, looking down on a tiny miracle, and if one miracle could happen so could another! She closed her eyes again, and seemed to hear dear Lionallo's voice as he peeled the orange, long ago, on a cliff in Famagusta. "And one day you will wake up and it will be ...

Monday, June thirteenth, eighteen thirty-one.

Mistress Lightfoot stood at the front door of Stoney Meadow Farm, in the Bowcombe Valley, on the Isle of Wight, England, a fine Cashmere shawl protecting her plump shoulders from the early morning breeze. She smiled as Lucy climbed from the white-washed mounting stone, by the gate, into the saddle of her restive chestnut hunter. With loving pride, she watched her pretty daughter ride down the lane and out of sight, and, had she but known it, out of her life, forever.

Epilogue

THE GRASS BEYOND THE DOOR is based on historical record. Sir Edward Estur is an actual figure, whose carved wooden effigy still lies in the tiny church built by his twelfth century ancestors at Gatcombe, Isle of Wight, in the south of England. The sword that now lies clasped in his oaken hands is carved from wood, a replacement for the original that was shattered so dramatically by lightning.

The Great Storm of June 13, 1831 remains, more than a century and a half later, the most severe storm ever recorded on the Isle of Wight. It is also a matter of record that the storm occurred simultaneously with a total eclipse of the sun that plunged the whole area into darkness for hours.

Lucy Lightfoot grew up at Stoney Meadow Farm on the Isle of Wight. She was the only child in a family that was prosperous, loving, cultured and indulgent. By all accounts she was a normal young person for her time and circumstance, except for one peculiar idiosyncracy — an infatuation with the crusader Sir Edward Estur. Lucy visited Sir Edward's effigy at St. Olave's Church, Gatcombe, virtually every day; the visits, which were well known throughout the parish, were the object of considerable amusement even to persons who did not know the Lightfoot family well.

On June 13, 1831 Lucy left her house to visit a friend, Marjorie Braithwaite, with whom she was planning to observe the eclipse that would reach totality at ten past eleven that morning. En route to her friend's home she stopped for her customary visit to St. Olave's Church. As witnessed by George Brewster of nearby Chale, Lucy hitched her horse to a railing and entered the church.

After the storm, the vicar Henry Worsley found her horse still tied to the railings. The church was empty. Nothing had been disturbed or damaged, save that Sir Edward Estur's sword lay in shattered fragments, and the chrysoberyl that adorned its handle had totally disappeared. Of Lucy there was not a trace. There was no sign of a struggle or foul play. She never arrived at her friend's home, Chillerton Farm, and was never seen again.

Lucy's frantic parents brought in notable detectives from the mainland, but neither their combined efforts and investigations nor the considerable reward offered brought any results. From the moment Lucy entered the church, she seemed to have vanished from the earth. After two years of fruitless searching, her grieving parents sold up and left the Island. Stoney Meadow farm later burned to the ground, but Chillerton farm, the home of Lucy's friend Marjorie Braithwaite, survives to this day. My sister was stationed there with the Land Army in the Second World War.

And that would have been the end of the story but for a strange quirk of fate more than a third of a century after the great storm. Until 1865, very little had been known of the Estur Crusader except his name and the fact that he had fought under Pierre de Lusignan in the Holy Land. Then, 34 years after Lucy's mysterious disappearance, a scholarly Methodist clergyman, the Reverend Samuel Trelawney of St. Mary's Church in the Scilly Isles, discovered an interesting set of ancient manuscripts. In these documents, Sir Phillipe de Mézières, chancellor to King Peter the First of Cyprus, recorded in great detail his services to King Peter. Included in the scrolls was a list of all the knights and their companions who had joined that particular Crusade. Among the Englishmen who (with the permission of their own King Edward) had pledged themselves to the cause was a knight from the Parish of Carisbrooke, Isle of Wight. The crusader's name was Sir Edward Estur. But what was indeed extraordinary was the name of Sir Edward's companion: a Lady Lucy Lightfoot. Moreover, as indicated by the documents, Lady Lightfoot was from the same parish in the Isle of Wight! De Mézières states that, according to the parchment, she was most anxious to go to the wars with her knight but he refused to take her, promising to marry her on his return.

It was not to happen. Estur was reported killed in action; in actuality, he received a severe head wound that left him in a coma for months. When he recovered from his injury he returned straight to England, where he happily lived out his life. All that had happened on Cyprus, including his betrothal to Lucy Lightfoot, was wiped from his mind.

Lucy, believing that Estur had died, eloped with a fisherman, Lionallo Momellino. They settled in Terra Vecchia on the island of Corsica, where she became a citrus farmer, lived to a great age and left an enormous family to mourn her when she died. She was buried in the Terra Vecchia churchyard.

Cicely Adams Veighey spent her early childhood in the tiny seaside town of Yarmouth, Isle of Wight. Tales of smuggling, hauntings and magnificently heroic shipwreck rescues – the stuff of local legend – inspired endless games of pirates, Roundheads and Cavaliers, and smugglers and coastguards, played on the beaches, on the common or, during inclement weather, in the dungeons of Henry VIII's old castle. She married David Veighey, a Northern Irishman, in 1937. After his discharge from the army in 1948, they emigrated from Ulster to Canada with their three small children and settled in Windsor, Ontario, where she still lives.